BANDAGES

Joe McClain Jr.

This is a work of fiction. Names, characters, places and incidents are either the product of the authors imagination or are used fictitiously. Any resemblance to actual events or locales or persons, lientirely coincidental.

DEDICATION

Dedicated to my Godson Darrell Anthony Nobles Jr.
Without you, I wouldn't be the man I am today.

ACKNOWLEDGMENTS

God Almighty first and foremost. Without Him, there is no me, no book, no anything. Chaz...I don't have to say words. Just look at your finger. I love you. My McClain fam, Washington fam, Cobb fam, Person fam, Dunaway fam, Pharms fam. The whole damn Alabama, Indiana, Michigan fam. Caujuan, you opened the door for me and I'm in the crib on the couch, eating good as hell. Stefanie, holla it out one time....UPROCK!!! Redlite, words can't explain, I got ya back any given time, any given day, night, whatever. D-Block, you aint on the way...you're there!!!! Keep killin em. BETA, you drive me to be a better man everyday. I love you nephew. Shawntae, big sis. I love you. Jasmine Willis, you've been my BIGGEST SUPPORTER from the crib. I appreciate the love!!! K.T., GUMP 5000, Jay Hall, Darien Matthews, Dennis Perkins, Darrell Nobles Sr. and Doug Jelks. Those seven men are my brothers. Point blank period!!! Veronica Cook...I can't even explain it. You have been a friend beyond the term. Lhea...woooo!!!! G-14 classified sh*t. We wrecked Asia together. You kept me from doing a lot of dumb stuff and always looked out for me. Thank you. To everybody who don't like me succeeding, you gone be waiting a long time for me to fall. Keep being mediocre in your miserable lives. Even y'all deserve a thank you. Your anger lets me know I am doing a good job. To the 503....Portland, Oregon. Y'all showed me a whole different aspect of life while I was up there. I look forward to many more trips up there. Carlos Cunningham, bro, I got you and the kids. Don't trip. Love you bro. 219, its all love. I'm holding us down on the West. To the whole Coast, all of Cali, I been here for over a decade and love it. Throw up ya W's from the 619 to the Bay and beyond. All my people in Reno, Vegas, Seattle, Texas, Phoenix, Guam, Japan, The Philippines, Australia and everywhere else I done been. I got mad love for y'all. To anyone who has ever supported me in anyway, its all love!!! Uprock!!!

CHAPTER ONE

<u>2010: THE BEGINNING OF THE REST OF MY LIFE</u>

"Blaze that shit up nigga!!!" That was my nigga Tez. All I could do was look at him and shake my head. This man was the weed head of weed heads. Hell, every nigga in here blew big except me to tell you the truth. Dante and J.J., well, they were the same way, but they took it more to the extreme with getting an ultimate rush.

If it wasn't weed, they wouldn't hesitate to pop a pill of X, snort some coke or whatever. Hell, if they could get high off sipping the oil from a honey badger's liver, those two negroes would do it. That's just how these two operated. I don't know why I jumped in the car with these niggas.

They were going to go hit a lick on some random person or people tonight, and I just tagged along for the ride. Whoever was on their dolo tip tonight was gone get it. Really, I didn't wanna be in the car with these fools mane, but I made the choice out of sheer friendship. I knew the type of lifestyle they lived, but fuck it. They were my partners from way back, so I had a sense of loyalty to em. They always had my back, so it was only right of me to have theirs, even if I knew what they were doing was wrong. I mean, that was just how things operated in the hood.

"Here Bones, fire up?" Tez Boasted.

"Naw mane, I'm good."

"Nigga quit being a bitch and blaze this shit up!"

Man, these cats knew I didn't smoke, but fuck it. Tez always had to egg some shit on, and the other two always co-signed and instigated everything. I was quite a drinker, as Crown Royal and Hennessey was my unofficial wife and side piece. However, as far as smoking went, that had never been my thing.

Oh well though I thought. You sometimes gotta do what you gotta do to get through a situation a lot quicker. In this case, I did it so I could shut these fools up and not hear em run their damn mouths. As I put that blunt to my lips and inhaled more than smoke, I really thought about what I was doing. They say weed gets your mind right and has you thinking outside of the box. So if it gets your mind right, why did I still know what I was doing was wrong? I inhaled one more time, and I freestyled a quick piece inside my head:

As fire burns in blunt form
fire burns in my spirit as well
I already see hell through a swisher
and right now
I'm defining what American society calls a nigga
As I exhale
I blow out my black skin
God please forgive me for all my sins

My name is Carl Jackson for y'all that don't know. Carl Lamell Jackson Jr. to be exact. I'm just your ordinary 6'4 , slender, but not to skinny chill negro with a head full of waves. I swear the United States Navy could sail their ships on my shit because they were so fresh. All of my partnas call me "Bones" because I was a twig sized kid coming up that could hang glide on a dorito, hula hoop in a fruit loop and walk thru the crack of a closed door.

Growing up here in Gary, Indiana was like growing up in a life sized hamster maze. One wrong move, and you may never leave out, whether that was being stuck here forever or dying before your time. It was truly a blessing if someone made it out of this city alive. It was top ten in murder rate damn near every year. Scary Gary, Gangsta Island, "Steel" City. Yea, this place had many nicknames because of it. There were no jobs because damn near all of the steel mills were closed. I mean shit, this place was a ghost town where the ghosts didn't even wanna stay. Damn near every other building you seen riding down the street was boarded up. Trees looked like ass, grass on the front lawns of homes were brown and dry, sidewalks and concrete structures were full of cracks as well.

Often times, I thought of this city as the place where the Devil would come and say "Naw, fuck it. I'm going back to hell where my shit looks like Beverly Hills." That's how ugly, run down and busted up my city looked. It was like the Hiroshima bomb had a duplicate and dropped down over here. Gary used to be a jewel of the Midwest decades ago. I use to hear all of the amazing stories about mighty, mighty, G.I. How Broadway was lined up with retail stores, and everyone and they mama came here to shop.

I know everybody knows about The Jackson 5. Ol' Michael and the crew, growing up at 2300 Jackson St, with those big ol negro fros and big ol negro noses. They were the jewel of the black community back in the 70's and early 80's. Hell I even kept a poster of Janet on my wall until one of my cousins ripped it down when I was 10. I know she didn't sing with em back when they were poppin, but catching old episodes of Good Times made her my biggest crush ever. Ol Penny was a dime piece, even though Thelma could get bent over as well. Yea, that was the Gary, Indiana that I could only dream of and fantasize about, because the Gary I grew up in was a nightmare. However, this was still home, and I was still very proud of where I came from. I grew up here in the TarryTown section of the city or, as me and my people from around the region called it, Terror town.

I was an odd ball kid at most coming up. I read books anytime I could get my hands on them, no matter what they were about. I loved them and they loved me. Words always intrigued me for some strange reason. I liked what you would call unordinary stuff for an inner city kid. I would go to the playground and play with rocks, thinking I would find a fossil or something crazy in the dirt. Sometimes, I'd make a hood telescope out of a shoebox, thinking that I would catch something in the sky that scientists hadn't yet discovered. Yea, that was me.

As a youngin, cats would attempt to pick on me because I was pint sized, but I always had something for em. See, I knew I couldn't win a lot of one on one fights because of my frail frame. Shit, I used to think if I thumped a bug I'd break my finger. Everyday before school, I found a huge rock, or some big object, and stuck it in my back pocket. It was my gun before everybody started carrying one on their waist in this pussified age of being scared to take an ass whoopin. One day in the third grade, this cat named Richard stepped to me on the playground during recess. I hadn't bothered dude at all, but because a girl he liked started talking to me, he got extremely upset. He stood at least an extra foot over me, so an even match was out of the question. He pushed me down several times, egged on by the surrounding kids in the yard. All the anger in the world all of a sudden built up inside of me. As I got up from what seemed like the 1,000th push, I snuck my hand in my back pocket.

"C'mon lil dude. I'll give you the first hit," he blared. That was the wrong idea, as I reached into my back pocket, clinched that baseball sized rock and hauled off on his ass with the most violent intent ever. All I remember was gushing blood coming from above his left eye. It looked like a red water spout as he rolled around screaming in pain, crying like the bitch that he was.

Richard didn't get up. He was out quicker than a negro who realized he rolled up on a Klan convention. The other kids on the school grounds were stunned silent, as they didn't know what to do. A minute ago, they were egging him on with every push, telling him to kick my ass. Now, they didn't wanna get their asses whooped, so they shut the hell up real quick. I was suspended that day for the next two weeks, but the message had gotten out: Leave lil Carl alone. Cats had learned to quit messing with me. When I returned to school a few weeks later, I was sort of a superstar. That's when I ran into Dante and J.J. They were some off the wall kids that I never talked too before the fight. I always seen them at lunch roasting some kid with some wack shoes or a screwed up haircut. Plus, they had the most foul mouth I have ever heard of any third graders in the history of mankind. However, we linked up and became friends ever since that moment.

My momma worked two jobs to keep me and my two brothers sustained, with my oldest brother being locked up in the penn. My daddy, he aint live with us, but he was around. He was from the Eastside of Gary, but he stayed in the neighboring city of Merrillville with the white folks. A Certified Vice Lord they called "Deuce," no one messed with him. He ran a lot of product in and out of this city, and surrounding areas alike. Anything you needed, Big Deuce had it. That's where I got my toughness from. He took care of his "soldiers" as he called us.

With pops, he gave us all we needed and we never wanted for anything. That was until that fateful day. It was the beginning of my sophomore year at West Side High school, when I got that call to the principals office. I hadn't done anything that I recalled, so I was scratching my head wondering what in the good hell did the principal want. As I went thru the front office door, I immediately saw my mama and a police officer buddy of hers they called "Mo" from way back.

"Mama what's wrong?" From the look on her face, I could tell the news was going to be bad.

"Baby…your daddy's dead." I stepped back, pretending like I didn't hear those words. I closed my eyes for a quick second, hoping that I was in class sleep and that my teacher would be shaking me telling me to get up. However, this was reality. My pops was found in an open field in North Hammond, Indiana. He caught 24 shots to his frame. Three to the dome and the other 21 all throughout his body. Pops aint give a fuck, but that mentality ultimately brought about his own demise. He was gunned down in a late night deal gone wrong with some Latin Kings, a large latino gang that was based out of neighboring Chicago. Why did he do business with those guys? I don't even know. I know they popped 5 like VL, but I never were too fond of them. I aint even bang at the time, but I hated every Latino I seen from that day on. If they wore gold and black, I hated them even more. Now, I truly realized how some white people felt when they looked at brothers.

Shit got real difficult after that. My older brother was already locked up in Michigan City, and my two younger brothers would both end up being sent off to juvenile hall before I even finished high school. I was the last one left with my momma. I had a choice. Do what I had to do for survival, or do what I had to do to ensure my survival. I chose both. However, like The Good Lord says, you cannot serve two masters. You will either love one or hate the other. I wasn't hearing that though. In school, I was the good student, keeping my grades up to par, putting on this great image for the teachers and staff alike. After school, I made sure Negroes knew what it was to be an Almighty Vice Lord. I didn't see it then, but I was slowly becoming my daddy's twin.

It was the second semester of my sophomore year and I was just starting to get back to normal. I had signed up for an English Literature class, and that choice would end up changing my life. We were studying this William Shakespeare cat. I didn't know much about him, nor did I care. All I knew was this was some ol roses were red, violets were blue shit. Hell by the looks of his picture, Shakespeare looked like he hugged up on men more than he did women.

My teacher, Mr. Wilson was a funny looking ass white dude, but he was very wise at the same time. He had these coke bottled glasses and had a knack for calling his students teeny boppers. It was easy to get fooled by his appearance though. That nerdy look was a disguise. He was the only white dude I knew

14

who could go toe to toe with a lot of these cats around here. He definitely had the respect of the student body, as he was known for being the one teacher who knocked a nigga out when a fight jumped off in his classroom. He gave us an assignment one day. It was to write two poems and present them to the class. The topic: LOVE.

"Man, aint no way in hell was I going to write some mess about no love Mr. Wilson!," I yelled out, as the class busted out in laughter. Mr. Wilson just shook his head as he continued to blurt out instructions. I was fronting though. I loved reading and writing. I couldn't let these hood fools know that. They weren't about to clown me.

As the rest of the class settled down and began to write, I twirled my pencil around thinking of ideas. That's when my mind and my pen began to collaborate with each other on a serious level. I had never written poetry before, even though I had read it often. Now, it was time for me to test new and unchartered waters. My first poetry piece was entitled "BLACK LOVE"

They say love is patient, love is kind and love is blind
what they fail to mention is that is simple love
cause real love is more complex, real love is more
than sex, real love is more than rings and I do's
and no one express it better than black folks, I'm
talkin bout real

love
where a man cares for you so much he'll paint yo
damn toes on the doorsteps and not care what any
other man think, real
love
while you at work and she up at four in the morning
cookin chicken and grits cause she know you gone
deliver that bomb love later, real love
where he tell the mail lady to get the hell off his porch
cause he don't want another woman that close to his
queen's palace, real
love
where she puttin couches in the kitchen, trash in the
bed and dishes in the bathroom because she steady
confused on a how a man can love this strong, real
damn
love
when he can walk in the store, grab her time of the
month gear, look at the cashier and tell him say
somethin nigga, real damn
love
see black men got it better than any cause our
choices are many,
red bone, yella bone, peanut butter, mocha,
chocolate, dark chocolate, so damn black that she
can lay on the street and look like a pothole but still
pretty,
but see its a reason God said out of darkness came
light

*thats why black love is tight, black love is right, black
love is undefined and perfect.
black love is worth it, see when they ask me bout real
love,
I don't tell em poetry lines,
I don't quote r&b singers, I simply say look at the
black man and black woman
and that's all the definition that you need*

Mind you, when I wrote this, I was on some Jodeci type stuff. I thought about a couple of bad ones I wanted to get in between, so I threw together some lies that sounded good. Maybe I could use this on them later. Really though, I aint think too much of this. I finished up my second one and turned it in, as did the rest of the class five minutes before the bell.

As it rang, I prepared to head off to the next boring mouth I had to hear for an hour. That's until Mr. Wilson told me to stay after class because he wanted to talk to me one on one. He had read my Black Love joint. He rapped to me on some real shit, telling me that I had a gift.

Also, he showed me that he had to give me an A- due to the fact that I dropped the N-bomb in the piece. I kind of chuckled at the notion that this was a gift of mine. Little did I know at that moment, he gave me the thumbs up on the gift that would ultimately end up saving my life, and giving it to me in the same token.

"A Dant, Jay, y'all remember this nigga used to be writing love books in school and shit?" All these fools bust out into laughter.

"Fuck y'all niggas," as I took another whiff of the blunt. I know they were just messing with me. What they didn't know though is how serious I took my craft. I had major plans to use my gift to take me far in life. Of course, you can't show it to ya partnas, as it made you look soft as hell. What hood nigga you know spits poetry? I just rolled with the punches and played along though.

"Y'all know I was doing it for the hoes man!" Them niggas burst out laughing, and we went back and forth. They was claiming I wasn't, and I valiantly proclaimed I did, even though they were telling the truth. We were now rolling down Broadway. It was 1 o'clock on this desolate and early Sunday morning, and we were all higher than giraffe pussy.

In the midst of all the shit talking in the car, I analyzed everything about Bloody Broadway. Everything, I mean everything was depleted. I heard my guys, but I didn't hear them, as I was in more than deep thought. All I could dream was that in a short time, I would be out of Gary, Indiana and onto a new chapter in my life. I would have the opportunity to become an asset to society and not just another black statistic. I was headed to Wayne State in Michigan on an athletic scholarship for football. Nothing was gonna hold me back I thought.

"A my nigga," Jay said in a silent voice. "We got us one." I turned quickly to look out of the window. Through the glare of the dim street lights, I could see that it was some middle aged looking cat. He looked about in his mid 30's, but no older than 40. He was stumbling around, looking like he had one too many hits of the liquor bottle. Everything was clear. We aint see no one else out round here.

"Let's get this nigga," whispered Tez. "Pass that blunt back nigga." I gave it too Tez so he could hit it one last time. I don't know what everyone else was thinking, but as my eyes locked on with this potential target, the little voice in my head said "You bout to fuck up, and fuck up bad." Have you ever had an out of body experience? That's exactly what I was having. Just then, Dante accelerated on the gas and sped up.

Dude took off running, but we cut him off as he hit a side street. As he rolled over the top of the whip, everyone except Dant, who was driving, jumped out of the car. We hauled ass on foot, as this brother was in Carl Lewis mode. As we inched closer and closer to this guy, my life felt closer and closer to ending, as if I was the one getting chased. I had a terrible feeling about this whole thing. This cat eventually fell and tripped next to an abandoned house.

"I AINT GOT NOTHIN MAN! I AINT GOT

NOTHIN!" he kept screaming. **BOP!** Tez hit him in his dome with his forty glock, and knocked him out cold.

"Check his pockets nigga!" We ravaged through his pockets, and him as a whole. This nigga had a wad on him, so we hit the right one. We popped his watch, his shoes and even his fitted cap all for the hell of it. Dant had pulled up next to us now and was shouting for us to come on.

"HURRY UP NIGGAS!" We cleaned this nigga off. As I turned back around and ran to the car, I heard **POP, POP, POP!** Right then and there, time stood still. I froze in mid run. My heart started to beat a million miles per hour, and I just said to myself "Lord, this ain't happening." Funny how we always wanna call on The Lord for a negative situation we put ourselves into.

The breath in my body stopped as I imagined those being the sounds of my pops getting shot years back. I turned around and was in disbelief with what I saw. This nigga Tez shot him point blank in the dome for no damn reason.

"C'mon nigga!" Dant yelled. **"All y'all niggas c'mon!"** Tez had to pull me, as I was dead stiff by the blood gushing from this mans head. We got in the whip and sped the hell off.

"The fuck wrong with you Tez?" J.J. screamed at him. "The fuck you shoot him for?!" Tez just started laughing, with no remorse shown at all.

"It's a rush nigga!" Them two argued all the way until we got back to Dant's house. Me personally, I was messed up by this. These were my day one niggas. I loved em like brothers. I was tough, but these dudes were on another level. We had all just graduated. These niggas were staying, but I was on my way to Detroit to play football for Wayne State University. I didn't need this shit on my conscious, or in my life period.

It was now 2:48 a.m. and we were all in Dante's basement counting up the bread. Three stacks this nigga had on him. That's a lil over $700 a piece, so we came up. However, I still couldn't believe Tez shot him. We all were well aware of everything we had just done, but it didn't sit well with me.

"Tez what's wrong with you?!" I aint even realize how loud I yelled at him until he gave me that stone faced look sitting on the couch.

"Nothin wrong nigga! Shit happens. Man the fuck up!"

"Nigga why...why...**WHY THE FUCK YOU SHOOT HIM FOR?** I bellowed out. Tez jumped off the couch and got in my face, as we had a verbal exchange for the ages. Our partners broke it up, and eventually, Dant regained control of everyone's emotions.

"A look," Dant said with a nervous tone. "The shit happened and its over with. Was it suppose to go down like that, no. But we all brothers. We keeping this shit between us. That's non negotiable. Now, yall two niggas good?"

I gave Tez a stone look. "Yea," I responded. Tez stared a hole through me as well.

"Yea." We all sat back down. We vowed to keep our mouths shut and act like this never happened. Finally, after recounting everything and passing one more blunt around in rotation, we all crashed. I was laying there in Dant's basement that night thinking everything was fine, and that we were getting away scott free. I thought this was like one of those bad dreams that would eventually go away. I started reciting some poetry in my head.

What's done in the dark comes to light
but what if light never arises
what if darkness becomes your new home
and light is a spirit trapped in another realm
your life at the helm of another ship
that is soon to be sunk

Those were random words I thought before I finally drifted off into dream world. I started off a little shabby because of the images in my head, but eventually I started sleeping good. Hell, we were all sleeping good. That was until seven o'clock Sunday morning hit, and we heard niggas kickin in the basement door.

"POLICE DON'T MOVE!" I was shook up on the couch. All I seen was guns in my face and my life gone. I thought about all those crazy ass gangsta flicks I had seen in my day like "Scarface" and "Dead Presidents." The first scene that came to mind was when they came after Larenz Tate and them at the end of the movie. He ran, but eventually he seen he was caught from all sides, and all those officers, and all those guns were just sitting there, ready to unload 100 pounds of lead into his ass. I damn sure didn't want that.

"Don't fucking move!" Those were the words of one of these officers who had snatched me off the couch and had me on the ground with a knee in my neck. I aint say nothing, but I could hear the rest of my partnas talking, yelling to the police "aight, aight," or "calm the fuck down." Talking shit right now to a bunch of nuts who hated us anyway wasn't smart. I just laid there and took it like a man.

They searched each and every one of us, and flipped the basement room upside down. Dant's mom's wasn't here, seeing that she was a fiend herself and was probably somewhere in the gutta passed out. The bright sunlight hit my face with authority as I was escorted out of the house and into the back of a squad car. I saw nosey neighbors, not moving past their doorsteps, as anything black inching towards the scene would probably be taken as a threat. In this country, if its black and it moves in the presence of the police, it usually dies. As I sat in the back of the police unit, I just tilted my head back in self disappointment. I couldn't cry, even though I had wanted too. That little voice in my head was talking to me all night, and all night I ignored it. Now, I was about to pay the consequences for ignoring it.

I glanced out to see J.J. being the last one brought out of the house. He was still struggling in handcuffs, until a baton was introduced into his rib cage. That was the end of that as he was keeled over and basically drug to a patrol car.

"FUCKKKKKK!" I yelled out from the back seat.

"Don't yell fuck out now son. You should've thought about that before y'all did what y'all did." I looked up to see an officer in the front seat. I didn't even hear him come in the car. All I could do was give him a menacing stare, even though I knew it didn't scare him one bit. Working for the Gary Police Department, I am pretty sure he had seen it all and heard it all, so this was probably a walk in the park for him.

In succession, we all took off to the police station. I was fucked and I knew it. Here I was, a kid from the inner city, who was about to go to a four year university. Fully paid for. Possibly with the potential of becoming a great asset to not only society, but to the black community in general, because Lord knows that Gary needed good examples of black men. Hell, the whole black populous of this country needed examples of good black men. Now, it was over. I could do nothing but lower my head in agony and self pity as the sirens began to blare throughout my ear canals as we took off. This car ride would seem like forever I know.

My mama all of a sudden popped into my head. I knew like hell she was gonna be pissed. Not for the fact that I had got caught up in a troublesome situation. She would be pissed because the last son that she had hope for all of a sudden turned into the biggest failure of all time. It was like I was Peyton Manning, and all of a sudden, one incident turned me into Ryan Leaf. Occasionally, I would pop my head up to just look out of the window. I don't know why, but I all of a sudden was having flashbacks.

Suddenly, the modern day 2000's Gary was looking like the 1950's. The first surprise that I seen were white people. That was the biggest shock of my life. Gary used to be largely populated by white people. I saw them outside watering their grass. Kids playing catch around their white picket fences. In another instance, I saw the inside of the legendary Palace Theatre. It was built in 1925 and was once the jewel of G.I. From the history I had read up on it, many, and I mean many entertainers flooded this place back in the days. From live stage shows to general movies showing, that was the spot to be back in the day. I could only imagine how life was back then. Things quickly went back to normal as that vision turned back into reality. I was back staring at ugly ass Broadway. This time, it was broad daylight, so nothing was hidden under the cover of darkness. I wasn't rushing this ride, as I realized that this may be the last ride I ever took. 5th ave seemed so far away, but yet so close. Aaah damn I thought, my life was over.

Immediately, I started to think about my younger days out here. Life used to seem so simple. Things weren't always so complicated out here. I think about when I was five. I couldn't even fathom the thought of truly living yet. But to me, being a kid was the greatest gift of all. The best gift we all had as children was innocence. We knew no better with most situations. We were just trying to have fun. Hide and Go seek, girls jumping rope, red light green light and many more games we played to pass the time by.

Tarrytown wasn't always something to fear in my eyes. I can remember my older brother TY, eleven years my senior, sometimes tooting me around as his lil side dude, making me feel tough hangin with the older guys. Of course I didn't go places with them, but just to be sitting with them on the front porch, or walking down to the liquor store with them to pick up some skins, a pop and some chic-o-sticks made me feel like not a man, but the muthafuckin man. Down the street from me lived my homey Ron. He was cool as a fan. It seemed like he was the swaggerific version of a six year old. How I met him was crazy. There was this one girl named Nicole that I liked a lot.

Well, one day, she chased me when I snuck a kiss on her cheek. I thought it was the funniest thing in the world. That was until I wasn't looking and I ran dead into a fence. As a five year old, that was the equivalent of getting hit by a truck. I withered with screams as I heard Nicole and her friends laughing at me.

"Are you alright?" Still groggy, but done screaming like a banshee, I looked up to meet Ron for the first time. His arm was extended out to give me a hand up. I grabbed it to pull myself up. He dusted me off as if he were my dad or something. "You hit the fence hard. I'm Ron."

From that introduction on, we were cool. We were normal kids who did normal things, until that fateful day years later. Ron was only nine when his life was cut short. He was struck down by a drunk driver after leaving a school function with his mom. The day his funeral procession passed by is a day that is forever etched in my mind. I watched from my mothers car as she was in the grocery store. I was nine as well, but didn't fully understand the concept of death as I do today. After she came out, we went by to visit my grandmother. There, I just dove into my grandmother's arms and cried. The reality of my good friend being gone had hit. How I only wish I could join him in death right now, as I for surely had just killed my life in the physical form.

The car had finally come to a complete stop. I hadn't even realized it at first seeing how deep in thought I was. "I hope you enjoyed your last ride as a free man son," said that prick of an officer. I just stared a hole at him. I couldn't stand this cocky son of a bitch. I was hoping he let me out of these cuffs so I could whoop his ass. On the other hand though, he was a big nigga. One of those big ass, Green Mile built ass niggas. I probably wouldn't have stood a chance.

I was escorted out the car and into the police station. Upon entering, I could feel the eyes on me. It was one thing to look at the people muggin you, but to feel their vision was a whole 'nother level. "Have a seat son. We'll be back shortly," that prick said again, as he un-cuffed me and left me in the room alone.

This shit was crazy. Just some days ago, I had the world at my fingertips. Now, all I had was a table, a chair, a surveillance camera and four white walls. I didn't know where the other three were being placed at and I really didn't care. All I focused on at this moment was my life. And hell, had I been focusing like I should, I wouldn't be in this messed up situation to begin with. I sat at the table and pondered the questions that they were going to ask me. We all seen those cop shows on how the police would steady try to bait you into giving up information, or beat the livin hell out of the suspect as crooked ass laws do, just so they can hear what they wanted to hear. I didn't know what the hell was about to happen. All I know is that I wanted it to be over with as soon as possible.

It's funny. Just weeks ago, I was on cloud nine, prepping for college as a full time student. I had dreams of being a Q dog. I had always been infatuated with George Clinton's song Atomic Dog, and it seemed like every black movie I ever watched had crazy guys in purple and gold, jumping around with their tongues out and going crazy. Yea, I wanted that. I couldn't wait for that. Now I could cancel that. Time can't be rewound, and I was stuck in a difficult place.

Neither writing nor reading could cure my woes. All I wanted was my mama and a bowl of Peanut Butter Captain Crunch. It seemed like that was my remedy for everything growing up. It just made everything go away. That was the joy of being a child. Simple things could cure the biggest woes. Now, simplicity wasn't even the answer.

CHAPTER TWO

BREAKING THE CODE

"When you're alone and all you have is walls to talk
too, you wonder will they listen.
You wonder did the men who scratched their names
in em scratch their spirits as well
I understood when they said walls could talk
but it seemed like they had fallen on deaf ears"

It was a damn shame I was thinking about poetry in an interrogation room, but I pretty much started to prepare myself for a lifetime behind bars. *Why the fuck did I jump in the car with them?* is all I kept thinking. This wasn't me, but I knew why deep down. I was leaving. and the fear of not seeing my partnas anymore was unbearable. I mean let's really look at this. I had an older brother in the system. Two younger brothers working their way towards the system. A struggling mama who lost all her kids but one. A dead father. Last, I had three niggas I called friends who just walked across the stage and didn't receive shit.

I felt alone. I needed that feeling of belonging to something or someone. Maybe that's why I jumped in the car. Damn this though. How the hell did we get caught? Then, I thought about it. On the way back, Tez was searching for his wallet. He had his and Dante's wallet in his pants, seeing that Dant had on some breakaways and didn't have any pockets. Shit I thought. He must've dropped em at the scene. **FUCK!**

"Alright Mr. Jackson. This is Detective Lewis and I'm Detective Davidson." I was screwed. I know they had already talked to my partnas and I was in deep shit. "Now, tell me the events that led up to yesterday's homicide?"

My head started sweating and my heart started pounding. I didn't know what the hell to do. "Do you need some water?" asked Detective Davidson.

"No Sir." I took a deep breath, contemplating whether to be honest, or hold tight to the code of the streets and not snitch. After a five second period that seemed like eternity, I gave em the full story.

"Well sir, Tez called me around 9 o'clock last night asking did I wanna kick it. I told him sure. I mean I'm bout to go off to college to Wayne State and play football on a scholarship. So I wanted to kick it with my boy before I left. Ummm he came and picked me up relatively an hour later. We rode to Sharky's. Got something to eat. A big ass wing dinner to be exact. Umm and then we went to our boy Dante's house. They started smoking and drinking, and around twelve or sometime after that, they started talking about finding someone to rob. I didn't wanna go but...I ended up jumping in the car with them, and that was my mistake I know. Next thing I know, they found someone and he got robbed and shot."

I can't believe what the hell I just did. I just ratted out my partners. I pretty much wrote my death sentence with this one. In the hood, snitchin was a no no, and I just committed the ultimate sin.

"How did the robbery take place?" Davidson asked. I took a deep breath and let it all out.

"Dante was driving and cut him off with the car. We then got out and chased him and caught him. Tez hit him with the gun and knocked him out. We found some money and started to leave. As I went back to the car, I heard a bang. I turned around and seen Tez shot him. I didn't wanna be a part of it and I fucked up sir."

At that moment, I just put my head down and pounded the table three times.

"Give us a minute okay?"

"Yes sir." Now, y'all can call it kissing ass or whatever, but I was trying to cooperate as much as possible to avoid prison time, even though I knew it was unlikely. About four minutes later, they came back in the room along with two uniformed officers.

"Mr. Jackson, you are under arrest and charged with first degree murder." I had nothing to say, as I was cuffed up in preparation to be hauled off to jail. "Before you go sir, there is someone here who has requested to speak to you." I kind of had this crazy look on my face as this officer informed me of this. Who in the good hell was here to see me I thought. The detectives left the room. All of a sudden, I looked up to face the most shocking moment of my life. It was my mom.

I don't know how in the good hell she found out I had been arrested, but she did. She had tears in her eyes as she approached me, reminding me of the only other times I seen her cry, which was when my younger bruhs were hauled away from her.

"Shut up!!!," she said in a muffled voice due to the tears coming down her eyes. She didn't want me saying shit.

"Now, I know I wasn't perfect. I know I made bad choices. I know I didn't give you boys the best choice for a daddy. But G** dammit, I tried. I tried so hard. After three failures, I finally felt I got one right. Now, I felt like I was all wrong. So either I'm a bad mother, or my boys just don't give a shit about life." It was hard for me to look at my mom crying while at the same time speaking in pure anger. "You made your bed, now sleep in it." *POP!* She slapped the shit out of me and then turned around, walking out of the room crying.

I couldn't help but to shed tears as I seen my mom run off. No hug. No kiss. No words of encouragement. Just a bitch slap to the face. It was like she told me goodbye without even saying it. At least that's how I felt. I was led out of the station to the police car. As the door was slammed behind me and we pulled out, I looked up at the ruins of my city. Much like these buildings, my life was now in the same depleted state. They say if walls could talk, they could tell you a million stories. Well, right now, I felt like they were telling me it was over.

A week passed before we all faced a judge. I didn't know, but we were all housed in separate cells. The day before we faced the judge, I was escorted to a closed door meeting with my lawyer and the DA. Sitting nervously in that room, I was given an option. Since all my partners had prior run in's with the law where their rap sheets were a mile long, including J.J.'s assault of a police officer during our junior year, and I was clean, they offered me a deal. If I testified against them, my charge would be reduced to manslaughter instead of capital murder. The most I would look at was two years. This was the hardest decision as a hood nigga I ever had to make. However, as someone who wanted to eventually make something out of himself, I felt it was the right thing. Hesitantly, I signed that plea deal and prepared myself mentally to never enter the city of Gary again.

Funny, coming up, we always talk about what we wouldn't do. Then, when we are put in that situation, we find out that what we thought we would do, it becomes irrelevant. I would be labeled a snitch, but I had to ensure the best possible outcome for my life, even if it involved me selling my friends short. Then, right before I was escorted out of the room, I asked myself. If they were really my friends, then why would they even put me in that situation, knowing that I had a different route that I wanted to go? I didn't know what to do. I was truly confused.

At the actual trial weeks later, I squealed like a pig at the slaughterhouse. I saw the looks on Tez, J.J. and Dant's face, all with the demeanor of dumping my body in the Mississippi River. I felt like the worse man alive, but a new man as well The trial lasted six days before the jury reached their verdict. My three partners were all found guilty of capital murder and sentenced to life in prison. I on the other hand, was found guilty of involuntary manslaughter and given two years in prison, with eligibility for parole at 18 months. They escorted us separately from the courtroom. This shit was the worst. School, gone. Life, gone. Me ever returning to Gary, gone. I was a rat. That's all I thought about. I actually ratted out my day ones. I know if my daddy was alive he would probably kill me himself. So much stuff was running through my mind in the van it didn't even seem real.

I pulled up to a minimum security facility days later in downstate Henryville, near the Kentucky-Indiana border. I didn't know what the hell a Henryville was, or what type of place it was either. It sounded like another one of those small Indiana towns where colored skin isn't allowed. The judge recommended this for me due to the fact of my outstanding education history, no priors and a little something I didn't know until later.

Mr. Wilson, my English Literature teacher from sophomore year wrote a letter to the judge explaining how great of a student and young man I was. Plus, he was related to the District Attorney. That helped out a lot, as the phrase "who you know and not what you know" was now proven as legit. It was the state's way of saying that they know I screwed up, but they seen me as someone who could eventually return to society and make something positive out of myself. I jumped out the van, shackled, under police escorts. I seen some of the prisoners tending to the outside grounds of the facilities stop their work to look up at me. In my head, I thought that even though this said minimum security, that big house shit still went down in here. My main focus besides doing my time and getting out was protecting my ass. Literally and physically. We all heard the horror stories about prison, and I did not want to become someone's bitch while in there.

I made it through in processing and was escorted to my dorm style accommodation for the next two years. Amidst the stares towards the new guy, everything seemed like peaches and cream. To tell you the truth, it seemed like I was at more of a country club than anything. A door was open, and I just stared inside for a minute, noticing the doubled up beds, with my cellmate taking his eyes off a book to get a glance at me.

"Welcome to your new home. Get comfortable." That was the guards final words to me as he locked the door behind me, sheets in hand. I said what's up to my celly, but to no response. He just looked at me and cut his eyes back to his book. Great I thought. I already made an enemy and I didn't even know the nigga. He was young just like me. I wouldn't put him over the age of 25. He probably was trying to have a big dick contest to see who was the baddest. I didn't want that though. All I wanted to do was serve my time and get on with life. Making this top bunk, he all of a sudden climbed out his bottom bunk and started talking out loud in spoken word form:

When you unite for a cause
they stop and pause
the best way to rip out a community's heart
is to take out his balls
cause balls contain seeds to form the next generation
and if they can't be formed from a proper father
that's when you have bastard seeds
birthed from the mothers
who let those bastards inside her walls

I had paused all I was doing and jumped down from my bed. Me and this cat was face to face, staring each other down. I noticed his demeanor. His fully tattered up arms told a story, even though I didn't know what was inked on him besides the huge black panther tattoo covering his left forearm with a five pointed star.

He stood about two inches taller than me, with Jesus dreads and he was pretty solid. So this is the life inside these walls I thought. It was like we were talking to each other without any words being spoken. Slowly, he threw up a Vice Lord sign, and I responded to it through speech.

"Born through CVL
in a hell that the devil would be jealous of
literature known of old essence
new generation has no essence or no discretion
never heard of Bobby Gore
to them he is just folklore, another name
lost my daddy to the gang
but he was lost as well
he didn't know unification of CVL, Stones and
Growth and Development
now we develop our minds to intertwine
and become one"

We just stared at each other. I slowly threw up the Vice Lord sign back and stated my peace.

"My daddy was CVL. I followed in his footsteps, but I respected the movements of all the organizations, especially ours. The true movement. Not the drug movement. Not the seek and destroy your own people movement. I mean what it stood for. I'm Carl." He extended his hands to shake up.

"Mike." I didn't know what was about to happen between us, nor with anyone else in the facility. However, I could see that I had found a brother who was intellectually gifted like myself. When I say that, I'm not talking anything from America's souped up textbooks. I'm talking about the knowledge that they didn't want us to know. We rapped for the next hour or so. I swear I had found my twin brother from another mother. Mike came out of Laporte, Indiana, about a twenty five minute drive outside of Gary. He was raised in Chicago for most of his life. At age fifteen, he watched his life flip upside down in one night. He explained how he was coming home from the courts in his Lawndale neighborhood, a Vice Lord haven.

He noticed the black smoke blocks away, but didn't think much of it. The closer he got to the crib though, he could see it was coming from his block. About two blocks out, he ran towards the crib, hoping his wasn't the one on fire. As he hit W. Roosevelt road, he was stopped dead in his tracks as he watched his grandmother's house burn. The rage poured as he tried to beat through firefighters and police screaming **"GRANDMA!,"** repeatedly. As the flames died and the smoked cleared, a new fire raged in his soul, as he eventually seen his grandmother's lifeless body wheeled out.

I knew how serious this affected him as his face became mixed with sadness and rage at the same time. As he continued, word got around that some GD's bombed his grandmother's house by mistake, thinking it was that of a rival they were trying to get at. He was associated with Vice Lord's at first. After that happened, he became full fledged and took it to another level. His first major initiation was getting back at the GD's for what they had done. The look in his eyes and the demeanor in his voice gave me a chilling tale of that fateful night.

"Imagine being fifteen Joe. Losing your grandmother. The woman who took you in. This after never knowing your father, and losing your mother to drugs at age eleven. Imagine you feeling like you have nothing else to lose. We crept into Englewood that night. I was the youngest cat in the car, with two other OG's. When they gave me that Glock 40, I felt like the power of the world was in my hand." Mike paused for a minute before he went on. I could tell this was about to get drastic.

"I...I don't know who was inside of me, but when we hit 61st & South Lowe Ave., I saw a gang of those niggas chillin, and I knew it was time. I cut loose and watched those fools scatter like roaches. Two of em dropped. I dunno about the rest cause we skidded off so damn fast. Whether those niggas were dead or not, I aint stay around to find out. I just felt like I was relieved for what those fools did. Then again now that I look back at it, it still didn't bring my grandma back. So now I ask myself. Did I really get revenge, or did I really hurt myself in the process?"

I stared at him for a minute. I was trying to comprehend what this man had dealt with. Hell, at least I had my mama and my daddy for some time. He never knew one, and the other passed on way too soon. He told the story how he dropped out and made his rounds around the Chi. Eventually, one of his partners got into construction in the LaPorte area, and he made that move. Construction was cuttin it, but to a street nigga, especially an 18 year old, it wasn't enough. He started to run weed up and down I-90/94, until he eventually got caught. He was ratted out by the same brother who got him in the gig.

Due to the amount of weed he was supplying and distributing, he was looking at some substantial time. However, a plea deal reduced his sentence to a measly two years, one of which he had already completed.

"So what's yo story Joe?" he asked as he leaned back in his chair as if to be entertained. What the hell was I gonna do I thought? I mean, I couldn't let him know I snitched out my partners. I know hood rules also applied to the joint, even if this was more of a country club.

"I got caught up in some shit. In short, I hit a lick with some of my partnas, things went wrong, a man got killed and we all went down. They doing life." That's when he sat back, rubbed his chin and looked like he was doing some serious thinking.

"So why you aint doing life?" In the quickest response of my life to a question, I told him.

"I had no priors. They all did. I was a 3.8

student. They made rocks look smart. I got recommendations from several people. They aint get shit. I ended up with a charge of being an accomplice to murder, but took a deal if I pleaded guilty to being there, I would get a manslaughter charge. Did that, now I'm here."

I said that cool, calm and collective. Inside, I felt like a punk. I lied to possibly avoid confrontation, and was all out bogus. Mike crossed his arms and just stared at me. I was sure he seen through the bullshit I had thrown at him. I knew he was just about to expose me.

"A Joe," he stated. "You did what you had to do. You took a plea. I took a plea. It is what it is. Now, we gotta make something better for ourselves." I was relieved by that, even though inside I knew I was a fraud. To be honest, I knew he knew that I was one too, but he more than likely had other plans on his mind than bringin the streets inside these four walls. We shook up and continued to rap with each other for the rest of the night until it was lights out.

That next year went by without incident. Over that time, I had taken some college courses, got into a spiritual revival group led by the prison Chaplain that discussed how to be positive and keep the Lord first, and continued to work my lil prison job of kitchen duty. Mike had bounced out a while ago and was now living in Naptown with some family members. From the letters that we wrote back and forth, and the frequent calls, I could see that he had rehabilitated himself to the fullest. He got his certification as an auto mechanic and had started working at a garage on the Eastside of town, making legal money. I was proud of him. He gave me the motivation that I needed to reach for my goals the minute I got out. My goals? My goals? Damn I thought. One night made my life take a turn for the worse. I was the lone star player on a high school football team that sucked.

I mean, Indiana is a basketball state, with some decent football teams. When it came to football, I aint gone lie, Gary sucked balls. A few athletes on the squads, but as teams, we were practice dummies to all other high schools. Especially to our main rivals East Chicago Central. In basketball, we always gave them a run. In football, the towel boy could rush for 150 yards on us with no pads. I really played to try and keep my mind focused on something positive, but I ended up being good enough to receive a scholarship. I would be playing Division II ball, but so what. That was gone now, and it was all my fault.

Now, I had a little under a year to figure out what I was going to do with my life. I was scared to return to Gary, because I know word had got out what I did. I wanted to go somewhere different, but I didn't have too much family in good areas. The ones I knew that lived in good areas, we weren't that close. I was really stuck between a rock and a hard place. I crept to bed one night and just pondered everything. 11 months and 17 days left before I was to be released, and I had no clue what I was going to do. Just then, I prayed to God.

"Lord, please open a door for me to prosper in life again. Allow me to correct my wrong." I closed my eyes and drifted off into my imaginary world. August 23, 2011. This was the next day.

"Jackson wake up." That was the guards words as he started beating on my door. "The warden wants to see you."

I slowly put my hands out of the mailbox sized hole in the door. Even though this was minimal security, they still had to take precaution when escorting inmates solo to the boss man. You never know with people. Hell, even people who were living in prisons version of a country club could snap off at any time. I took this long walk down these long halls wondering what in the good hell did the warden want to see me for.

I hadn't done anything wrong. I hadn't misbehaved, so I was truly confused as to why this meeting was about to occur. This was too much like when my daddy died and I got called to the principals office, so I knew it was bad news coming. We got to the Warden's door.

"C'mon in," he said. I mean damn, you can tell this guy was indeed from the backwoods by that heavy ass country accent he had. He had six deer heads lining his office wall, so I could tell he was an avid outdoorsman. Award upon award and three college degrees lined the back wall behind his desk. I had always seen "Johnny Poon" around the facility, but never once stepped foot into his office.

"Uncuff him Richard and step outside for a bit." Rich uncuffed me and I took a nervous seat. "Carl," in that country accent of his he said.

"You have been extraordinary in your time here. I have seen a lot of minor first time offenders come in, only to get out and end up in the real big house. However, I think you have what it takes to make something special out of your life. How's this sound?"

He handed me a brochure in an envelope. I held it in my hand as we locked eyes for about three seconds. In that time, I thought to myself maybe, just maybe it was a letter from Wayne State, telling me that they would give me another chance. Hell I was only 20, so I still had plenty of life ahead of me. I opened it up.

"The Navy? Why in the good hell did you give me a Navy brochure sir?" I couldn't believe this. A closed door meeting to give me a brochure to join the Navy. Was he serious?

"Sir, isn't this where all the gay men of America go?" The Warden burst out into a laugh as if he were watching a Bernie Mac stand up. What he didn't know is that I was dead serious.

"Carl, as he started to contain himself, I served six distinguished years in The World's

Greatest Navy. It opened doors for me that I could never have imagined. As a kid growing up on a farm in Frankfurt, Indiana, I would have never thought on my best day that I would one day become a warden over a prison even if it is quote on quote a country club. Now, I have a great guy who happens to recruit for this fine organization. They need good men to man these ships and we need forces to kick the asses of all enemies foreign and domestic. We need people who will be leaders and defend this great nation. We need people like you." He pointed his finger at me with that last sentence and just held it there. I didn't know what the hell to think.

"So what's the catch sir."

"Carl, there is no catch. Either you can agree to join and be released early, or you can finish out the rest of your time and try you luck in the world around July. April or May 2012 if you qualify for early release. Its up to you, but I see so much potential in you to become something great."

"What about my criminal record sir?"

"That will be all taken care of son." I really started to think now. I had never been outside of Indiana. All I knew was Gary and this hole I was stuck in down here.

"Tell you what Carl. I'll give you the night to think it over. You're dismissed. C'mon in Rick." Rick came in and cuffed me, escorting me back to my cell, which was more of a dorm room as I stated earlier. I laid on that barely bigger than a coffin bed and pondered the thought of military life. All the stuff I seen on TV. Hell, I ain't wanna be shot at. I aint wanna be gettin yelled at and spat in my face. I would be nuts to go put myself through that. Just then though, I remembered something an OG from back home told me. Actually, he was a wino, but it seemed like they gave the best life advice on how not to screw up, seeing that they screwed up so much.

As I came out the liquor store one day as a youngin buying some chic-o-sticks, he said "Baby boy. Do what you don't wanna do to get where you wanna go."

I remember him taking a hit of the bottle after that and passing out right there on the curb. Funny how something you thought was so meaningless could become meaningful later on in life. I ate dinner, wrote some poetry and drifted off into the night contemplating this decision. The next morning, I was escorted into the Warden's office at my request.

"Sir, I'm ready to take the next step." As I finished spewing out those words and observing the smile on "Johnny Poons" face, all I could think was one thing. *What in the good hell did I just do?*

I started my process to join the service. Ol Johnny brought the recruiter in and talked to me about the life. It sounded good, but I was boo boo the fool to believe everything he was telling me. I heard how they yell at you, spit at you, slap you and all that. He wasn't preaching none of that. He was spewing out that one team, one fight bullshit. I wasn't buying it, but I damn sure bought the idea of getting out of here early. I took an asvab test about the second week of August and scored a 76. From what he explained, that was high and qualified me for a lot of jobs. However, I guess due to their quota, I was offered three gigs. A nuclear technician, a cook or a welder. I hated the kitchen, and I didn't wanna radiate my nuts so I couldn't have kids later. I took the welder job, even though I didn't know a damn thing about that either.

Over the next few weeks, I completed my physical evaluation at the military entrance processing station. I swore in and was due to ship out to boot camp on October 29, 2011. It seemed so far away, but the time ticked down. Until then, I was still a product of the state, so I couldn't slip up. I managed to increase my workout regimen all the way up until the final few weeks of October. Even the warden gave notice one day when he seen me in the prison gym as he made his rounds.

"Damn Carl! Look like you getting those GAINZ!" When you first came in you looked like a weiner dog named Justin who humped bear feet for a living. Now, you look like a stacked shit of a brick house that was built in Tuscaloosa, Alabama." I don't know where the hell he developed that crazy logic from, but I nodded in agreeance and kept going.

The time was finally here. October 28th, I was granted my release by the State of Indiana. I was driven off prison grounds for the last time to the hotel which would be my final rest place before I would fly out tomorrow to Chicago. My only thoughts were that it was great to sleep in a real bed before I left. I did nothing much that night but savor that moment. Oh, I also smashed a thick white girl who I met at MEPS. I hadn't had no ass in about two years, so to get that nut off felt great. The next afternoon came with the quickness and I was taken to the airport.

I was flying out of Indianapolis to Chicago O'Hare. Once I arrived, I was greeted by three gentlemen in uniform. In a nice way, I was pretty much told to follow instructions and shut the hell up. I ended up sitting butterfly style with a bunch of other future military men and women, waiting for the bus to arrive. It seemed like eternity, but finally it showed. We were escorted on to the bus, told to remain quiet and we took off for Recruit Training Command Great Lakes. Again, I started to think: *What in the hell did I get myself into?*

CHAPTER THREE

<u>RECONCILIATION AND REVENGE</u>

Boot camp went by without major incident. I mean, I had stressed myself out so much thinking that it was going to be hell on Earth, but it turned out that it wasn't that bad at all. I mean really, all you had to do was be everywhere on time, listen to orders, fold your clothes, make you bed and you were good. Sure, you dealt with the occasional ass chewing to your face or some other crazy ass physical training session, but besides that, that shit was cake.

Some good stories did arise out of that experience though. With me included, there were five bruhs in my division. This cat named Boston from Georgia. Gladden from North Carolina. Geter was from South Carolina.

Burwell was from Jersey. Anywho, so our division commanders marched us to the store from time to time. Well, on one trip, we all got us some du rags. I mean they had these damn Filipino barbers fucking our fades up, so we did what we had to do to get our waves back. Man one night, we threw our joints on as usual, but we forgot to take em off in the morning. Our Chief, a brotha from Florida, came in, caught us and drilled our assed for what seemed like forever.

We also had this one chick from New York who was supposed to be on security duty one Saturday night. Well, she got caught writing her boyfriend a letter instead of being at her post. Our female division commander woke us up at the crack of dawn and exercised all of our asses, male and female, until we were damn near blue in the face. That was really the worse shit that happened. Besides that, like I said, it was cake.

After those nine weeks finished up, I went right across the street to the Naval Training Command to start school, learning how to become a welder. I would be up here for about six months, so I had to make the most of it before I really had to get on official military duty. In that time, I completely cut the damn fool. I swear this was more like college than a military installation. I mean we went to school for 8 hours a day, and after that, we were free to do whatever we wanted. We had a club on base, a bowling alley, a few more kick back spots, not to mention Chi-town was just a train ride away. When I say it was party central up in that joint, it truly was. I don't know how many fine sisters from every corner of the world I met, but I do remember how many of em I knocked down. Being cooped up in a prison for over a year, my sex drive was on a hundred thousand trillion. Everything had looked good to me.

If it had a pussy, I wanted it. Well, not everything. I mean there were some straight ducks walking around that joint as well. Not to mention there were just some chicks who looked like they should've been pushed back in after their mama squirted them out. The women, that was just one part, like I said. There was also the typical hood nigga shit that occurred.

There were fights in the club all the damn time. You woulda swore wasn't none of us in the military as cats scrapped like they were back home. This is what happens when you take every brother from every hood and put em in one establishment. You were begging for confrontation.

There was even a drug bust in there one night where they let the dogs loose. It was like Gary, Indiana, except it was surrounded by barbed wire. Gary, Indiana damn. I wish like hell I could go back. I wish I could just go see my mama. I knew I couldn't though. People were probably waiting on me to come back, just so they could separate my skull from my spine. I hadn't spoke to my mom in damn near two years. She didn't call or visit me while I was locked up. I knew she was pissed, but it really did hurt. I needed her love because she was all I had left in this world. My mama really did the best that she could with all of us. I mean, for a woman to face the predicaments she faced, she did a damn good job.

What happened with all of us wasn't her fault. As young men, we were all well aware of the decisions that we made. Sure, you could use age as an excuse, but that wasn't the case. The listening factor is what got us in the mess that we were in. Trust, its a difference between listening and hearing. Me and my brothers, we heard a lot from the elders. We just didn't listen.

The beginning of May rolled around and I was about a week away from graduating weld school.

"Jackson," my instructor barked out while we were lined up in formation one day. I stepped out of line to grab the papers he had in his hand. As he gave them to me, he bellowed "Congrats, you're going to Cali." I had to let those words sink in to my head. *California? Did this man really just say California?* After we dismissed from quarters (formation), I calmly walked to the corner of the classroom, took a seat and read over everything. USS NIMITZ CVN 68. That was my future destination. I didn't know what it was, so I decided to look it up. I went down to the computer room and googled it. Lo and behold, it was one of those big ass carriers. It said it could hold somewhere close to 6,000 people. What the hell I thought? Why in the good hell would I want to be on a steel ship with 6,000 other men? Man, I know they say The Navy was full of homo juice, but I damn sure didn't wanna sip that shit.

My day had completely been shot. This was that bullshit. I didn't want to go to a huge ass ship. Furthermore, I didn't want to go to California. On our request sheet they gave us about 3 months in, I picked Hawaii and Florida. I wanted to be in the tropical part of the world. I knew Florida would be full of women, so a brother had to get down there. Cubans, Dominicans, Ricans, all of that was down in the Sunshine State. Hawaii, well, who didn't want to go to Hawaii? All the commercials that I seen on that place. I was anxious as hell to get there and get with a few of those girls in coconut skirts.

I wanted to travel the beaches of Waikiki, eat me some good ol pulled pork and I wasn't an avid swimmer, but a brother wanted to surf at least one time on the legendary North Shore. However, the Navy decided to stick me in California. What in the good hell was I gonna do out there? All I could think about was Bloods, Crips and Mexicans with high ass white socks and dickie shorts. I would have to change colors everywhere I went. I aint wanna deal with that, nor no undercover brothers. I heard about Cali dudes in San Francisco. The way I seen it, that's how they all were. I kept reading further to see that my ship was homeported in San Diego. It didn't matter to me, because if Frisco was full of gay dudes, Diego would be full of the same. I didn't want this shit. This was gonna be miserable I thought. Besides that though, I had bigger fish to fry.

My ship was deployed to the Persian Gulf already for some of The United States usual, which was taking care of things overseas instead of on the homefront. I would meet them out there. That wasn't my biggest personal battle though. It was only May 29th, and I wasn't scheduled to leave on a plane until June 20th. The question that was pondering inside of my head was how would I go home and enjoy some much needed down time, when probably the whole hood would be at my head for doing what I did?

I lied in my bed and thought long and hard about it that night. It was one thing to be going into a war zone for the first time in my life. However, I may not survive the urban war zone if I went back. My mama probably wouldn't let me back in the house, and the only other family I had out there that I could call were a few cousins out in East Chicago on my daddy's side. I had my mama's peoples out there too, but our relationship was off and on, seeing that mama usually kept us away from her folks. Some shit had went down way before I was born, so me and her side really didn't get to kick it like that. This was gonna be something to really ponder. As I drifted off to sleep, I started to recite another piece in my dome.

"Bullet fragments and gunsmoke
cause a cloudy haze that covers the sun
which once rose to give life
but also sets when darkness lurks around the
corner
the corner isn't safe anymore
as days of sidewalk tic-tac-toe
were replaced with chalk outlines
of the ones that were financially declined
but inclined to poverty"

The following morning I made a call to my cousin "Snap" out in EC (East Chicago). He was surprised like hell to hear from me. He knew I was in the joint, but he didn't know I had been released, nor that I snitched on my partnas. We chopped it up for a good while, well over an hour and a half to be exact. I told him that a brotha was about to head off to The Middle East real soon and that I would need a place to crash, seeing that my mama was still upset with me for getting into negativity. He agreed, and he was gonna pick me up from the South Shore station on June 1st. I was relieved like a live chicken that didn't get picked out at a black folks bbq to go swimming in the fryer. I could lay low in EC and just be easy until the day I would fly out of O'Hare and begin my new life. That's if I made it through the next twenty something days.

The 1st came around with no qualms. I spent my last night on base kickin it with homies I went to school with, saying my goodbyes and all that other shit. I was pretty sure I would see them again, since my instructors constantly beat into our heads that the Navy was small. I arrived at the South Shore station in EC a little after 12 in the afternoon. I didn't mess around in this city too much, seeing that I was damn near stuck in Gary 90% of the time growing up. Even so, I knew EC wasn't a place to mess around in anyway.

These fools were just as crazy as Gary niggas, if not worse. They were right on the Indiana border, mere minutes from big city Chi, so they had the same mentality. Hell, they had an even worse mentality being the city in the middle of Chi and G.I. They felt everyone overlooked them because they weren't considered major. However, if you fucked with them, your family would find your body buried under one of the mills. Trust me when I tell you that East Chicago was not to be fucked with.

"Cuz whats good," Snap greeted me with some dap and a negro hug.

"Aint shit cuz. A nigga just happy to be on chill mode." He took one of my bags as we went to the car and just chopped it up bout the Navy life. I told him bout the little stories on base, the hoes and he just cracked up.

"A lil cuz, lets roll to go get something to eat. Catch up a lil bit." That sounded good with me. We rolled over to a joint called Petros out in neighboring Hammond, not to far from the train station. I had been here a few times before. As a youngin, my daddy would take me here. He always had two or three others bruhs with him every time we came. Being grown now, I knew that was his drug connects. As a youngin, I just thought they were cool partners that he had always rolled with.

I really missed my dad. I mean, I know he didn't exactly live the holy roller life, but he was still my pops and he still was there for a brother, even if we didn't have the typical father-son relationship. Me and cuz ordered some omelettes and got to choppin it up. I told him about how Henryville was more of a country club than a prison. I went through the whole spill about everything, from meeting Mike, to the warden getting me out early to join the service. In the midst of me giving my story, cuz stopped me in mid sentence.

"What I wanna know is how did you get out of a life sentence and those other three niggas didn't?" I just paused. In my head, it seemed like time stood still. I had kept what happened inside of me for quite a while. It was time to finally get this drama off of my soul.

"Cuzzzz?," Snap motioned. "What happened? And be real with me. I'm yo cuz nigga." I took one huge ass gulp of that omelette and just came with it.

"I'm a rat cuz. I ratted on my partnas and struck a deal." Snap drop his fork on the plate and gave me this look of disdain. He literally was piercing a hole thru me. Snap was seven years my senior and certified out here. He was from The West Calumet Complex projects, a Vice Lord Haven. Those boys didn't play over there. To them it was the W-C-C. To outsiders, it stood for "With Caution Complex," cause that's exactly how you entered if you went over there. With caution.

"We'll talk about this when we get back to the house cuz. These white folks in here don't need to hear this shit. Gone finish up and tell me bout those hoes in yo school." I could tell cuz was upset. He lived by the code of the streets. However, he still knew I was family and cared enough to want to know what was steady going on in my life. We talked a lil more, he paid the bill and headed out that joint back to EC. The car ride back to EC felt like more of a drive to my death sentence.

"Cuz, I love you, but you in violation like a muthafucka. You know damn well if y'all all get caught, y'all all take the fall. You ratted. You copped the plea. You wasn't an innocent ass on stand by who just seen stuff go down. You wasn't none of that. You was **A MUTHAFUCKA involved!**" I was feeling terrible, but cuz wasn't through.

"Hear me my nigga. **YOU WAS INVOLVED!** I can't co-sign the shit at all, but you still family. You were young and scared. I get that. Know though, just know if we weren't famo, I'd greenlight ya ass on sight. And that's on **ALMIGHTY!**"

I felt the biggest knot in my throat at that point. This nigga loved me, but I know he wasn't bullshittin. We were almost back to the projects, and all I could do was look out of the window. Even my own flesh and blood looked at me as a soft ass. This shit was irking the hell out of me. I felt like I wasn't even what I thought I was. Gangstas don't snitch. Gangstas take the charge.

How could I even claim some shit and I didn't live it properly? Just then, I thought about Mike and the look he gave me when I first told him the story. I knew he knew, but he didn't wanna put himself in a position to get his time extended, so he left it alone. We finally got to cuz crib and pulled up in the driveway. He shut the car off and began to talk.

"Listen lil cuz," in a soft, yet somber voice. "I love you. I do. That aint gone never change. I knew ever since you were a youngin, you were a lil smart muthafucka. I mean shit..I had a feeling you would try to emulate your daddy, but you gotta realize, everything aint for everybody. I don't like this life I'm in. I gotta look over my shoulder everyday. This drug shit can only get you so far. I wanna get out of this area one day, on some real shit.

Right now though, this is what's keeping me eatin. This is what's keeping my son fed. I don't want him to know his daddy as a dealer. He only three, but he gotta grow up sometime. Remember what I'm tellin you. Be about the life you living now. Don't try to be about something you think makes you tougher. It only gets you in the grave or sent upstate, downstate or wherever the fuck they put the jailhouse at, I can't count how many funerals I seen. It's crazy too.

All these niggas were just like me. At the funeral though, ahh shit, all those niggas is angels. They didn't do no wrong. Everybody crying and shit like the muthafucka was an innocent bystander or some shit. Same nigga they crying for is the same nigga I rode out with when we hunted our enemies and knocked em down for permanent dirt naps. No matter how gangsta I am, I recognize this shit. When the last time you talked to you moms?" I paused and took a deep breath.

"My moms aint talked to me since I left. Even when I called for the last year and some change, she never would pick up. I think she hate me." We stared at each other for about a good ten seconds.

"C'mon cuz. Let's go put yo stuff in the house." We got in the house and cuz escorted me to my upstairs room which would be my crash site until I bounced. I pulled out everything I needed and just relaxed on the bed for a minute. I thought about that talk with cuz. I thought about my life in general. Just then Snap holla'd,

"CUZ COMMERE!" I walked downstairs to see cuz holding his phone out. "Here, someone wanna talk to you." I grabbed it.

"Hello?" There was an eerie silence. "Hello," I said again.

"Come see me baby. It's been long overdue." I just burst out into tears as cuz grabbed the phone from my hands. To hear that my moms wanted to see me meant the world to me. She was so distraught from me getting caught up in bullshit that she completely cut me off. Now, she was willing to reconcile and see her son. The only son she had that wasn't in some type of institution right now. Cuz helped me up and whispered lets go. We headed to the car and my heart didn't stop beating under 150 miles per hour. I was on the way to see my mama. I wondered how this shit was gonna go.

Time waits for no one
Unless you are that no one
you aint think bout that

We hit that long stretch of road between East Chicago and Gary. I hadn't seen this in such a long time. It was damn near like I was entering a foreign country. The Gary/Chicago airport still sat there on the right side of the road. I swear as long as I lived here, I never remembered anyone ever flying out of that thing. It was like they just put it there for decoration to say, "Here, we got something every major city got, but we don't use this muthafucka."

We kept rollin on past the airport. As I looked to my left, I saw the remnants of the old Club Tops. That was one of the strip clubs in my city. All I could do was laugh, cause I swear it was everyone's first experience in seeing a naked girl shaking their ass. Me and a few cats from high school went up in that joint my junior year of high school.

We were so excited that we forgot that this was Gary, Indiana, a.k.a. Scary Gary. The strippers looked very scary and like they had caught bullets in their ass cheeks. Some of them looked like they hadn't seen a dentist in some years, as rows of teeth did the electric slide in their mouths. That was the young days, and I missed em dearly. We kept rollin until we were rollin past 4th avenue. My heart started to beat heavily. I was nervous as hell. I had the feeling like a million eyes were on me, even though I really didn't see anyone outside. I was just waiting for a bullet to come flying through the window. I tried to block out the negative thoughts inside of my mind and just concentrate on seeing my mama, but it was damn near impossible.

Finally, we turned down the street where Tarry Town liquors was at. I was almost home. I was almost back on the block. I was almost dead in my mind. We got to the front of the house. Immediately, I noticed two tinted out cars a few houses down. Everything pretty much looked the same, but that shit was weird.

"Cuz," Snap said. "Dont worry bout shit. I got my partnas in these whips in case some shit pop off. Gone in there and make amends with ya mom."

I remained cool on the outside, but inside, I took a deep sigh of relief. At least I know someone was watching my back while I was over here. I stepped out the car, looking at this beat up green house I spent my entire life in. The steps I took leading up to my mamas front door seemed perilous. As Snap led the way, I turned around to notice one of the cats in the tinted out chevy has his windows down now. He nodded his head up at me as if to say,

"I got you." I turned back the other way and saw a crib across the street boarded up. It probably was a crack house that the police shut down. I looked the other way and saw another abandoned home. Damn, shit had really changed. I aint saying the hood wasn't already fucked up, but it looked like in the last two years, someone came thru and let off a mini nuke. Vines were growing up the sides of some houses and many of em just looked lifeless from the outside.

Snap rung the doorbell. No answer. After bout 20 seconds, he rang it again. Suddenly, I saw the door knob fiddle. The door opened, and it was my mama. We just stared at each other. There she was, all 5'3, 139 pounds of her. She was in her typical house wear of sweats, an old T-shirt and a scarf. She had a cigarette in hand. They say a person's eyes can tell a story, but the look we were giving each other told many stories.

"Hey mom," I let out in a faint whisper. She put the square to her mouth to take another puff. She looked me up and down in the process. *Great* I thought. *I came all this way just for my mama to ignore me.*

"You've grown a lot I see," she said. "Gotta lil bit of muscle on you keeping those men off your ass in there I see." Just then, she flicked the cigarette into the lawn and extended her arms out towards me. We embraced in a hug that said more than any conversation could ever say.

"C'mon in baby." We all followed moms into the house. "Snap baby, there's some fish, spaghetti, greens, cornbread, some turkey necks smothered in gravy and some grape kool aid in the fridge. Make yo'self at home baby."

Snap darted into the kitchen without saying a word, and left me and moms by ourselves. I was acting nervous as hell. She looked me up and down with a typical mama look.

"C'mon downstairs boy. Let's talk." We walked down to the basement and immediately memories started to come back into my soul. I remember I got my first piece of ass down here when I was fifteen. Moms was at work one evening, and it was this cold freshman cheerleader. We had chopped it up for a while. She was a virgin. I was a virgin. That was all we needed to know and I got my first piece. She also domed me up that night.

I also started to think about all the time me and my brothers would be down here wrestling on old mattresses. Like I said, we aint have much, but we made the best out of everything that we had. Knowing that none of them were around kind of hurt. I sat on the couch and the converstation started.

"So baby, what's been goin on? I heard you going to the Navy," as she lit up another square.

"Yea mom. I got a deal to let me out early if I joined so I took it." She nodded her head up and down, square pressed firmly to her lips as she took another puff.

"Mom, can I ask you something?"

"Go head baby." I took a deep breath.

"Why didn't you reach out to me while I was gone? It was like you abandon me and forgot I was your son." She nodded her head up and down as she took one last puff of her Newport, then put it out. Then, she would give me the motherly rant that I would never forget.

"Put yourself in my shoes Carl." That's when I knew she was about to say something relevant because she called me Carl and not baby.

"You raise four boys. Four young men. One daddy for all of em. Not the best choice, but you deal with the decision you make. I can't lie, your daddy had me whipped. Even though I knew he did what he did, that man had me gone in the head. I think it was his charm that kept me around. I mean, he never abandoned y'all, and he was there. I will give him that. However, I know I could've chosen better for my sons. Anyway picture the four best gifts you ever received, ever.

Now imagine them getting snatched away from you over time. Ya older brother in the Fed system. The other two knuckleheads in juvie. Wait, take that back. One is in juvie and now the other, ya brother Curtis is headed to the big house cause he couldn't get his act together. I looked at you and thought maybe, just maybe, this one gone make it. Carl, my lil skinny man Bones Carl Lamell Jackson. You had it all. I seen you when you was lil. Reading all those books and shit. I don't even think you knew what you were reading half the time. But you loved to read. I saw something special in you. You kept ya grades reasonable for a boy whose daddy wasn't in the house and whose mama seemed to be always at work. You did all that. Went to parties, hung out with friends and I never heard anything negative come out of anyone's mouth about you.

I saw you sometimes with ya hat broke off to the left, thinkin you were a big bad gangsta, Almighty Vice Lord, but still, I never thought much of it. I thought to myself..my son he is bigger than that. He wont get caught up. Then in one fell swoop...*pow* (claps hands), one mistake. One damn mistake, and the one with a gift has ruined his whole life." She puffed her square again.

"I was mad. Oh boy was I mad. I couldn't believe it. I thought to myself...*the boy is about to go to college.* I aint never been to college. I know I wasn't book smart on the level you were. I said wow, my boy is gonna make it out of Gary. He wasn't going to IU Northwest or some Ivy Tech bullshit. He was headed out of state. Full ride." She took another puff of the square.

"When I got that call that morning, I felt like a complete failure. I cried and cried because I thought I had at least got it right with one. But it didn't happen. I felt like you abandoned me." As she puffed the square again, she then continued.

"Then, I thought about it after I left you at the police station for the last time. The parent sets the example for the child. I failed you. I failed you in so many ways. Worst than that, I gave up on my child when no parent is supposed to ever do that. Because no matter where you go, or how successful or messed up you end up, you still my child, and I still love you dearly. So son, mama apologizes for leaving you behind these last two years. It will never happen again. I am proud that you got the chance to bounce back. All I ask is that you learn from my mistakes and continue on the path you on. Mama living her life. It may not be the life I want, but its the life I'm living and I have to deal with it. Now, you gotta do what's best for Carl, and only Carl."

I sat in awe at everything my mama had just said. I soaked it in. This woman, with all she had went through, did her damn best. Everyone has breakdowns. I was no longer upset that she didn't wanna talk to me for the past couple of years.

"Mama…all I can say is I'm sorry. I'm sorry." We looked at each other. More so, she looked like she was staring a hole in me. Moms took a puff of her square, closed her eyes and nodded her head.

"I forgive you baby. It's done, and we moving on." She put her cigarette out and we embraced in a hug that reconnected our spirits more than our souls. We talked for about a whole 'nother hour. I also had my first home cooked meal in two years. I swear my moms made the best damn spaghetti on this side of the Mississippi. After a few more hours of chillin, along with my mama going off on Snap for going in the cabinet and eating her last pack of Ritz peanut butter crackers, we rolled out.

We got back to Snap house 'round 7 that evening. It was a chill summer evening. This felt great. I was back in the 219 chillaxin. I had reconnected with my moms, cuz let me in his home and I was on my way overseas real soon. We sat back for the rest of the night just choppin it up while watching Menace to Society. The sounds of negroes blasting their music outside took the air over. I didn't know the group, but I remember one line vividly.

"I'm shootin at every car that look suspicious I aint bullshittin/I'm high powered/giving yall chill like yall ass took a cold shower/we devour you cowards with big guns."

I don't know who that was, but that shit went hard. Snap was blazin up. It smelled good, but it wasn't no way in hell I was gonna screw up my chance at a new life. Hell, I never cared for smokin' to tell you the truth. Eleven o'clock rolled around and I was dead tired. Snap had already passed out on the downstairs couch. I headed upstairs to drift off into dream world myself. As I lie under the covers, I could do nothing but smile. God has an amazing way of restoring things. My relationship was rekindled with my mom. This was the joy of my damn life. I didn't have much close fam around, seeing that a lot of em were on the wrong side of the law. To have her and Snap again though, I was gravy like smothered chicken. Speaking of family, I wondered what the hell the rest of them that weren't in jail were doing. I closed my eyes to indulge in a great sleep.

"WAKE THE FUCK UP CUZ! NIGGA WAKE THE FUCK UP!" Snap was shaking the shit outta me and just yellin. **"WAKE YO ASS UP NIGGA!"** I was groggy as hell.

"Nigga what are you screaming for?"

"AMBULANCES ALL AROUND YOUR MAMA HOUSE! YA MAMA BEEN SHOT NIGGA!" I shot up out that bed faster than Carl Lewis outta the blocks. Snap was struggling to get his shoes on. I was so nervous that I had put on my jeans backwards. Ahh man, this was the worst thing imaginable. All I could hope was that my mama was aight.

"C'MON NIGGA!" That was Snap screaming from downstairs, and I came running. I damn near fell down the stairs trying to get to that door. We raced out of West Calumet and shot towards Gary. I swear the way cuz was driving he could've won every Nascar Sprint Series. He was steady on the phone with someone whom I didn't know. Inside, I was dying a slow death. All I heard was the word "shot" and the word "my mama" together in the same sentence. I stayed calm on the passenger side as cuz kept screaming at whoever he was talking to. This car was racing down the road at over 90 miles per hour, but it seemed like it was going no more than ten miles an hour. This shit was nerve wrecking.

I flash-backed to the night that I got caught up in, the worst moment of my life. How I seen my moms in the police station as she gave me her final words and left me to fend for myself. I sucked as a son, I thought. She gave all she had for four boys, and neither one of us had amounted to shit. Yea, I might've been in the service now, but I still felt like my life's purpose was incomplete and that I was a complete failure. Now, the failure to protect the one woman I loved had hit my soul something fierce.

We finally arrived in Tarrytown. I could see the flashes reflecting off the houses as we turned the corner. Cuz had gotten real quiet and started to creep thru the streets. That's when I saw the white sheet on the ground.

"CUZ, CUZ WAIT!" Snap was shouting, but I hopped out the car while it was in motion. It seemed like the longest run of my life.

"Sir, calm down! Calm down!" One of the

officers on the scene was clutching me and holding me back.

"MAMA! MAMA!" That's all I shouted. I didn't give a damn about this officer. I wrestled with him until a few more cops came and manhandled me. I felt a knee in my back, a knee in my head and only heard

"CALM THE FUCK DOWN!" Tears rolled down my eyes as I had no choice but to remain calm, seeing that I had damn near 1000 something pounds holding me down. I don't know where Snap was, but I figured they had whooped his ass, too. That's what the police was good for around here.

"Let him up. I got him," a cold deep voice bellowed out. They snatched me up and dusted me off as my head stayed hung low with rage, hurt and anger.

"Hey, are you calm now?" I looked up to see Detective Davidson. Man this was like a family reunion of two estranged family members who couldn't stand each other. He was the same detective who interrogated me two years ago.

"Hey? I'm talkin to you," as he nudged his hand to my chin to lift up my head.

"Yea," in a faint whisper I responded.

"Alright. I'll take him boys." They kinda pushed me into his arms as I stared em down grudgingly. I swear they were lucky, cause I'd whoop all they bitch asses if that uniform was off.

"C'mon and lets go look." I mean he was straight forward. No am I ready to see it or nothing. I guess he figured that I knew what had happened, so he said fuck it in his mind. As we both lifted and ducked under the caution tape, my heartbeat felt like it was on a hundred thousand.

"You ready son?" I just nodded my head in agreeance. As he bent down to remove the sheet, I looked up to notice Snap behind the caution tape shaking his head at me as if to say I'm sorry bruh. Sadness was written all over his face.

"Hey," that voice from down below beckoned. I looked and was instantly frozen. There was my mother's lifeless body. All I could see was blood and a nasty neck wound. I couldn't even cry. I was just stunned more than anything. I suddenly felt like all of the life was sucked out of me. He put the sheet back over my mama.

"C'mon son. Let's walk." Detective Davidson walked with me to the opposite end of the street. "First off son, I'm sorry. I truly am. I lost my mother some years back, so trust me, I know the pain that you are going through right now. I have to ask you something though, and I need you to be straight up with me. Did you come back home to see your mom since you've been in the area?"

I paused for a long minute, knowing damn well he already knew the answer. He just had to make sure.

"Yes sir," in the faintest voice I think I ever produced. He stared a hole through me. "Carl, you know I was born and raised here just like you, down some ways in Glen Park. You know these young niggas out here don't forget anything. I heard how you conducted yourself downstate and how you went into the Navy and thought to myself, wow, this kid got another shot. Good for him. However, in the back of my mind, I knew somebody would be waiting. Just waiting for you to show your face around here so they can get some payback for putting your boys away. I don't like how the streets operate, but that's how they operate, which you know all too well."

I couldn't say shit. I just stood there looking at this man in a different light. I thought he was some square ass suburban nigga. This dude knew the real.

"Don't worry. We gone do everything in our power to find who did this. On another note, I wanna say this to you man to man. Do not, I repeat, **DO NOT** go out and hunt for your own justice. I got this. I know life ain't gone be easy to continue on, but you have to do it. Here."

Just then, he gave me a pocket watch out of his slacks. "Keep this young brotha." All I could do is stare.

"What's this?" With a deep breath he explained.

"My mama always looked at this clock when I was out of the house. If I came in late, I walked in and she said nothing. She just flipped open the clock. I knew that was my ass, and the belt and I were about to have our what seemed like usual family reunion. I want you to have it, as a connection of sorts. Furthermore, I want you to remember that time is precious. Make the best of it."

As his words echoed in my head, he rubbed my shoulder and slowly turned around to head back to the scene of my mama. I stood in awe. I couldn't move. I sat back just looking at the lights, the caution tape, the white sheet over my mama's body, all the nosey neighbors I knew and didn't know.

"C'mon cuz. Let's roll." That was Snap talking, as he grabbed me and we headed back towards the car. This was all my damn fault. I came home to make amends and I did more damage than I could ever imagine. Somebody saw me. Somebody remembered. Somebody paid me back in a way that I could never imagine. This shit was for the birds. I was so happy to see Gary once again. Now, I could care less if I ever saw this shit hole for the rest of my life.

That night, when we got back to Snap's crib, he just left me alone. It was me and four walls. I wondered what the hell they were saying to each other about me right now. I couldn't sleep for nothing. I mean hell, my mama had just been found murdered in cold blood outside of her own home. If this was God paying me back for the life I helped take a few years back, then he was a cold hearted God in my eyes. I couldn't think that, though. The Good Lord got me through my situation. He gave me another chance. I couldn't be mad at him. I decided to get up and write. I looked at the time. 3:43 a.m. That's what I titled it.

3-4-3
The Holy trinity
that avoided four brothers
three failures born of one mother
one escaped his past
but didn't get a pass
as death passed him
and grasped onto his mother
at 3:43
came the death of one brother
the author of this poem

I wrote that and just looked at it. I would rather have done life in prison than to see my mama lay under a white sheet. How the hell would I recover from this? I truly had no idea. I attended my mama's funeral the next week. Seeing that it was a lot of bullshit in the air, you would've sworn this was the funeral of a gangbanger. Every Vice Lord you could imagine was there. I already knew Snap arranged this. I knew deep down cuz was upset at me for breaking street code, but he always stayed loyal to family no matter what. It was about 70 of these niggas. Most of em, I didn't even know. All I knew is that only a fool would try something at this homegoing service. I heard the pastor preaching, but I wasn't really listening to him. Nothing he said could take away my pain. All I wanted to do now was leave. I wanted to go and start my new life overseas, wherever the hell that ship might've been. I needed it. I was just tired of everything in my life.

My chance to start anew was coming soon. I just wished I didn't have to wait days to begin that new life. I wish my brothers could be here to send me off, and most importantly, our mama. I wish like all hell that my daddy was here. Then, it really hit me. My daddy was who I wanted to be all my life. Yet at this point in time right now, I truly realized that I wasn't him. I wasn't a real banger. I wasn't that crazy street nigga. I wasn't made to be a drug dealer, thief or just common crook. I was made to be Carl Lamell Jackson.

I often tried to imitate what I had seen from my upbringing, but all that did was bring me nothing but grief and mischief. A year and some change sentence for what? Trying to be something that I wasn't? I slapped the hell outta myself about 15 times in my head. Truly, I had finally realized that I needed to be my own man, and not what the world thinks I should be. Just because you come from the hood doesn't mean you have to embrace the stereotypical bullshit that comes along with it. Also, I didn't want to be known from the hood. I wanted to be known as a man from TarryTown, a solid neighborhood. I thought about something at that very moment. Why do we call it a hood and not neighborhood? It's simple to me. We don't look at each other as neighbors. We look at each other as enemies.

We appear to be close knit because we all grow up in the same area. However, if push comes to shove, most if not all, will step on your neck to ensure their family eats and the next man starves. I was tired of this boy mentality and ready to step into the mentality of a grown ass adult. I felt I was ready, but only time would tell. The funeral finally ended and we proceeded in the long drive to the cemetery. I just calmly leaned my head back and zoned out as Snap drove. Poetry in my head accompanied me on this drive:

*Out of a mothers womb comes a gift that
sometimes turns into a curse
yet what happens when the curse has to watch his
gift ride in a hearse
what happens when life wants to be switched with
death, what happens when you breathe yet still only
want to take your last breath*

what happens

We got to the cemetery and I watched my mother's coffin slowly lowered into the ground. I shot my eyes up and around the crowd to see the reactions on others' faces. Neighbors, close friends, old heads from throughout G.I., all paying tribute to whom I considered a warrior. Me, myself, I shed not a tear. I just stood there in silence, with a vision to jump on top of the casket and have the caretaker bury me along with mom Dukes. I couldn't cry. I couldn't show emotion. This was my mama, but I was too mad at myself for my shortcomings.

I felt the reason she was gone was because of me and my brothers. Four of us, gone. Members of the fraternity Jail Phi Nigga, better known as the ignorance breeding business. The billion dollar prison business. I wanted this to be over with for good. As the pastor said his last words, I made a silent vow to my mama that I would make her proud in all that I do. If I had to damn near kill myself to achieve this and make her smile, I would. Snap grabbed me and we headed back to the whip. The old Carl was dead. The new Carl was here, with more life than ever before.

The days finally passed and June 20th was here. I asked Snap to drop me off at the bus station. I wanted to just marinate on my life and think to myself while being surrounded by complete strangers. He dropped me off and peeled out into the street, chuckin a deuce at me, followed by a VL sign. I nodded my head up at him and followed him with my eyes until I couldn't see him anymore. I went inside, got my ticket, and just zoned out. No music or anything. Just the sounds of Northwest Indiana. This would be my last time around here for a while, so I had to enjoy it.

"The Bus to O'Hare Airport is now here for boarding." That was my cue. I grabbed my bags and walked outside. The clouds looked different for some reason. Maybe it was because I was thinkin that my mama was sitting on one of those clouds rooting me on. I just stared up there for a good minute.

"Sir? Are you going to give me your bags or what?"

"Oh, my apologies sir." I was zoned out so much I ain't even hear dude asking me for my baggage. I went all the way to the back of the bus. I wanted to be alone. This was it. I didn't know what was waiting for me, but whatever it was, I know it would be better than the first 20 years of my life. As we took off for the airport, I whipped out my notebook and went into my poetic zone:

Life

Spare me time with weak hearts and minds, I don't need people who are gonna bring me down in life, cause life, unlike what they say is long, only those who don't live to the fullest consider it too short, so I court this experience with their life experience of others who want the same thing I do, progress and success, cause many people just want sex, but life fucks you over enough, so I'll just stay a virgin, and this new 50 inch, the picture I paint clear, life with fear is life with regrets, and better yet, life without the balls to take risks, just leaves you with a dick, you can't create life in anyone else, life is here for the taking, sort of like the man who is ridiculed for wanting to win, and took his chance, standing as his own man to make something happen, while the rest of the world scoured and soured at his own decision, see men do what they want, and boys, just wish they could be in that position, 'cause instead of worrying about a man who plays a forward position, they need to position themselves out of minimum wage and video games, cause don't no woman want a half ass male, and I don't think God made us to be 50 percent, 'cause its the small percent that have the rest of the world lookin at me as if I ain't worth a damn, cause regardless of how many times I go to defend this flag, I'm still a nigger in their eyes, 'cause they're so accustomed to hearin out cries from watchin people behind caution tape, and then the same ones that's cryin. glorify the ones that's dyin with old pics full of gang symbols, but then they holla they want peace, major contradiction is what I see, but a lot of folks are blind to their own faults, quick to point out that it's someone else's fault for the ways we stuck in, this life is full of people, who don't take responsibility for their actions, major actin with no action is common cause for today, cause here today, gone tomorrow is the new slogan, screw YOLO, cause you don't live once, not if you play your cards right, and I ain't just talkin about the day you embraced that saved life, and I would explain what I just quoted, but I'm a let y'all marinate on that and really think about those words, life is to be made, taken in stride with a partner who gone ride for you at all costs, no billing or unnecessary fees, cause ya partner in life should be willin to do all things for free, the only thing you need to pay is respect and love to ya significant other, see life is like a cover, you can either lay under it and hide, or lay on top of em, willin to mess up your bed, cause when you make something up on a daily, and put it in its best form, then, you will really understand, what life is all about

It's amazing how words can express life in either its roughest or greatest forms. I was just ready to live life. I closed my eyes and just imagined everything that was about to come for this young brother. Before I knew it, I was sitting at my gate, staring outside at the plane that was about to take me on this new and unknown journey. This was flight 3900, heading to Virginia, followed to the next destination, in which I did not know yet. I said a quick prayer, and boarded my flight. It only took an hour and some change to get to Virginia. When I got there, I walked to baggage claim, passing by some stallions that attended Norfolk State University. To hell with catching another plane. I wanted to catch them in a dorm room by myself. I walked thru this damn airport, tired and hungry. Finally, I got to baggage claim to get my stuff. A huge sea bag full of uniforms and a duffle bag with all my personal gear up in it.

"Fireman Jackson," a voice bellowed out from behind me. I turned around to see a clean cut brother, tall as a damn giraffe. This dude had to be at least 6'7.

"Yes, that's me." "How you doing? I'm Petty Officer Barnes and I got you from here." That was a relief for me. Getting to somewhere foreign and having a brother pick me up. That was coo beans for me. I mean, I wasn't a racist or anything like that, but having someone you could possibly relate to as a first impression seemed to make things a little bit easier.

We rolled up out of the airport and headed on our way to base. We chopped it up and I found dude to be a legit brother from our talks. He was from Gould, Arkansas. Country ass dude with a country ass accent. He was keeping it 100 with me on what to expect out there in the fleet. Fam told me I was about to feel like a gazelle in a middle of a bunch of caged lions that were about to be released for the first time in a week. Damn, I thought. Was it gone be the good cage where all the women would be after me, or would it be a bunch of niggas trying to test me out, seeing how hard I was? Then I thought about it. I hadn't heard anything about females being on this ship, so right then I knew I would have to deal with the latter. I aint wanna deal with no Mickey Mouse shit, but it looked like that's what it was gonna be.

We finally arrived to the air station base. Kinfolk got me checked in, dapped me up and rolled out. Here I was, back in another airport terminal. This time though, I wasn't headed to anyone's boot camp. Naw, I was going to the real. This was it, I thought. I looked around to see a bunch of other folks who looked around my age waiting as well. I didn't know where they were going, but I really didn't care. I was just ready to start my own journey.

The time ticked down and after two hours of sitting around, looking like some miserable puppy dogs, we finally boarded this behemoth of a plane. I had never seen anything this damn big or luxurious in my life. Flat screen TVs, tables on the flight, all sorts of other crazy shit. If this how the government was treating their folks, I was damn sure glad to be on the winning team. Just then, the stewardess came across the speaker and said some ish that made my mouth drop. We were flying to Bahrain, but we were having layovers in Spain and Italy. I just clasped my hands together in my own little world of excitement. This time, there were no thoughts about women at all. All I could think was that a few years ago, I was stuck in Gary, Indiana, worried about my future. Now, I was on my way to Europe, about to see the world. Time damn near stood still as I soaked in the news. *Why me*, is all I thought...*Why me?*

We took off on an eight hour flight to Rota, Spain. Everything was gravy as I chopped it up with folks headed to other destinations. Some of these cats were headed to Spain for good. Others were on there way to Italy. The rest were either going to Bahrain, or with me on The Nimitz. Eight hours and some change later, I was here. It was late evening in the states. Here, it was a lil past seven in the morning.

I finally stepped off the plane and inhaled a whiff of fresh air. This wasn't that Northwest Indiana air, breathing in smog and whatever else was in that dirty air. Naw. This was official countryside; pure, breathable air. To me, I felt like I died and went to heaven. Never in my life could I have imagined seeing something like this. We had a five hour layover, so I had the opportunity to see a lil bit of the countryside courtesy of a homeboy named McNeill I had met at Great Lakes. He was from North Carolina. He graduated way before me, and got stationed out here. With the limited time I had, he took me out into the city for a minute. We stopped at a simple little spot and got our grub on. I couldn't pronounce nothing on the menu, so I let him order what he thought I would like. When it came, my stomach started throwin up gang signs from that good eatin. It was something with veal, and that shit was hittin like a muthafucka.

Mac showed me around a little bit more and we were back on the road. He showed me a few more sights, including those sexy ass Spain women. I mean I loved my sisters, but these women over here were just pure beautiful, if there was such a thing. I would definitely have to roll this joint up a lot longer in the future.

Bruh took me back to base and dropped me off at the terminal with about an hour to spare. Sitting there alone, I started to think about my mama. It was sad that she was gone, but I had a feeling that she was looking down on me watching. I wondered if they caught her killer, even though I knew it was highly unlikely, seeing that 90% of the murders that occurred in the inner city went unsolved. It was a sad statistic, but it was one that sadly would probably never change. Everybody, especially my people, always talk about things have to change, yet it will never come because of us and us only. We do shit for a day. Temporary is our middle name. We never wanna do shit until shit happens. I noticed that in my so far short life. And when we do finally make an attempt at something, we always gotta bring each other down. That's us though. Not all, but most, and it's sad. Finally, it was time to board again for a two and a half hour flight to the Island of Sicily. Now I was gonna touch down in Italy. Man, what a rush this would be. I decided to just take a nap on this flight. Rest my eyes and just enjoy this new life of mine.

The flight attendant woke me up when we were about 30 minutes out from landing. I adjusted my groggy eyes to the outside as heaven seemed to be blingin on this day. I was still stuck in a major trance as I couldn't believe that I was actually on the other side of the world. I didn't know what to feel really. We finally landed on the island of Sicily, having a three hour layover to chill. I know I had just ate not too long ago, but I had to go get me some authentic Italian food out here in Italy.

I stayed on base and went to some restaurant to smash some real ass spaghetti and meatballs. Folks might think its simple, but can't everyone who's from where I'm from say they've eaten spaghetti and meatballs in Italy. Time flew by quickly as it was well into the late afternoon now and we boarded the last flight which was headed to Bahrain. Truly, I started to get nervous. I had nothing against Muslims, but the way the world was depicting them, I was skeptical about going into Muslim territory. I didn't know what to expect. The excitement had disappeared. I was now really reevaluating my decision. My God, again, what did I get myself into?

"Welcome to Bahrain." I totally ignored the other words made by the captain or whoever. All I heard was welcome to Bahrain. It was now dark out, and well after nine at night. It was six of us, and we were escorted into a room by some senior officers and given a quick brief on Bahrain, the good and the bad. Soon after, we were bussed off to our hotel.

Five guys, one girl, and I noticed she hadn't said a damn thing the whole time from Virginia to here. Maybe she was feeling the same way I was. This was a wake up call to anyone. Finally, we arrived and were booked in for the night. The next morning, we would be flying out to the ship. I walked up to my room to crash for the night. As I retrieved the key out of my wallet, I seen the adjacent door open. It was ol girl that I had flew in with. The quiet one.

"Hi," I said. She looked at me with a lil discontent and then shut the door. I didn't emphasize too much on it, seeing that I probably wouldn't have said anything either realizing the circumstances. I walked in and noticed a normal hotel room like anywhere else. With a quick shower, I cut on the TV and flipped through the channels, getting a chuckle out of some game show on TV. I didn't know what the hell they were saying, but they were being goofballs, so it kinda put me at ease. I cracked open my notebook and just stared at it for a minute. I went to sit over by the window, looking out into the Bahrain night. It seemed so peaceful and calm. However, I know that looks could be deceiving, much like this setting. I knew tomorrow that my calm nature would dissipate, as I would land on the deck of an aircraft carrier, in a foreign world, with foreign people. As I was about to lay, I thought about the ultimate price I could pay being out here, so I wrote my final piece for anyone to see should I never leave this region of the world again:

DEATH

I wonder if the world would miss me if I died,
would the same words that did damage be idolized in scripts and songs,
causin sing alongs mixed with send my baby home tunes,
see I watched death in HD courtesy of LK and GD,
pop shots had cats droppin on pop rocks while kids stuffed their mouths with pop rocks,
doing double dutch, immune to the cobra clutch violence had on inner city folks,
so when you see my casket, leave it open as you throw dirt and water me up,
allow me to sprout up out of the same ground where the richest reside,

rich ideas, rich dreams, rich amounts of love, all
taken away because of poor mindsets,
let me come back a ghost, haunting those and
scaring bullshit out of em,
allowing only greatness to exist

It was now no turning back. I was here, in this moment, in this time, prepping for my biggest challenge yet. Either I could suck it up and get it over with, or I could moan, bitch and complain, making it seem long and drawn out. I went to sleep that night as if it would be the last normal night of my life.

CHAPTER FOUR

THE START

Thump!!! That was the sound of the aircraft as it hit the flight deck of my new home. Crazy thing was though, we didn't land. We were back in the air, doing Lord knows what. Inside, I was shitting bricks. I wasn't an aviation expert, but I know when planes hit solid ground, they are supposed to stop, not keep flying. I couldn't see anything in this little ass plane, so I just bowed my head and said a silent prayer to God.

At least if this was my time, I was just hoping my death could be instant and I wouldn't have to suffer by getting eaten by some sharks or some unknown sea creatures. ***THUMP!*** Again, that sound commenced. This time though, I heard the landing gear sound afterwards and felt us come to a complete stop. Here we go I thought. I was here. The door opened, and we were met by a brother in a funny mask, a long yellow sweater and some camouflage pants on.

"Follow Me," he barked out over all the noise. One by one we filed out until all seven of us made it out. Hot damn, it was loud up here. In following my mans, I took a glance around. All I seen was a bunch of folks in crazy masks and helmets staring at me. Yellow shirts, Green Shirts, Blue shirts, Brown shirts. You name the color, and they had it on. Man these fools looked like they were headed to a skittle convention up here. We made it to a room with some black benches and a little TV.

"Aight everybody. I'm Petty Officer Miller. Welcome aboard the Nimitz. We'll have our personnel men up here shortly to come get you and check in. Welcome aboard."

He bounced out and went back to doing whatever he was doing before. I don't know what everyone else was thinking, but I had butterflies inside of my stomach. In that moment though, I noticed something. Ol girl who looked pissed a day earlier in the hotel was here. I had just realized females were gonna be on this ship. That was a big sigh of relief I'll tell you that. The waiting process continued, as one by one, seven dwindled down to two. It was me and the girl left. Talk about an awkward moment.

"Hi, I'm Carl." No response and no movement

at all. She sat there as if she was made out of stone. Arms folded like she didn't have a care in the world.

"Excuse me? How are you doing?" She slowly turned her head my way.

"If I wanted to talk to you I would have addressed you. Thank you."

Damn, what the hell was wrong with her? I mean she was pretty, but her attitude was shittier than a newborn baby's pamper.

"Jackson!" I looked up and seen this tall, skinny brother in the doorway.

"That's me sir."

"How you doing mane? I'm Petty Officer Taylor, and you aint gotta call me sir. C'mon follow me so we can get you situated."

This was cool. Once again, I felt comfortable. A brother came up to get me. Hell to the yeah. As we were walking to wherever, I was just amazed by how big this joint was. I was walking, but in awe at the same time. We got downstairs to the hangar bays where the planes get repaired at, and I swear to you these shits were longer than at least two football fields.

I caught the stares of everyone. They knew I was the new guy by my civilian clothes. Everyone else was in their work coveralls doing whatever. Me and Taylor started to chop it up as we hit one more ladder well downstairs to the main deck. As we passed the galley, my mind yelled *"Oh Shit."* Man, I swear on everything, I loved the Nimitz. They had some pretty jokers on it. Just was my luck that while we were walking, I seen a big booty light skinned. She had to be from the South. Hot damn, my young ass would have to contain myself if I was gonna make it through this deployment without impregnating somebody.

We made it to the personnel office. Just like earlier, the minute I stepped foot through that door, the stares had started to occur once again. I wasn't intimidated, but I was wondering whether or not these were what the hell are you doing here looks. I know I was new, but I was already feeling like public enemy #1. We sat down and went over all my information. We chopped it up a lot as I told him about my past and all that good stuff. Where I was from, who my peoples were, all that. I kept it to the basics, because I was skeptical to share personal info with someone I barely knew. He seemed cool though, as I learned he was from Texas and loved the hell out of the Dallas Cowboys. Me personally, I couldn't stand those clowns. Just then, someone came in the office and didn't say a word.

"What up Nobles?" Taylor exclaimed.

"Aint shit mane. This the new dude?"

"Yea. I got em all checked in. He's all yours." I sat back and observed this dude. He just looked like he was just fresh off of whooping somebody's ass. Nappy head, about 6'2, looking like he didn't have a care in the world. I got up and introduced myself, extending my hand to the brother. He just looked at me. No extension of his hand back.

"Follow me man." *Man this ol salty ass, jim crow nigga* I thought. I'm trying to be cool, and I run into primary asshole number one on the first day. I got down to the shop to meet me new LPO. He was also a brother. This was definitely cool seeing that in my field of work, there weren't a lot of blacks. I was the only one in my class at A school, and just totaled 8 in the whole entire school. This even gave me more motivation to do my best while here.

The boss laid down the ground rules for me and just chopped it up with me for about the next hour. He would officially introduce me tomorrow at our morning quarters, seeing that work was done for the day. For now, he just told me to head to the berthing, chill out and get something to eat if I already hadn't ate. I went back out the shop with Nobles. He led me to the berthing where we sleep. On the way there, I passed by the other galley. It was some more folks eating up in there.

What I caught in my eyesight truly astonished me. I observed four girls at the table, and we were having corn dogs for dinner. One of em put the whole thing in her mouth and her girls were screaming, laughing, all that. Others might have seen a hoe. I seen me a potential victim. We headed down the stairs, or ladders as The Navy called it, and into the berthing. *Damn* I thought. These were some small ass beds to sleep in. They were called coffin racks. They were about the size of one, and it looked like I wouldn't get any good sleep.

"Here you go nigga. Rack 87. Clean sheets and shit in the linen locker. We muster up at 645 in the morning. One of these fools will show you where the shop is if you forgot." He turned around and walked off, going to do whatever. Damn, that was one helluva first impression to have for a first night on the ship. A few more cats came through and showed me love. It was cool to see that there were actually some fellas who were attempting to make my welcome feel as pleasant as possible.

I laid out my sheets that night, got all my goods unpacked and placed in my rack. I really was hungry, but I didnt wanna put on any coveralls and walk out into a sharks pit. I would save that for tomorrow. I just pulled out a box of pop tarts I had purchased in Bahrain and smashed those. After a good shower, I got my bed ready and prepared myself to savor this experience.

I laid down and adjusted myself properly. This was gonna be very difficult I see, seeing that I maybe had 2 ½ feet of bed to move across. I was 6'4, so this thing was just long enough for me to stretch my body in without having to bend my knees. I cut my rack light off and simply stared into darkness as I closed my curtains behind me. I simply just laid there, eyes open, listening to those around me. I was trying to prep myself for everything that I thought I would encounter. I slowly but surely started to drift. I drifted until I was completely out. A few hours later, I was awaken by a prayer over the ship's loudspeaker.

"Shipmates, in the book of James, it states: Consider it pure joy, my brothers and sisters, whenever you face trials of many kinds, because you know that the testing of your faith produces perseverance. Let perseverance finish its work so that you may be mature and complete, not lacking anything. During this time away from our loved ones, we need to rely on the support of each other to make it through everyday trials and tribulations. God gives you strength, but he also gives you your fellow man to exercise His strength through others to help yourself. Demonstrate God's strength on a daily. Let us pray."

I heard nothing else. I listened to the prayer, but I was so mesmerized by the Chaplain's opening statement that I felt a renewed sense of pride within myself. Immediately, I thought about my mother. In this case, she was my trial. I was over her, but then I wasn't. In the most important time of my life where I felt I needed her, she wasn't here. I still was battling myself because I took the blame for her death. It was me coming home that eventually sent her home with the Lord. I started to shed a tear, as emotions overcame me. Difficult wasn't the word. I felt like writing my feelings, but I couldn't muster up the strength to get my notebook. I just lie there until I eventually fell back asleep. That night, I had a dream.

I was back in Gary, walking the halls of West Side High School. It was completely empty, but I could hear the noise of 2,000 other students as if the halls were full. I walked around everywhere, looking for somebody, but I could find no one. I seriously walked past every classroom. I was hearing noises, but not seeing anyone. What the hell was this meaning I thought.

I came back around until I finally reached the locker I had my senior year. It was cracked open and I saw a ribbon sticking out of the bottom. I opened it up to reveal a blue notebook, with a red ribbon hanging out of it. I bent down to pick it up. I opened it to the page where the ribbon was placed and started to read. It was a letter from my mom.

CARL,

You will never understand the hurt a mother has when all of her blessings are all of a sudden disappeared. I thought I knew the meaning of hurt.

but when you went to jail, it felt like someone had ripped my heart out of my chest. I must have smoked about three packs of squares that night. I was trying to smoke my lungs totally black until I was no longer breathing. That's all I wanted to do was die when you left me. I felt hopeless. I felt lost. I felt like the worse woman on Earth. Rather, the worst mother that ever lived. I don't know why I am writing you this letter, because I don't have plans on sending it to you. I hope you do find this one day to understand how I feel. It is hard right now to just live. Maybe you can find this when you are old and grey, and I am no longer existent in this world. Know I am dead inside. Don't blame yourself though. Just blame me. I am the failure who allowed this to happen. If God made one mistake in this life, it was me. I hope you make it to be something in life. Please, pretty please, do not end up like you mama. I love you.

-MAMA

Right after reading the letter, everything got intensely bright and a huge burst of light appeared. I damn near went blind. it was like staring into the sun. With my hands over my eyes, the light started to dim down and I fully stared into it.

"MAMA!" She was there. Staring at me, smiling, yet saying nothing back.

"Mama, mama, mama!" I kept shouting for her, but she said nothing back. All she did was smile. I began to walk towards her, and in a flash, the scenery went from her draped in pearl white cloth, to a murder scene. No, it wasn't her murder scene. It was the murder scene I had left over two years ago, as me and my friends left a man dead.

No one was there. Not even the police. All I seen was caution tape and a white sheet. I stood behind the caution tape for a good ten minutes, staring at the white sheet. I finally mustered up the courage to go under the caution tape. I slowly walked over to the mans body. I was scared shitless. I didn't know what to expect. As I knelt down to raise the sheet off, my heart began to beat at about 1000 miles an hour. Just then, out of nowhere, I heard police sirens, only to turn my head around and see two squad cars racing down Grant.

I whipped back around, took a deep breath and lifted the sheet. It was the ugliest sight of my life. This man…did he really deserve this? Half of his head was damn near separated from his skull. I scanned his body to observe two more bullet wounds. One was to his neck and the other one was to his back. I shook my head in awe, as all I could think about was why did we do this to this man? Why did I involve myself in such fuckery? Just as I was about to place the sheet over him, he whipped around and grabbed me by my shirt. I was frozen solid as I looked into his lifeless eyes. They looked like cataracs covered them. Blood foamed from his mouth and his mouth trembled. I couldn't believe this.

"W-W-W-W-W-Why? Why did you do this to me?"

I shot up in my bed, bangin my arm against the top of my rack. Luckily, I didn't wake anyone, as I still could hear a rat pis on cotton. My breathing was deep, heavy and I was lost in my head. I laid my head back on my pillow and just tried to calm myself down. I was regretful and remorseful for what happened that night. However, it sucked that my mind still had to remind me of the events. I learned something with this. You may be over something in life, but outside forces that you can't control may remind you from time to time what you went through.

I didn't know if this was God showing me to remind me of what not to do again, or the devil just messing with me as he is good for. This was more than I could handle. However, I was in a different world, so I had the chance to make a different outcome of my life. After a good thirty minutes, including a pis for the ages where I fed every salmon on Earth, I drifted back to sleep, thinking bout the next step in the life of Carl

Jackson.

DUBAI

It was August 15th, the night before my birthday. We were officially in the richest city in the world. Man, I couldn't have pictured this in my wildest dreams. We had pulled in at around nine that morning, and it was hot. Im talking crazy hot. I mean it was so hot that the sweat on a rats ass would boil if he was out here. I was super anxious to get off and do my thing. After hooking up sewage connection from the ship to the trucks down on the pier, I was free to do what I wanted to do.

Yea, I know that sounded nasty, but that was the job I signed up for. I was called a HT, short for Hull Technician. In lamen terms, I was the ship's plumber. Yea, I did some welding from time to time. On this big ass floating city though, I chased shit. All kinds of shit.

The worse was dealing with the triflin females who flushed tampons and all kinds of other nasty shit down the line, clogging it up and giving me more unnecessary work to do. I guess that's the nature of the beast though. I rolled out with a few of the guys from the shop I had gotten cool with. We caught the bus in Jebel Ali, the port city about 45 minutes from Dubai. The drive was amazing. Here I was, cruisin thru the United

Arab Emirates on my way to see Dubai. Along the way, I seen some of the most amazing shit a man could ever see. A six door Lexus. Crazy billboards which I couldn't read, but were tight as hell. We even passed by the camel track where they were racing camels. Yes, I said camel racing, just like we have horse racing in the United States. All they needed were squares in their mouths and they would officially be Joe Cool.

This here was amazing. Finally, we got dropped off at the Ibn Battuta Mall. This however wasn't a mall. This was a monstrosity with stores in it. When I first entered, I was just amazed. They had a setup in there where it literally looked like a night sky was above you. If I woke up from a dream and ended up here, I would swear I was outside. We walked around the mall, amazed at the architecture and everything it had to offer. Being a typical negro, me and the partnas walked into Foot Locker. This joint was about the size of a mansion though. This was by far the biggest Foot Locker I had ever seen in my young life.

Holy shit! I couldn't believe it. Further along, we found a full blown ship structure inside. How they built this and who in the hell built this, I will never know. I had to give them major props though. We strolled through the mall for about another two hours, eating and looking in amazement at the beautiful women this city had to offer. I mean I saw Russians, Ethiopians, Asians and African sisters. Every breed you could think of, they were here. **THEY ALL LOOKED GOOD!!!** Shit, I wasn't even concerned about no American booty after seeing these beauties live and in the flesh. After bouncing out of the mall, we aint know what to get into. We hopped the cab, and fortunately, he spoke English.

"A man, where is somewhere fun around here?" I clamored to him.

"Haha. I got something for you." I was cool with it, the partners were cool with it, so we sat back and enjoyed the ride. It was early afternoon, around 2:30, and we pulled up to this joint called T.G.I. Thursdays. Yes, I said that right, T. G. I. Thursday's.

"A, man. Aint this supposed to say T.G.I. Friday's?"

"Haha. No my friend. T.G.I. Thursday's. You can thank me later." It was whatever. We jumped out the cab four deep and headed into this place. **"What the fuck?!"** That was what my boy Harv from New York shouted. He was fresh like me in the service, and none of us could believe this shit. It was like a restaurant. I mean, a legit restaurant, except it was full of women. Lots of women. More women than usual. It didn't take rocket science to realize that these were prostitutes. I'll be damned though. They were fine ass frog legs. We sat at a table and were soon joined by six of 'em. Convos started to flare up, as a waitress came over and got our orders for a boatload of hot wings and some beer. This here was cool to me. Booze, buffalo wings and bitches. Me myself, I had a fine ass Brazilian baby on me. Her ass was so phat if she bootied bump a cancer patient, all the cancer would be knocked out of them. My partnas were satisfied, and I was too. I started to smash some wings when she reached her hand down and grabbed my dick.

"You wanna have fun baby?" Oh man, that voice sounded sexy as all to be damned. I looked around at my partnas. It seemed like they all got told the same thing by their chicks. With smiles on our faces, we paid for our food and agreed to meet in the lobby when we were all done. We didn't have to be back to the boat until 11, so we had plenty of times to get "acquainted." The next thing I know, I was upstairs in a room, knocking down some Brazilian culo. Aww man is all I could think. My first real port and first international piece of ass.

Yea, I was definitely loving the Navy right now. Trust, it cost me some dough, but like one of the elders in my life had once told me: "You gone either pay for it directly or indirectly. But either way, you will pay for it." He was damn right too. We ended up meeting back in the lobby at a little past six o'clock. None of us came down at the same time, so it seemed like a few of us were maybe making love to these chicks instead of just knocking the dust off the kuda snap. We made it back to base at around 7:20. We boarded the ship and went our separate ways. I dropped my stuff off in the berthing, changed into some basketball shorts, a T-shirt and went right back outside to an area outside of the ship called "The Sandbox." It was pretty much a giant sandpit with eating joints, several stores where you could buy anything you want, a few basketball courts and one helluva beer garden for drinking. As long as we were in this area, we could stay out until damn near three in the morning, no matter what your rank was.

I had less than five hours until my 21st birthday and I definitely had plans to be faded beyond belief. I went over to the Popeye's stand to cop me a two piece dinner. This wasn't like the states, because crazy as it may sound, it actually tasted better. I guess those Arabs had some magic in their spices, cause this shit was the bomb. After finishing up the grub, alone I might add, I waltzed around, drifting to every corner of the sandbox, observing everybody.

I was still virtually unknown except to a select amount of people. It was gravy though, cause I knew in due time, I would leave my mark with everybody. I got over to the basketball court to see the boys from the ship finishing up a game.

"A new blood. You wanna run?" That was a fellow damage controlman named Marlin

Jackson. He was from L.A. and was a cool dude.

"Yea man. I'm down." I walked out to the court to be met with daps from everybody. It amazing how basketball can just draw cats to you. What was even more amazing is that a brother was about to be hoopin in the Middle East. It was hot as shit, about 95 degrees, but still yet amazing. Me and Jack were on the same team.

The game started and quickly turned into a typical game from the hood. Bruhs started arguing calls, shit talkin commenced and we battled literally. It got to 7-4 in the game. We were running to 16 and we were down. A few of the bruhs were arguing a call when I just glanced to the side. A group of females from the ship had gathered on the side lookin at us.

"Aaah shit. Two Jacksons out there." I don't know who she was, but she was fine as frog legs and thicker than a pot of Louisiana Gumbo with crab claws. Me and Marlin looked at each other, nodded our heads in agreement and thought the same thing.

When the game resumed, we started gunnin our asses off. Naw, we didnt end up taking every shot, but we damn near took about the remaining 90% of em. We propelled a comeback and ended up winning 16-14. After the game, an ol' light skinned shorty came up to me on the court.

"So where you from Mr. Jackson?" I wanted to

smile from here to Japan, but I kept my cool.

"I'm from Gary, Indiana baby." I could see her homegirls out the corner of my eye gettin geeked when I said baby. *Here I go* I thought. A nigga done got in there. We chopped it up til the next game started.

"I'm Tasha by the way." She shook my hand, I cracked a smile and said back

"I'm Carl. We gone get up." I turned around and ran back to the court, listening to her and her homegirls making their lil noises like you go girl. Yea, I was that nigga. Even if no one else said it, hot dammit I felt it. I finished up hoopin about 10:45 when we finally lost a game after winning five straight. I headed back to the main area of the sandbox to find my division all drunk at a table.

"Heyy, Jackson? Get your ass over here birthday boy!" That was one of my Chiefs yellin, as the rest of the drunks followed behind with **"wooooooooos."** I tell you man, when white boys get drunk, it is truly a sight to see. I immediately went over and cracked open a Coors Light and went to town.

For the next hour or so, I just kept going and going. Before I knew it, I had drank a good 16 beers in that time frame. It was now 11:58 and two minutes til my birthday. Just then, I got the shock of my life.

"A?!" It was Nobles. He stood up on the table holding a beer in his hand. "Its new booties birthday, let's count this shit down for this young ass!"

Damn near the whole area of the sandbox we were in held their drinks up and came over to where we were at. It seemed like a million people were introducing themselves to me, but I was damn near incoherent, so I know damn well I wasn't gone remember half of those fuckers.

"Here we go!!," Nobles yelled.

"10…9…8…7…6…5…4…3…2…1…HAPPY BIRTHDAY!!!!!"

The whole damn sandbox counted down as I chugged two beers at once Stone Cold Steve Austin style. This was damn great. I had survived Gary and prison, only to be in The Middle East drunk as shit on my birthday. I was alive and I was blessed, no matter what the hell had went on in my life. The next thing I remember was waking up in my rack with all my clothes on, sweaty as all to be damned. I had the hangover of hangovers, but dammit, I felt good. Happy 21st birthday Carl!!!

CHAPTER FIVE

FINDING MYSELF

Our next stop was the country of Bahrain. I was once again back. This time however, I was on an exploratory mission. Leaving the ship, I didn't think nothing much of this place, as it was too damn hot and just looked like nothing was here. The van dropped me and a lot of the crew off. We didn't need any liberty buddy off the ship just going to the base, so I did my thing dolo.

I walked into the two story Navy Exchange and was actually impressed. They had everything from the bank, local craft stores and a huge gym where a brother could get his hoop on. I went into the exchange part and picked me up some basketball shorts. It was early, like 10 o'clock early, so I was in and out very quick. I went up to the gym hoping to catch a game.

"A Carl, we need one more. You wanna run?" That was my dude from Chitown Greg. He was from the South Side. We called him Megatron because the dude was just big for no reason. I swear it looked like he ate concrete cinder blocks and drunk Hulk juice for a living. He was also a Q Dog, as you couldn't miss those two huge ass brands that he had on his arm and his chest.

"Yea dude. I'm in." The hoopin was on. It was hot outside, but in here, it was good and cool, allowing you to actually run some games without damn near passing out like in Dubai. Shit, we were getting it in so much, by the time I looked up, it was 2:30. I didn't even know it had gotten that late into the afternoon.

We were all pooped by this point, sprawled out across the bleachers, seeing that the same ten were the ones balling for the last four hours. I was about to chalk it up and head back to the ship, but Greg had different plans.

"Whatchu bout to do man?," he asked me.

"I'm just gone head back to the ship bruh. I'm tired and just wanna chill." He wasn't hearing that though.

"Naw bruh. Gone downstairs to the bank, pull you out bout a G stack and come with me. I gotta partna who stationed out here who got the connects on some good suits."

Suits I thought? I wasn't really into that type of

dress yet. Hell, I was just 21 and still in my tennis shoes and white tee phase. However, that inner voice in my head kicked in and said go. Greg was a lieutenant who came from the same ranks I once was. I figured he was trying to teach me a lesson in being a grown man.

"Aight cool bruh. Where ya boy at?"

"We gone meet him at his crib about five minutes from the gate. Don't worry, we can shower up there and get out of these funky hoopin clothes."

That's all I needed to hear. I hated going anywhere smelling like a sewer rat. I hit the bank and checked my account while pulling out a wad. **"Hot damn!"** I shouted out loud and didn't even realize it. The teller kind of chuckled at me as I took my money and rolled out with my mans. I was looking at my bank statement. $8,276. I had never in my life seen that much money at one time. The only niggas in Gary who had that type of bread were the dealers, hustlers and pimps. It felt good to know that I was getting legal money from being a productive citizen and not a destructive one.

We stopped by the little eating joint in this two story mammoth building and got some food. Afterwards, we made the twenty minute and some change hike by foot to Greg's homeboy house. It was hot as shit out here, but this tea I was sipping on was hitting. I felt like Kermit the Frog in this bitch. I took in the surrounding area.

There was a lot of dirt, and the apartment buildings weren't what you called extravagant looking from the outside. *How is anyone living in this places* I thought? I didn't see any A/C units from any windows, so either they had some Central Air, or they had some past time Ancient Kemet type air duct system providing some good ventilation for them. Finally, we got to his homeboy building, clothes in hand.

"BOOM BOOM BOOM!" Damn, I knew Greg was strong, but I swore his knock was gonna break the door down. The door creaked open.

"What's good nigga?!" They dapped up and chopped it up as I sat back just chilling.

"A Terry, this my mans from the boat Carl."

"What's good Carl?," as he dapped me up.

"Yall niggas come on in mane and sit down for a minute." I walked in too a hot damn palace. If this is how the government treated their sailors in Bahrain, I needed to get stationed over here as soon as possible. This dude apartment was laced. Hardwood floors, big ass flatscreens, marble countertops. I mean, this boy had it made.

"A how much you pay for this bruh?," I asked him. He laughed hysterically at me.

"My nigga, I don't pay for shit. Uncle Sam handles this shit. I just sit back and stack my check, making that bank account rise." I was impressed something serious. They paid for it and you basically chilled. Oh yea, I would have to keep this in mind. Maybe I would get stationed over here in the future. Maybe here or Guam. Naw, here would be more appropriate. Who the hell would wanna get stationed in Guam? I couldn't even see myself being stuck on an island. Never that.

"A, y'all boys hungry man? I got some left over cabbage, salt pork, roast and cornbread from last night." Man I know I had just ate, but I couldn't turn that down. Greg went to go take a shower as I commenced in warming me up a plate and going ham on this salt pork, no pun intended.

Me and Terry chopped it up and he was a cool dude. I found out he was from Texas, D-Town to be exact. I expected him to be the typical Cowboys fan who only talked about the three super bowls from the nineties, seeing that they couldn't win shit since. However, to my surprise, he was a diehard Steelers fan. The dude had Steelers mugs, plates, flags, all that. I wouldn't be surprised if I walked into his bedroom and seen that he had Steelers sheets.

I finished up and walked into the second bathroom to take my shower.

"A Carl, The Guest Towels are under the sink If you don't know. Use Anyone Except For My Steelers Towel!" Man, this dude was serious bout those damn Steelers. I showered up real good, thinkin about the only other time I showered in Bahrain. It was when I first got here, staying in my hotel. I remember there was a big window that exposed me from the neck up. It was great for a view, but it was scary at the same time. Now, I was here again, doing the same thing, but at peace with this place and myself. I finished up, put on my clothes and walked back to the living room.

"You ready mane?," Greg asked.

"Yea, I'm gravy. Let's do this." We mobbed it downstairs to Terry's car. We took off and hit the road heading to I don't know where. I just sat back enjoying the ride. While Greg and Terry was choppin it up, I was just sitting in the back seat, analyzing my life and the place it was in. I slowly started to feel like that I was on my way to becoming something great. I just had to remember three key things.

One, align myself with good people. You hang around trouble, you will get trouble. You hang around positivity and success, and the same will follow. Two, always analyze everything you encounter fully. Don't just jump into a situation because it sounds good, or if its a female, because she looks good. Make sure it can upgrade you and not downgrade you. Third, and probably most importantly, do not be afraid of what life throws at you. Everything eventually passes. If it aint God, it has no reason to be feared. As long as I remembered those key principles, then I would be good.

"We here y'all. Let's roll." Terry was quickly out

of the car after saying that, as we pulled up at a joint called the Gold Souq. The name was obvious, so I had to see what they had to offer. I wasn't a big jewelry man, but I didn't wanna ruin Terry's gratitude by just looking around. We got to one section of this place and I swore it was the biggest watch collection I have ever seen.

"My friends, my friends, how are you?" That was the Arab behind the counter greeting us cheerfully, probably for a sale. We scoured around, browsing for jewelry. Well, to be real, Greg and Terry were already trying on watches, while I sat back trying to make sure they didn't notice.

"Come here Carl?" Greg told me.

"Sup bruh?" He started to explain the fine art of jewelry selection.

"When you get a good watch or any piece of jewelry, don't be like most of these young boys and go for a million diamonds. Its too flashy, kind of tacky and it draws too much attention to yourself. You see this?" as he held up a solid pearl white Concord with a sleek design. "This is something that is different, unique and can compliment any outfit because it's a neutral color. That's how you do it as a grown man bruh."

Shit, I was honestly amazed. I always figured that a watch is a watch, but even then, a watch isn't a watch.

"Now, you pick out something?" I searched

around and searched around, and then I found it. It was a medium face, outlined in gold, with a kind of pearl face and a tan leather strap.

"How this you think Greg?"

"What do you think?," he asked me back.

"I mean…its a nice design, and the leather is a good offset instead of having a whole band made out of gold. Greg looked at me for a quick second before he nodded his head in agreement.

"I see you learn quickly young boy. Gone get it." I purchased it and didn't even break $100. Our money stretched over here and that was gravy for me. We walked out immediately after my purchase following Terry. Greg looked like he knew where he was going. Me, I was just wondering what was next.

"You were suits bruh?," Terry asked me.

"Nah, not really."

"Well today you grow up my dude. Trust me, you will thank me later."

Greg laughed as we began to walk down a side alley. Gone were the flashy buildings selling jewelry. We were now in what seemed to be the alley heading to hell. There weren't any doors. There were only curtains with lights shining through them. About halfway down the alley, we stepped through one of the curtains.

"Terrryyy."

"Ponytaill" They dapped it up.

"I see you brought ya two brothers with you?"

"Yea mane. They looking for some good custom made stuff to separate them from the rest." He walked over to us and introduced himself.

"I tell you two. I will get you looking right. You're brothers, so I will take care of you. See, we have no problem with you, as the black man has experienced the same struggle and rejection that we have. We have no problem with you. As far as I am concerned, we are all brothers. Now, lets get you two looking good."

That shocked the shit out of me. You would think the way the news portrayed the Muslim culture on television, that they were all some extreme radicals who wanted us dead. Nah, they were normal people like us with a few bad seeds. I mean hell, you see all kinds of black rappers on television promoting any and everything. That still doesn't mean that every one of us is a damn ignorant person.

I felt more comfortable now. That was humbling and enlightening to hear. All three of us started getting our body measurements taken. This actually felt good in a strange sort of way. I was so used to going in the store and buying something oversized and baggy. Now, I was on the way to possibly look like a man. Hell, I was 21, so I needed to start switching up my style.

"Go around my friend. Look and feel what material you want." I really didn't know what to look for in quality material, so Greg helped me out. I ended up picking some high quality Italian wool and cotton.

"So what's my limit Ponytail?," I asked him.

"My friend, you are a brother of one of my good brothers. I make you three custom made suits, 10 dress shirts, 10 pairs of slacks and give you three ties for $600. My goodness, that was a fucking steal I thought. Damn, dude really did look out for the brothers. I had one three piece made in cream, and another in a forest green with olive pinstripes. My last suit, which was a two piece, was Navy blue with light blue pinstripes. The good thing about the stripes is that they weren't a blaring light blue that stood out.

When it came to the slacks and shirts, Ponytail let me know that he would put together some good custom combinations for me that he knew I would enjoy. He would give everything to Terry and he would ship it to the boat when it was ready. I gave him the $600, he gave me the receipt, his e-mail, and we were all on our way. It was early into the evening and we didn't have to be back on the boat until 2 a.m. We went back to Terry's house to eat and got in a good nap before we headed back out for the evenings festivities. We were gonna hit the town, but we just decided to head back to base and party in an area they called The Desert Dome. It was straight over there. You could get you some grub, some drank, sit down at some table to enjoy it and they had enough room to get ya dance on. It didn't take long for us to get in the mood for the evening. We got some drinks in us with a lil bit of grub as Young Jeezy was blaring through the speakers. The whole damn ship was in this joint and we had the intent to tear this place down. I'm telling y'all, wherever the Nimitz landed, it wasn't the same after we left.

Once I hit the dance floor, it was on. I was getting juked up something serious out here. I may have been sweating in this hot ass heat, but bending females over on the dance floor was the lick. The night was going well. It was about 15 minutes till midnight. The placed was packed, the music was blaring, and then...all hell broke loose.

You just seen a mob run to the other side of the joint. I couldn't see what was going on from where I was, but somebody was rumbling. I started to see bodies end up on tables and the MA's came in running towards the entrance. Finally, I managed to jump on a table and see what was going on. Greg and Terry were looking from the inside of the food area I seen. It was a gang of niggas fighting. Then, I seen the sight of my life that let me know the Nimitz was not to be fucked with. The girls from the ship were fighting the MA's. These nutty bitches were actually fighting the military cops. Oh shit that got me geeked the fuck up. I don't know what started it, but dammit these broads were gonna finish it.

Before we all knew, military police vehicles were pulling up like a muthafucka. They had to throw tear gas into the crowd for us to disperse. I ran the fuck up outta there with the quickness and just waited outside for my peoples. By the time the smoke cleared, me, Greg and Terry were back together. We were teary eyed like a muthafucka, but we were cool. About 20 folks came out handcuffed, still shouting, talking shit. One group from the boat was screaming **"Fuck the Police!"** from the inside. How they were doing that with tear gas everywhere, I have no idea. All I knew is that The Nimitz was not to be fucked with. We were lucky. Me and Greg had a personal connect, so we immediately got driven back to the ship. I don't even wanna imagine what happened on the vans that were driving back to the ship. I got back to the ship that night and just fell asleep with a smile. Yea, tonight was fun. I could only imagine what the next night would be like.

That next day came about quick. Greg had duty CDO, but I was scotch free. Greg pulled some strings with my chain of command and got me overnight liberty to stay the night at Terry's crib. Not having to go back to the ship in the morning was cool beans for me. I mean even taking that nap at his house yesterday felt like a relief. You will never truly appreciate a bed until you sleep in a 6 by maybe 2 and a half to 3 foot space with a mattress made for prisons.

"What's crackalacking man?" Terry blurted out as he pulled up on the pier. I jumped in, bag in hand, ready to get this day jumpin.

"A man you gone love it today. I'm gone meet a few of the fellas over at Johnny Rockets. We gone eat and smash out to the water park." I looked at him strange.

"Water Park? Aint that some shit for kids?"

"Trust me my dude. You will thank me later."

"Aight," I said. I took his word for it. Maybe it was just me, but those funky waterparks I went to as a kid growing up in Northwest Indiana weren't shit. That's why I was so damn skeptical. We got down to Johnny Rockets. I had always heard of it, but we aint have any in the Midwest. At least around the parts I grew up in. It honestly looked like one of those old 60's diners that I had always seen on TV with some of those old television shows. We walked up in that joint and met up with two bruhs in one of the booths.

"Rick, Pham, this my mans Carl." We dapped each other up and just got to chillin. It was real cool as I enjoyed the waitresses stopping every now and then dancing. Plus, this fucking peanut butter milkshake I was slurping on was awesome!!!

"A Rick, I told him about the water park. I don't think he believes me." Rick put his burger down and just laughed.

"I see its about to break you in to." I guess this shit was off the chain. I still wasn't convinced though. Hell, they were stuck over here, so maybe they had duck vision going on. If y'all don't know what that is, that's when ugly girls start to get cute because you have seen em for so long, you start to find qualities about them. After about an hour of chillin, some picture taking, including flashing that Arab money, we took off towards the waterpark.

There we were, pulling up to the waterpark. The Lost Paradise of Dilmun Water Park to be exact. We walked in, and it really didn't look like anything special to me. That's until I turned my head to the right when I was putting my clothes in the lockers.

"HOT DAMN!" I shouted that shit out loud and didn't even realize it. There they were. Four of the baddest damn Ethiopian chicks any man could ever lay eyes on. I looked a lil bit past them, and there were some Brazilian chicks going to war in one of the pools. I knew they were Brazilian by the obvious Brazil flag tops and the one who was climbing out of the water with an ass phatter than Jupiter.

We went around this park and damn near broke our necks. I however was the only one who was damn near droolin. This was the Bahrain that they were used to. For me, not exactly. This however was a great reintroduction. We blazed through the whole day here. Drinking, chillin and damn near shittin myself on the tallest, biggest and longest waterslide I had ever got on in my life. I swear I made my peace with Jesus when I slid down. 5 o'clock rolled around real quick and we were jettin out of this place. Rick and Pham got dropped off back on base, and then we headed back to Terry's crib. I was chillin on the couch, watching a lil television, when Terry came out from the back room.

"A bruh, rest up. We gone head out at about 10. Its an all white party at the club tonight. You gone see some bad ones."

I took heed to that. I was already wrong about the first jump off, and I learned my lesson quick. Terry went to the back room to get some sleep. **"I'M WAKING UP AROUND 9! IT'S FOOD IN THE FRIDGE BRUH. HELP YA'SELF!,"** he yelled. That was cool with me. I was a little exhausted and hungry at the same time. I raided the freezer and popped two hot pockets in the microwave. As I brought em back to the living room, I sat em down and pulled my notebook out of my bag. I didn't really have anything in particular on my mind, but I did have the urge to write. So that's what I did.

SHADOW OF A MAN

I hide my thoughts in a vault that cannot be penetrated by anyone but myself, I take my feelings, crumble them up so that the only ones satisfied with them are the birds, see my words take on a whole new meaning too many others, and as much as my book is open, I close it off to avoid hurt, it's like sometimes, I'm alive yet buried under mounds of dirt, just so no one will find me, what is general is sometimes taken as subliminal, and was is subliminal is not said because I don't want to live with the emotions that come after, I myself am a disaster, one that exists in the midst of triumphs, I'm never enough it seems for myself, and I think there is a major problem within myself, bi polar is an understatement, because I can't even make a statement without suffering the consequence, so I keep my thoughts confined to notebooks with blue bars as if I have given my pen a life sentence to write sentences, all this until the death of me which occurs when ink is no longer present, I present my spirit to my soul, hoping for acceptance, knowing that if I say something to it, he won't backlash on me, see I have hidden the key to this lock, I want no one to even know I exist at times, these rhymes are just my coming out, when I really don't want to come out and be seen, I wish I could say it was all a dream, but I can't, it's reality, so I have to man up and face it head on...

CLONE

Clone me into your ex boyfriend, but don't give me his heart, I just wanna be his spirit so I can sit back and really observe what the hell went on, see I don't fall for the he did me wrongs, I mean, it happens sometimes, but not all of the damn time, let me be his ghost so I can disappear when you nagged at everything, when you questioned where he'd been during normal working hours, let me see how you rejected his flowers because they weren't your favorite color, see its more to keepin a brother than some good ass and good head, you say you want that crown on the top of your head and wanna be treated like a queen, well quit trying to be the king, wanting to run the household when you bring scraps to the table, see we simple, we want the ish that we aint able to do, and I aint talkin bout boys, I'm talkin bout men, and if you stay around givin your all to a man who aint worth two dimes then it sounds like you had bad mate selection, don't try and blame it on him because your dumb ass stayed around for an erection, and thats sad when a dick is the hardest thing on a man, but you wanna take that grief out on your next man, saying he has to earn his way, he gotta prove to you he's worthy of treatment, well baby girl, you aint God, so I aint gotta prove nothin, as you don't have to prove nothin to me, but best believe, if your past turns into my problems, I got an easy way to solve em, you'll be dismissed to the next chick, cause life too short to be suffering from what he did, see the problem nowadays is too many women think their cooch is golden, when it aint nothin but nickel plated, cause you can find silver everywhere, but gold is rare as hell, and if you think I'm a go through hell for you because of what he did, then you crazy as hell, see when I asked to clone me into your ex, I wanted to just see myself from the outside to make sure I wasn't trippin, and I wasn't, so enjoy your lonely nights, enjoy your fingers and DVD's, enjoy setting yourself up for unhappiness again, cause aint no real men gone take that shit

I managed to write two pieces to my surprise. I was happy than a mutha, cause I hadn't did that in a good while. I went to sleep, only imagining what the madness was going to be tonight.

Nine o'clock rolled around more than quickly. I jumped up to iron my clothes. I aint have an all white fit, but I did have a white polo, so at least a brother would be fitting in some kind of way.

"A boy, now this is how we get down out chere." The boy was fly I must admit. He aint come out with the typical all white Dickies fit. He came out dapper. He got clean with an all white, 100% Italian cotton fit. No poly or no ester in that joint. Slacks, dress shirt, shades with white trim, white ostrich skin dress shoes and a fresh cut.

Now, that is how you did it big.

"Well damn my nigga," I told him. "We aint going to church our we?"

"Naw foolio, but I'm going out there looking like a grown man. The fitted caps and shoes are nice, but fuck all that. When I step, I step correct." Damn, it seemed like everyone I was meeting was on a grown man dress game. Not knocking it at all, but I knew it would take me some time to adjust myself to that type of wear. It was cool though to see I must admit.

We headed out the door and hit the car. The club ended up being a quick 5-7 minute drive from his house. The joint was called BJ's. You know the first thing that came to my mind right? I was hoping that this wouldn't turn out to be another T.G.I.Thursdays like in Dubai, and we got cleaned up for some hookers. We stepped foot in that joint and it was far from T.G.I. Thursday's scene. Yep, this was a pure club atmosphere. Yep, this joint was full of beautiful women. Yep, it was one big ass white out. Yep, the music was on point.

Terry started walking me around the joint, introducing me to a few of his partnas and some bad ass females. Good thing about it is that I aint see nobody from the ship in here. This is just what I needed. I loved my bruhs, but it was good to get away from em. We walked on over to the V.I.P. section, where they already had bottles of Goose, Cognac, Hennessy and Patron on ice for us. I licked my chops, as y'all know Mr. Henn and Mr. Coke were about to mix into my system very well.

"A BOY!" Someone shouted that from the VIP area right next to us. I turned around.

"BONNET! WADDUP NIGGA?" This was my dude Bonnet (pronounced BO-NAE) from down bottom. He was from the backwoods of Louisiana. The boy had a permanent gold up front and was louder than a freight train. Man was he funny though.

"A MAN...I'M FUCKED UP HOT DAMMIT, BUT GONE GET YOU ONE OF THESE BAD THINGAMAJIGS IN HERE MANE! DON'T LET ME HOLD YOU UP!" All I could do was laugh and dap him up with nothing but love and respect. He may have been loud, but he was one of the most down to Earth cats on the ship I knew. He knew his shit work wise. I was never too fond of Boatswain Mate's in The Navy until I met him. I called them sea going janitors, cause I swore all they did was paint bulkheads and polish brass.

He showed me a whole other side to his job though. That's how we all were though. We made fun of each other's rate at a constant in The Navy. I was a HT, a.k.a. a plumber, so they called me a SHIT CHASER. Boatswain Mate's were sea going janitors. Fucking Yeoman's weren't nothing but paper chasers. HM's, known as the ships doctors were called "Handout

Motrin" techs, because that's all they ever gave you if you got sick. I didn't care if you had been shot four times, stabbed through your eye with a pick and lost your hand. They would give you some motrin, some water and tell you to go to sleep. Yea, that's what HM really stood for. Handout fuckin Motrin.

I could go on. We all had our fun talking about each other, but we all knew that we couldn't do our job without each other. As I enjoyed the music, Hennessey and a few bad ass women Terry brought up with him, I looked over a Bonnet living it up. I started to just look around the club in general. I was seeing people have fun, be free, cut loose, but keep it classy at the same time. Yea, the other night, the brawl was on. Tonight, I got showed something very, very different. It was possible to go to a joint with a lot of black folks and not worry about the joint getting shot up. It was possible just to live period. I was slowly changing my thought process inside. The old ways of me were slowly fading and a new wave of thinking was slowly creeping in.

"A BOY, FILL YA GLASS AND LET'S MAKE A TOAST!!! EVERYBODY HOT DAMMIT, WE TOASTIN!!!" I grabbed my nearly full glass of Henn as both VIP sections came towards the railings that separated us. Bonnet then began to speak, and trust, no music needed to be lowered at all for us to hear him.

"A LOOK HERE! WE IN FOREIGN LAND, WE FUCKED UP, WE GOT A DJ, THIS SHIT, THESE MUTHAFUCKAS DOWN BELOW US AND THE WORLD IN OUR HANDS! NOTICE SOMETHING THOUGH...WE ALL BLACK. WE ALL FROM DIFFERENT PLACES. ME I'M FROM THE MUTHAFUCKING BOOT! WE HOLDING EACH OTHER DOWN. SO BEFORE WE LEAVE EACH OTHER FOR GOOD, LETS TOAST TO MUTHAFUCKING LIFE!"

The biggest shout I ever heard in my life came out as we all snapped our heads back and took down our drank. Bonnet was taking a whole bottle of whatever the hell champagne to his dome. I learned just from this moment how valuable life was and had become. This was definitely a place that I would never forget as long as I lived.

SINGAPORE

Singapore was next on the agenda. We had left the Persian gulf a few weeks earlier and I for one was glad. I was so sick and tired of the blistering heat. It was 140 degrees topside on the flight deck. It was 160 degrees down in the pump room. Being an engineer over there sucked, but we were finally done with it and now in cooler weather around Southeast Asia. This was my first trip to Asia and I was very excited. I didn't know much about the place except that they were good for handing out some ass whoopins. I remember some years ago they caned the hell out of some white boy who went over there spray painting cars like an idiot. I'm pretty sure after catching that bamboo across his back he didn't ever wanna see another can of krylon paint ever again.

We got there on a rainy Sunday afternoon. I didn't have duty until our third day in, so it was time for me to get down for the get down. I had a partner I was cool with named Reggie. He was from Nashville, Tennessee. He was an older cat, about 5 years my senior. I know that wasn't much of an age difference, but it was big in the maturity department. He had a wife and kid back home, and he kept himself in line, ensuring not to do anything that would risk taking food out of their mouth. He had been here before, so he was gonna head out with me to show me the flare to this joint. We headed off the ship around 11 o'clock that afternoon, taking a taxi towards the shopping district.

"See that boi? That's where we gone be tonight!," as a happy go lucky grin appeared on his face from ear to ear while pointing at this huge building.

"What's that mane?" He even got happier with his response.

"FOUR FLOORS OF WHORES BOI! The name says it all!!" I just kinda leaned to the side and looked at him. A place called four floors of whores? Really? Now, I was all down for meeting women and doing what I do. However, this didn't sit well with me. I wanted to have fun, not go to a four story whore house. That just wasn't in my fortay. At least Dubai we were in a hotel. That place didn't look much of anything from the outside. *Oh well* I thought. I might as well roll with it.

We got dropped off right outside the Louis Vuitton store and got to walking. Man, these Asian folks really loved luxury. Prada, Gucci, Michael Kors. You name the designer, and their store was here on the strip. I didn't too much care for all that high end stuff. I was more of a simple guy when it came to dressing. Give me a polo, some crisp jeans, or a fine tailor made suit now and I was good. Reggie however liked the upscale things. We ventured into every designer store until he found what he was looking for.

"See this right here youngster," as he adjusted the collar on a button down Burberry shirt. "You gotta be diversified."

"Man you aint see those tailor made suits I got made when we were in Bahrain? You trippin bruh." That's when Reggie hit me with truth.

"Looka here," as he took the shirt off and neatly folded it up. "That's nice. You got one suit. Maybe more. Look what else you bought with your money though boi? Jerseys, jordans, all other sorts of bullshit. I understand its your first deployment. But your usual crew of friends are around your age. You going back to California bro. Out there, they dress. Its high end. San Diego is a money city. Hell all of Southern California is for that matter. You aint gotta look like you came out of a casket all the time when you go out. However, you do wanna diversify yourself. You a grown man now boss. We had our talks. We both from the hood. But you gotta expand ya horizons. Aight?"

I shook my head up and down as he began to walk to the register. I then thought about the lesson I just learned. Just because you are from the hood, it does not mean you have to constantly conform to the hood way of life. Reggie was right. The t-shirts, jeans and timbs were ok. However, I needed to learn how to dress properly. A few suits I thought was an accomplishment. However, a predator isn't satisfied with just eating one type of animal. It adjust itself to its environment. If the wildebeest are gone, then it has to hunt other animals that are available. It can't just rely on one animal for feed. The same lesson applied here.

I couldn't rely on one look to carry me through life. Lord knows my people were already known for walking around with our pants hanging half off of our ass, wearing t-shirts as long as dresses and all other sorts of bullshit. Yea, they were stereotypes, but they were ones that a lot of my people fed into. I was clamored to be the change.

"That will be $730 sir." My eyes got big. Damn, this dude just dropped seven bills on a shirt. I asked him as we walked out the store how much that was in American dollars.

"$600 boi." Damn. The price you paid for quality was amazing, even though I shouldn't have been shocked, seeing that I just dropped that in Bahrain for some clothes. We hit the streets once again, got some grub at Mickey D's and eventually met up with some of the ship bruhs at a hotel a few of em were staying at. After kickin it for a few hours over some beer and spades games, we all headed down to Orchard towers, a.k.a. Four Floors of Whores. Oh boy. I was about to get the experience of my life and I didn't even know it yet.

It was eight o'clock on the dot when we walked into this place. It wasn't as bad as I thought it would be. I saw a hell of a lot of women, but I also saw a good number of men. I thought it was one big whore house. Come to find out, this was a mall. What was the big deal these dudes were making out of this place I thought? Then, we kept walking. We hit the second floor. It was still a mall, but there were two bars on the floor, music blaring out of the speakers. You could tell it was full of squids, as you heard the screams and sounds that only Americans could make.

"A my nigga," Reggie said. **"Fourth...floor.**

We bout to get it in boi! Welcome to overseas niggga!!" He was loud as all to be damned as one of his boys hit me on the back as if to say it was time to break me in. We hit the third floor, and it was the same as the second floor. Then, we got to the escalator. These fools were making hella noise now. As we hit the fourth floor, the top of the building, I read two words: CRAZY HORSE. Oh shit. Here we go. We walked up in here and it was indeed crazy.

I saw everyone and they mama from the ship. I walked in feeling like a stranger of sorts. I was still fresh, but random girls started hugging me saying hey boo. Cats were giving me dap. I guess now I was officially apart of the ship family. It's crazy how much a difference a few months makes. Just a little over two months ago, I was a complete stranger receiving mean mugs. Now, I was officially part of the crew.

The dance floor was packed as Ying Yang's "Georgia Dome" was blaring through the speakers. Reggie and us all split up in here. Most headed to the dance floor. As for myself, I headed for the bar. After weaving my way through this madness, and a bunch of Asian women grabbing on me, I got to the bartender.

"A lemme get a Hennessy and Coke bruh?" The bartender took my Singapore dollars and proceeded to make my medicine. This was cool. I was vibin, chillin with my ship family, in a foreign country and life was good. I looked around real quick. Dance floor packed and a few bruhs with some girls on their laps. Even though some of those girls necks were kinda hefty, I guess the liquor had kicked in. I just hope they realized a he she before they got completely naked later. As I turned to peep the side opposite of the dance floor, I saw that girl I had flew in with, sitting by herself at a corner table, kind of twiddling her thumbs. It was kind of shocking, but then it wasn't.

Shocking for the fact that everyone was having fun. Not shocking thinking that no one wanted to mess with her because of her stank attitude. I had remembered how she had talked to me when I attempted to strike up a conversation. However, it could've just been a bad day. There was a lot of stress coming over to a foreign land. *Screw it* I thought. I'll go chop it up with her. The bartender gave me my drink and I headed over to the table where she was.

"Do you mind if I take a seat beautiful?" She just looked at me, blank stare, until she finally spoke.

"It's there aint it?" Oh my damn goodness. This girl was making me want to choke her ass. All I was trying to do was be cordial. I thought about turning around, saying screw it and just heading to the dance floor to get juked up. However, I decided to maintain my composure and sit.

"So let me ask you beautiful. Why are you so

anti-social to someone who is just trying to say hi?" Again, her stare appeared once again. This time, it was putting a hole through my face I felt.

"Why do you keep calling me beautiful?" I kinda threw my head back like what the hell. I wasn't expecting that. I sipped my medicine real quick.

"Well I just call it how I see it." She paused for a minute. I thought this time I would get something intelligent said back.

"Sorry, I'm not interested in talking to you." By then, I got the hint. The way I am though, I had to get the last word in.

"Ok miss lady. I apologize. I'll be on the dance floor if you would like to dance later. However, I just want to tell you that you are a beautiful person. But your soul makes you ugly as shit."

I got up, stared at her as I took a huge gulp of Henn, slammed it down on her table and walked the hell off. I know in her head she was probably saying a million curse words, but I aint even care anymore. I was being nice, but I damn sure aint about to kiss no ass. I scooted through to the dance floor to see Reggie getting his groove on with a shorty.

"Waddup boi?," as he slapped me some dap and kept receiving an oh so graceful juke. Twista "Slow jamz" was bumpin now and I was enjoying my drank, just vibin. All of a sudden, a nice lil Operational Specialist I saw around the ship backed that thang up on me. I damn sure accepted. The OS's in my opinion had the sexiest group of females on the ship. We grooved and it was nice. This was the life and everything was going great. The DJ went right into some old Do or Die. "Po Pimpin" to be exact. Ahh man, this was my shit growing up. I was definitely getting it on this one. Just as Twista got into his verse, I heard a loud glass shatter, followed by a vision of a fist flying through the air.

Everyone all of a sudden was getting knocked back and falling on the dance floor. I managed to grab shorty I was with and pull her off the dance floor before we got crushed. There was a fight and it was a big one. I couldn't see who it was, but it wasn't Reggie, as I seen him on the floor scrambling to get up. I made it through the ruckus to help him up as these niggas kept brawlin.

"You good, you good?," I asked him as I pulled him up and moved him off the dance floor. He was straight and we dipsetted towards the entrance. I saw all of Reggie's partners from the hotel outside the entrance as everyone started to file out nervous and confused. Just then, I saw a cat from the boat stumble out with his eye cut open. The gash was at least 2 inches long as he was drippin' blood everywhere. A few girls went to help him as I saw my mans Black from New York coming out, being held onto by three people. He was blaring a bunch of shit at ol boy on the ground.

"New York Nigga! We Dont Play That Shit Son!" His partners were telling him to be easy and to keep cool as they took him down the stairs and away from the situation. I was just looking like damn, he fucked that boy up. I recognized dude too. He was a cat from Florida who boasted and bragged like he was the thug of thugs on the ship. One of those air wing cats who worked on the flight deck. I aint know what part he was from, but I could see that mouth had wrote himself a check his ass couldn't cash.

"A y'all, Singapore police coming thru. Let's be out." That was one of Reggie's partners letting us know, and we proceeded to head down the stairs calmly, but in a quick manner. By time we got to the first floor, the police came through storming through there. The whole ship was damned near all filed out and concerned about catching cabs. The scene was tense outside, as we seen police sitting and waiting for someone to act up.

We all kept it moving, eyes locked on us like a hawk on a mouse. This damn near felt like America right now, except the cops weren't white. We had to consider ourselves lucky. We would've probably all got gunned down back in the states for walking while black. We found some cabs down the street and headed back to the ship.

Back on the boat, shit had gotten crazier.

Black ended up bangin with some of ol boys homeys in his berthing. He wasn't no easy win. Dude was 6'5 and could hold his own. We had sprinted down there as soon as we got the word. By then, all hell had broken loose. It was at least 10 niggas going at it. We were all trying to break it up, but it wasn't happening. Next thing you know, the ship's MA's came storming through the berthing 7 deep. Led by MA1 Turner, a big built brick of a brother, they quickly got things under control, and cleared everything and everybody out.

Things were crazy. I knew Navy life was wild, but now I seen it first hand. It was true what they said. In the Navy, you get drunk, screwed, tattooed and you fight. Three of the four were down for me, and it was only a matter of time before I started looking like Lil Wayne. I had enough excitement for one night. I walked towards the mess decks to get me a pop real quick from the vending machine. Everybody and they mama was out there, talking shit and trying to recover from the drunkenness that occurred.

I got my drank and was headed back to the berthing. As I rounded out of the p-way to walk through the forward mess decks, I bumped into someone and dropped my drink. "Aah damn!," I said as my pop fizzed all over the deck, some also getting onto my clothes.

"I'm sorry." I looked up to see who it was. It was her, miss funky attitude from the club. The same one whose attitude stank worse than pig shit. It had been a long night and I had just wanted to get some sleep without dealing with anymore drama.

"No worries, it's cool." I walked away pissed, but not trying to think too hard on it.

"Star." I turned around. This girl had actually talked.

"Star," I said.

"Yea, Star. That's my name. You wanted to know my name right?" I was astounded. This girl actually said something. All I could do was stare as she cracked somewhat of a smile.

"Just know you're the first man to ever say I'm beautiful." She spoke those words and continued on her way. I tried not to dwell too much on it, but I always appreciated talking to a person, whether it was just a simple how are you. I headed back down to the berthing to shower up and drift off into dreamland. The next morning, we found out liberty was secured because of the brawl and the Singapore government wanted our happy go lucky asses out of there.

Our CO was pissed the hell off! We were supposed to be there for a few more days, but that shit wasn't happening. This dude came over the 1MC, which is our intercom system and lit into our asses. It was funny, but not funny at the same time. I mean, this dude was a gangster. Hell I remember one night, a man overboard was called. From the flight deck I believe, someone tossed a chem light (glow stick) into the water. Those things are located on the life jackets so just in case someone falls overboard at night, we can spot them. Come to find out, no one fell over and the CO just warned us to be more careful when we were topside.

The next night, someone did the shit again. Again, the CO came over the 1MC and stressed the importance of not being clumsy up there and dropping stuff in the water. The next night, for the third straight time, someone did it again. This time, ahh man, the old man was pissed and the evil came out of him over the 1MC.

"Listen up you son of a bitch! When I catch you, whoever you are, I am going to keel haul your ass!" I know it was early as all hell in the morning, and we were all dead sleepy at our mustering station, but we had no choice but to laugh. Yep, that was the mighty USS NIMITZ. What it stood for you asked? Never Imagined Myself In The Zoo. This was indeed a zoo, with a bunch of untamed animals who got their joy off kicking ass and acting a fool.

<u>HONG KONG</u>

Singapore was now a distant memory as we now were anchored out in the waters of Hong Kong. It was kind of a gloomy day pulling in, so only remnants of its Jupiter sized skyline was visible. From looking over the side of the ship, I could see the waters were rough and rugged. *How in the good hell were we going get to land?* I knew the answer, but I still asked myself.

Two o'clock came around and liberty call was dropped. Usually, I would be on the first thing smoking off the ship. This time though, I had actually decided to switch things up. About two days prior to pulling in, I signed up for a community relations project. This was something the Navy did to either give back to the host country, or allow the host country to treat some squids to a good time. I signed up for something simple. Some random family offered to cook us an Italian dinner at their home. All I had to do was catch a cab over once we reached land. I was free for the first day in country before duty blues struck, so I decided to use it wisely. I just didn't know how great this decision would be.

I rolled out to the liberty boat round six o'clock with an air wing brother named Darien. He was from Georgia and was damn near one of my closest friends on the ship. We always talked about college football. I swear, you would've thought we were an old married couple when we talked about that shit. He was an avid Georgia Bulldogs fan. Me, I rooted for those Michigan Wolverines. It was always Big Ten vs. SEC talk. I guess it could've been worse. He could've been an Ohio State fan. I would've thrown his ass overboard had he been a Suckeye fan. The liberty boat ride was a good half an hour, and we were the only two on this boat, seeing how everyone else was already on land getting slizzard. The choppy water sound immediately got drowned out by our conversation.

"A mane. You think one day you gone settle down with that Star chick?" I looked at this dude with the most what the fuck look ever. I looked around to make sure wasn't nobody else on the boat with us, in case Ashton Kutcher was gonna jump out of a crack and say **"You've been punked!"** I turned back around to Darien and told him **"NIGGGGAAAAA PLEASE!"** We both started cracking up, but he kept on.

"Naw forreal my nigga. I mean, think about it? She was so uptight when she came to the ship. Then, you told me what you told her ass in Singapore about her being ugly as shit. Then, the incident where she made you spill your soda. Ever since then my nigga, she has been a totally different person." I kinda leaned back.

"What you mean?" That's when Darien went in.

"My nigga I'm tellin you. She been different. She actually smiles sometimes. She's trying to open up to folks. Hell, she used to walk around like her pussy stank. Now, it's like a gynecologist cleaned that shit out and said 'Here you go. You got a brand new pussy.'" I cracked the fuck up, as only Darien would say some shit like that.

However, I paid attention to him. I was actually glad shorty had started to act human. I wasn't trying to get with her or anything like that, but I did feel more at ease when I knew everyone around me was human. We chopped it up about everything until we finally hit the pier. Immediately, we saw a cab once we hit the street, as we told him the address given to us on the e-mail we both received.

"One Robinson Road," I told him.

"Oh yea. You're going to the money," the cab driver responded. Me and Darien both looked at each other with that alrighty then look. The city was lit up now. Hong Kong had turned into a gem. This city was amazing. 7 million people, and it seemed like it was 1 million lights for each person who lived here. We headed over the bridge and continued our journey. We finally seen the sign to Robinson Road as the cabby exited the freeway. The road got dimly lit, but it didn't look like anything we didn't want to walk through.

"Here you go. One Robinson Road."

We paid the cabby, got out and he sped off. We both stood there for a minute, looking at all these high rise buildings.

"Aight my nigga. Let's do this." Darien said. We were trying to figure out our way into the building. Finally, we seen a Silver Rolls Royce go into the building. After we finished picking our jaws up off the ground, we followed our way in right behind it. The Rolls was out of sight, but hot damn, this place was full of luxury cars. Ferrari, BMW, Rolls. Man, you name it and it was there.

"Man nigga," Darien blurted out. "They can dip me in chrome and put me on the front of this Rolls."

That boy was wild and bruh always provided me a good laugh. I pulled out the piece of paper with the address on it. We hit the elevator and were headed up to the sixth floor. As soon as we hit the sixth floor, the elevator doors opened and it just smelled like money. The door to our hosts was the first one as soon as we stepped off. We were both nervous as hell, as we didn't know what to expect from these Chinese people. The door opened.

"Hello! Are you the guys from the ship?"

"Yes ma'am," we both said together.

"Well come on in." I thought we had died and went to heaven. Man, this house was like walking into a live version of MTV cribs. I don't know what Darien was looking at, but the first thing I noticed was the huge bar that was full of every drink known to man. As the host, who introduced herself as Michelle continued to tour us around, I saw a cat on top of a plush couch inside of the living room. That couch looked like it cost well over $5,000. I mean this cat was laid up like he had been on vacation his whole life. Most of the times, cats were territorial and didn't like anyone in their space. However, he looked like he had an attitude of fuck it. *Damn, so this is what the other side of the hood looked like* I thought. Michelle eventually told us to make ourselves at home with whatever drink was available and some cookies as she finished up dinner. Immediately, I saw something that a lot of boys in the states hadn't ever seen. Hennessey White. I had always heard that this shit was smoother than a hairless ass. Steady scanning as Darien went to fill our glasses up with some ice, I saw something else that caught my eye. Gem Clear. I never seen it anywhere, so I put that on my list as well.

"Dinner will be ready in 15 minutes," Michelle yelled.

"Yes Ma'am!," as we stepped out onto the balcony. We were both in awe. The view of Hong Kong from the sixth floor was magnificent. I took in all the sounds, which was nothing but the sound of the wind. Up and down the street, the lights of the cars heading to wherever simply amazed me. Darien was busy downing that white. I didn't know what he was thinking, but I'm pretty sure we had the same thought process.

"We had achieved success." A black man making it from where we were from to the streets of Hong Kong. Tell me how many cats can say that?

"Dinner is ready gentlemen!" That was our cue to smash as we stepped back in. As we went back in the house, we were greeted by Michelle's husband John. We sat at the table, marveling at the masterpiece that Michelle had created. Eggplant, meatballs, fettuccine alfredo, garlic bread, two more dishes that I couldn't pronounce and a huge bottle of wine imported from Ireland.

As we ate and conversed, John let us in on his life. He was a profitable business man, whose company grossed well into the hundreds of millions. He took his company, which did major work with famous designers such as Louis Vuitton, from San Francisco to out here. Continuing eating, he showed us his collection of cigars from around the world, as he handed both of us authentic Cuban cigars that he had obtained while on his travels. I marveled at this man's story, as I imagined myself in his shoes. From the sounds of it, it sounded like he didn't work hard to achieve what he had. It seemed like all he did was listen, observe and copy a blueprint of one that went before him.

That was one gift that I did have. It was the observation and dissection of people. I could tell a lot about someone just through their speech and tones. There was no hardship in his story at any point. This man was an example of how to achieve success. It wasn't putting in long hours and pushing yourself to the limits. It was simply learning how to follow before you could lead. This was even further more solidified after dinner, as we were shown the numerous collection of cars downstairs, one of which consisted of a Ferrari. Now, the Ferrari wasn't the impressive part, as this whole underground garage was filled with luxury cars. it was the fact that he explained it as him and his wife's whatever car. Well shit I thought. If that was their whatever car, what the hell was their specialty ride? I didn't know, but me and my partner left with a renewed sense of goals. We headed back to the ship. Darien went to his berthing, while I went to my supervisor's office to check my e-mail and write. The title was simple:

LIGHTS

Dim lights bring out your worst fears as going into the darkness presents the unknown
Bright lights give you hope yet disguise trouble through vivid designs blinding people to the truth but what is the truth? you ask sometimes truth is disguised in the biggest lies

Duty went by quick the next day. When I got off that following morning, me and Darien headed off to Ocean Park amusement park. I really didn't know how to describe this place. Just picture Sea World mixed with Six Flags, mixed with an Aquarium on steroids. We kicked it here until about mid afternoon and then headed to Hong Kong's Wai Chai district. This was the party spot out here, as any and everything you wanted was here. Yep, if you lost your pinky toe in an accident, you could probably find it on sale over here.

We stepped into a joint called Joe Banana's and caught a few of our homeboys from the ship. It was amazing how this organization was nothing but a big melting pot. We sat around a table, choppin it up for a good while. My dawgs Malcolm and JD were both from the LA area. My dude Chris was from the Chi Blocks. Throughout our talks about gang culture, city life and whatever else, I was more so focused on the fact that we were all from different backgrounds, coming together and just learning each other. Eventually, as with brothers, we got tired of the tough talk and got hungry. There was a buffet down below and we didn't wanna waste any more time starving.

"Man what the fuck is this mystery meat?" JD boasted.

"I dunno playa," I replied. He had a point though. Nothing was labeled food wise, but everything was recognizable except for this meat. I could tell fried rice was fried rice. I could tell egg rolls were egg rolls. What in the good hell was this mystery ass meat they had on the line? It looked like a big ass pan of grease. Now I knew what Chris Tucker meant in Rush Hour when he told Chan "that was a big ass box of grease." We all said screw it and threw it on our plates. We got back to the table and commenced operation indulge. At the same time, we all sampled this mystery meat. While chewing, we all looked at each other. No words, just chewing and stares. We were all waiting for someone to say something.

"MUTHAFUCKA! This Shit Here!" That was Darien going off as he stabbed his fork in for another bite. We were all nodding in agreeance.

"Nigga," I said with a full mouth. "I don't know what kind of meat this is. Bear, lion, crossbred horse and baboons. But whatever it is, they put their foot in this shit. Niggas must of seasoned this with some Ancient Chinese pepper or some shit."

"I co-sign famo," Chris replied. We all started to just max out now, feeling good and getting back into our talks since we were getting our food fix. After all of us went back for seconds, including JD who got a whole separate plate of the mystery meat, the waiter came and asked did we need anything.

"Yea sir," Malcolm asked. "What kind of meat is this?" Immediately, the waiter started to chuckle.

"Do you really want to know sir?"

"YEA!" Malcolm screamed. Hell, to tell you the truth, we all wanted to know. With one last chuckle the waiter replied to our request.

"You all eat dog meat. Very good." He chuckled and walked back down the stairs as we all just stared at each other in amazement.

"Third plate nigga!" yelled Darien as he got back up. Hell, we all did. I don't know if we were eating pitbull, weiner, rott, shitzcu or what. All I knew is that dog was high on my fuck up on sight list from that moment on.

After stuffing our faces and washing it down with every liquor imaginable, we went down the street to a hotel a few of our partnas were at. As soon as we hit the floor they were on, the first thing we all noticed was our man's Mace pissing right in the middle of the hallway. As we all laughed hysterically, he kept feeding the imaginary fish. I knew we were all a lil tipsy, but this fool was dead ass drunk and it wasn't even eight o'clock at night yet.

We entered the room to the smell of damn sex and liquor, as Mace finally sat his ass down. It was a shorty in the bed under the covers, and one girl from the air wing aboard the ship chillin on the second bed. She didn't budge as we all walked in, so in my mind, I kinda figured out what she was on. Just then, the bathroom door flung open.

"Man, my dick won't go down. This shit won't go down!" That was the homey Ranger from the ship.

"Nigga what the fuck you do?," I asked with a crazy look on my face.

"Man, me and the lady was chillin. I copped one of those Viagra pills just to see how it was. Man, we was fucking forever. Bruh, I mean, my shit stood at attention longer than us at quarters. Now my shit stuck! **FUCK!**"

We all burst out into laughter as this nigga let out fuck you after fuck you after fuck you. While we were entertained by that, Chris and ol girl from the air wing had been conversing with each other. Now, he was on the bed, slobbing her down. I mean, you could tell this girl had skut bucket written all over her. We looked around at each other as her shirt came off. Even Ranger girl had a "damn bitch" look on her face. JD suddenly pulled his camcorder out and placed it on the hotel room dresser. Before you knew it... yea.

Say what y'all want, but being young and not giving a fuck goes together. Especially with Navy dudes. Now, it was back to Joe B's. Our nuts were empty and the liquor was out of us. We had to refuel. As we walked in, we saw that the whole ship was in here, along with a few cats from the USS Princeton. Hell, they lucky they even got the chance to get in. I immediately jumped into the crowd as Three Six Mafia's "Who gives a **** where you from" shook the place. We were in this hoe beyond crunk. It was crazy how the Navy was. The entire world swore up and down we were so professional. Then, we hit these foreign ports and just act an ass. Every time a hood song comes on, you saw a million gang signs go up in the air. Lords, GD's, Bloods, Crips, Latin Kings, 13's, everybody set was repped. It was cool, but it wasn't cool. Bringing the hood into something it wasn't meant to be could backfire. You just hoped that it didn't.

After dancing and drinking about half of the liquor supply in the world, I took my tail back to the area where we were eating earlier. One of my mans from Milwaukee was up there kicking it with a lil shorty from the boat. I was about to sit down, til I noticed a shorty all by her lonesome. She was on the ship and she was dead on ugly. I mean, she had a face that only a mother could love. I recognized this, but the liquor in me said this was an easy target. We'll just call this shorty "Mrs. B." Trust, the B damn sure didn't stand for Beyonce.

As I started talking to her, you could tell her ugly ass was on ten, as she wasn't used to men talking to her at all. We talked about shit I can't even remember. I kept drinking my Henn and talking to this ugly ass thang. That was until I started to cop a feel and kissed this ugly ass mudduck dead in her mouth. Oh we kept kissing too. I couldn't stop, as the liquor was telling me to keep going. I looked up to see one of the Boatswain Mate chicks from the ship look at me and just shake her head. I aint give a damn. Hell, you only lived once. Plus, she had a big booty. Just then, some drunk white dude came up and started talking crazy to my mans from Milwaukee. I mean seriously, he just came up and got in his face for no reason. The liquor quickly brushed out of my system and the grown mature man came out of me.

"A man, just gone back and chill," I told him as I nudged him back towards the three stairs.

"NIGGA FUCK YOU!" he shouted back as he pushed me. Just as I was about to come back at him, out of nowhere I heard someone yell

"Carl bout to fight!" It was my boy "Slim Cutta" from Cleveland. He used all of that reach of his 6'7 frame to snatch dude and commence a vilified ass whoopin. Soon, the music stopped and the whole USS Nimitz was fighting each other just to get a piece of this cat. All this was going on while two partnas from the ship were keeping me at bay. Cats from the Princeton were trying to sneak out, but they eventually got caught and took an ass whoopin themselves.

This brawl, if you wanted to call it that lasted a good ten minutes, as the 6-8 bird gang thugs took it from the inside to outside the club. Eventually, things died down, as everybody from the ship was now back inside of the club getting crunk as if nothing had even happened. This was the Nimitz for you. Thugs, lowlifes, crazies, people with half of brains. All brought together in a one thousand and ninety two foot piece of steel with the sole purpose of kicking the ass of enemies foreign and domestic. Now, you could add different ships as well to the list of those who could get their asses kicked. These were my brothers and sisters, and I wouldn't trade them for anything in the world. As I calmly hit the bar for another drink, Pastor Troy's "Vice Versa" hit. I seen Darien wilding in the corner with some oriental chick.

"GEORGIA MY NIGGA!," he shouted as I laughed my ass off. This was Hong Kong, this was life and this was me Carl, loving every bit of it.

CHAPTER SIX

HEALING THE HEART

HAWAII

When you start a journey
the destination is unknown
stuck in a parallel universe that inhabits success
yet we are sometimes too fearful to visit
because to us success means gains
financial, mental, physical
when deep down we forget the most important one of
all
and that's life
if your destination is life
you have achieved success

I wrote this as we were almost complete with this journey. I had totaled 4 and a half months of this six month deployment. The day I flew out of Chicago, I thought my life was completely over. Going into unknown circumstances after leaving unknown circumstances. Now, I was truly smiling. This was the last stop before we headed home to California, and that would be part three of my journey. Life hadn't even begun for me and that was the scary part.

I had duty this October 30th, 2012 day. We had pulled in at about twelve o'clock in the afternoon. You would think I would be upset having duty the first day back in the states. Contrary to belief, I was happy. I used this day to indulge in cable TV, with BET being my default channel. I hadn't been up to date on all the latest music, new artists and all that. First vid I seen was something with 50 cent. I didn't know if it was brand new, old or what. All I know is that it felt good to hear some music I could relate too.

I sat in the office all day, preparing for the next four days off in Hawaii. I had gotten me a hotel room at The Waikiki Wave. It was right off of the Waikiki strip, so I assumed it would be cool. This was my first time to Hawaii, but from what the cats on the ship told me, it was easy to navigate. It was one looping highway around the island, so it was damn near impossible to get lost. Even though I was chillin, I was bored as hell. I was the only cat in my shop who had duty, and wasn't nobody to talk too. TV was eventually boring me even more, so I decided to get up and head outside to one of the ship sponsons. I just stood there, leaning against the lifelines, thinking about life. Truthfully, I was thinking about my mother. It still seemed surreal to me that she was departed from this Earth.

Deep down, I still felt like a failure. I was the reason she was dead and gone. Had I not went back to G.I., she would still be alive. This was a wound that would run deep in my soul until I was six feet under. My grandmother used to have a saying. She would say that bandages can cover a wound, but the healing process was determined by the body. I never got that until now. A tear or two trickled down my cheek as I looked out into the grassy and cloud covered mountains of Hawaii. I was just hoping that I could get this right. I hoped that I could make something out of myself and not let her down. I was hoping to find my bandage to cover up the wound on my spirit and soul. Hopefully, one day, I would be able to take it off and be completely healed. Right now though, it was still fresh, bleeding with every breath I took. Death had to be better than this feeling. I calmly took in another five minutes of the scenery and walked back to my shop to chill for the remainder of the day.

The next day came along with a breeze, as I was ready to tear Hawaii up from tha roota to tha toota. I meant that literally too. I had heard how good the pork was here. They cooked the pig underground in a process the island folks called kahlua. I was dying to try this, along with just wilding out on the island. It was Halloween, and I heard the stories about how this day on the island was their Mardi Gras. I never experienced a Mardi Gras ever, so I wanted to see what it was about.

I caught a cab to the airport from base and rented me a simple Ford that had some knock. I know I had tax free bread in my account, but I didn't need to stunt in a Navigator or an Escalade for the next four days. I pulled out that Jeezy Thug Motivation 101 and started to shake the island through these speakers. *"I told 'em straight drop this and ziplock that/Right on my waistline is where I kept that strap (yeahhh)/I remember nights I didn't remember nights /I damn near went crazy, had to get it right (that's rightttttt)"*

Man this shit was thumpin. I loved the music of The Snowman. It was perfect riding music on this lovely 80 plus degree day. The sun was out and beaming as I hit the H1 highway, headed to the Waikiki strip. I had never seen anything like this in my entire life. I mean, the scenery on this drive was just breath taking. All I saw were green mountains and low lying clouds. This shit was amazing. I exited off towards Waikiki. All throughout the streets, folks were starting early as damn near everyone was in some type of crazy ensemble for Halloween. All I could think was that tonight was gonna be wild. I made it to the Waikiki Wave and checked in. Room 404 was to be my dwelling for the next few days. I expected it to be a normal room with the usual amenities. As I entered though, my mouth dropped.

"I'LL BE HOT DAMNED!," I screamed out loud. Now, this was luxury. Straight through the door was my 'frigerator, with personal sized bottles of liquor. I aint see my medicine of Henn Dogg, so I knew I would have to make a run by the store. To the right, there was the private bedroom with sliding doors, just in case you wanted to make the walls sweat with a female. The living room ahead was huge. There was an oversized sectional sofa and another bed by the patio window. What the fuck? These niggas was on one in this telly I opened the patio door to see that it led right out to the roof.

Yes, the hotel was bigger than four floors, but my room on the corner just happened to allow me to walk out and just look at the strip. I proceeded out and let out a whale of air. I got to the edge and just looked up and down the street. It was poppin right now, so I could just imagine how it would be tonight. Life was indeed coming together. At this moment I realized, another wound had been healed. I could take the bandage off the scar left on my mind that I called Gary, Indiana. I made it out. I was halfway across the globe. When you come up in an open wound called poverty, it festers and gets infected until you one day make it out. There are many consequences that come with leaving, but most of them are good and better for you. I just smiled, walked back in and decided to take a nap for a while.

I woke up around six that evening, sleeping longer than what I expected. I immediately took a hot shower, brushed, listerined the teeth and got my fit ready for the night. Y'all know me. A simple blue polo, some heavy starched charcoal jeans and some blue and grey timbs with my named etched on the side of them, courtesy of my mans Eric from Minnesota. I ditched the car and proceeded to walk towards the elevator. As I was heading down the hallway, I saw an OG from the boat named Mac. He was an engineer like myself and dude was hella cool.

"What's crackin Mac?"

"Aint nothing young blood. Tryna enjoy myself just in case this my last time." I gave him a side eye.

"What you mean bruh?"

"Step in the room young blood. I'll explain everything." I stepped into his room concerned like all hell, but trying not to show it.

"You want something to drink youngster?"

"Naw man, I'm good." I sat on the couch as Mac went to the cabinet of his kitchen and pulled out a bottle of Southern Comfort, Hypnotiq and Vanilla Coke. He sat it on the living room table and went back for a glass and some ice.

"I'm gone mix this up and make what they call Tennessee Swamp Water. When you mix it together, it turns a murky green color. That nigga Reggie you hang with showed me this shit, and I fucks with it."

I just let out a chuckle as he was so adamant about this drink. He took a quick sip and put his drink down. "Do you remember when they called that medical emergency two days before we pulled in to Pearl?"

"Yea man. I didn't respond 'cause I was on watch, so I don't know what went down."

"Well youngster," as he took another sip of his medicine. "It was me. My heart spazzed out. I don't know what happened. I just got up and it was racing. I been dealing with heart problems since I was twelve years old. Actually, nine. I got a waiver to come in the service, and I was actually straight 'til about four years ago. I started getting chest pains every now and then. I thought nothin of it as my heart always seemed to beat normally. Now, I can't take this shit no more."

I was stone still, keyed into the look in this mans eyes. He really didn't know me personally, just mainly from the training he gave me on the ship. However, to hear him opening up his soul to me was humbling.

"I thought they were gonna fly me off the boat since we only a week and some change away from home, but they diagnosed it as anxiety. I just feel weak at this point. And now, I'm gonna sit in this room tonight and just drink. At least if I die, I'll die on a mattress with the least amount of pain as possible."

He sipped one more time before he really hit me with the realist shit I ever heard. "Remember this young blood. Sometimes, it takes you dying inside…before you really start to learn how to live."

I processed those words as he extended his hand. I grasped it and with a firm grip he looked dead in my eyes. "Go out, enjoy this thing called life. If I don't make it through the night, just remember what I told you."

He ended with a grin as we embraced in a quick hug. As I exited the door, I looked back at Mac one more time. He held up his glass and shouted,

"Heaven better have a bar!," as he smiled and sipped again. I shut the door, leaned my back against it and shed a few tears. I didn't like to think negative, but I knew that was the last time that I would see Mac alive. I headed out the hotel and proceeded to walk the strip until I came across something that caught my eye besides the numerous amounts of ass that was walking up and down the street. Man, there were women in every skimpy costume you could imagine. After walking a few blocks and crossing over to the next street, I stumbled upon a joint called Dukes. It looked chill from the outside, so I said why not. I walked in and headed upstairs. Boy oh boy, this was definitely the right idea. They had a big ass bar, and the joint extended outside to the beach. I actually held off on the liquor for a minute and got me a simple orange juice. I walked outside to the beach and just looked around to see if I seen anyone I recognized.

"Carl!" That was my boy BJ from Fresno. I sat at the table and we chopped it up for about an hour on good times and just life in general. It was a cool convo with no distractions, except when one shorty walked by and we had to eyeball those cheeks until she hit the water. I was definitely impressed, seeing how I was a booty man myself. I swear it looked like someone was smuggling two beach balls full of cocaine on her backside. We both cut out around 9:30 and headed to club Zanzibars together. It was right next to my hotel, so that was a good thing, cause I could get tore back and just stumble to the hotel elevator.

We walked up the stairs to the club and seen that this place was packed more than flat titty women with kleenex in their bras. Everybody and they mama from the ship was there. Jukin was at an all time high. Women were in every costume you could imagine, including a few who decided to come in just lace thongs. (Yes lawd!) I was peepin' everything up in here. I even seen UFC great Chuck Lidell in the corner chillaxin. Man I hoped no one would get some liquid courage and try to mess with him. I would hate to see a grown man get his face bashed in.

Eventually, I got into the party. The whole ship was gettin it in!!! Of course I had to get juked up a few times. Get in my groove like a G was supposed too. After a good two hours in, I finally sat my black ass down for a minute, Hennessey number four in my hand. I just wanted to get a good buzz so I could walk straight to my room and pass out later. As I chilled out vibin, sippin and listening to some classic Domino that the DJ was spinning, I heard a voice.

"Is it okay if I sit down?" I looked up to see Star. I didn't know what to expect, but it seemed like ever since I told her that she was ugly inside, she was trying to change how she was, or maybe she was bi-polar as all to be damned. I didn't know, but I was surely about to find out.

"Yea sure. Sit on down. Let's rap a taste." She sat down. Blushing, but with a sense of nervousness on her face. I started off with a simple question to get convo started.

"So aint you gotta be back to the boat by 1?" I know it was corny, but it was all I could think of. She chuckled and responded.

"Naw. I got overnight tonight with a friend, across the street in The Island Colony." I let out a little chuckle and took a sip.

"Cool, cool. So lemme ask you something? Why is someone so beautiful filled with so much animosity in her heart? Once again, her famous pause came into play. She kind of chuckled and put her head down for a minute. I was now confused. "Did I offend you with that question?," I asked. Hands folded, she raised her head back up.

"Naw...naw you didn't. You just brought back old wounds that I need to heal." A smirk came over her face, as you can tell all of a sudden that she became very uneasy.

"Well Star, if you need an ear, mines is open. My grandma always said you have two ears and one mouth, so you should listen twice as much." She smiled, placed her hand on my hand and simply told me "Let's worry about that later. For now, it's time to enjoy this time."

I could feel the emotion behind her voice, as I wholeheartedly agreed. Ironically, we didn't even dance or anything. Our night continued on with great conversation until the club closed around three. No personal trials were disclosed, but I slowly started to feel that she would be my balance of some sorts. It was a crazy feeling, but indeed a legit feeling. I walked Star back to The Island Colony, and got back to my hotel after heading to the nearby Jack in the Crack. I swear they had some cocaine in their Supreme Croissants, and a brother had to get his late night fix on. I walked in my room with a new feeling of accomplishment. The crazy part about it is that I didn't know what I accomplished. As I got to the fourth floor of my telly, I stopped in front of Mac's room. I stared at door number 416 for about a minute before I put my ear to it. All I could hear was a TV and the ramblings coming from it. I just hoped that wasn't the only noise being made in his room. I hoped his breathing was still making a sound. At this precise moment, I did something that I wasn't accustomed to doing. I got down on both knees and just prayed right in front of his door.

I mean, it wasn't that simple "Lord heal him prayer." Naw. I really put my heart and soul into this prayer. I was in front of Mac's door for at least eight minutes, praying for a miracle. Finally I got up, touched the door with my hand and walked off to 404. As I pulled my key card out, I looked down at my watch. The time read 4:16. It was the same 416 like Mac's hotel room number. I didn't know what to make of this, but I felt God was telling me that he heard my cry, and this was a sign of it.

I walked in my room and sat at the table, eating my Jack in the Box. I pulled out my notebook of words and was about to write. Suddenly though, I couldn't. Everything in me just up and left. There was no energy. I was once again facing death. This time, it was someone whom I felt didn't deserve it just yet.

The same way my mother didn't deserve to die over my misdealings in life. My tears formed a lake in my hands as I couldn't believe this. There was nothing I could do but take my weary eyes to a mattress until they closed. I prepped myself for bad news later today. That's a part of life though. When one wound closes, another one opens. Our souls are nothing more than human bodies. It gets cut, stabbed and burned. However, it must heal. How long it takes to heal...well that is the question that cannot be answered off top.

The next afternoon came around. I woke up feeling great. I brushed my teeth, showered and prepared myself for another day on the island. The swap meet was at Aloha Stadium today, so I figured I'd swing by there and see what I could cop for the low. As I exited my room, I immediately remembered Mac. I didn't hear any commotion in the hall while I was sleep, nor did anyone knock on my room door with any bad news. However, I was worried sick.

I walked over to 416 with an urgency as if it were two miles away. *BOOM BOOM BOOM!*

"MAC!!!" I called out. No answer. *BOOM BOOM BOOM!*

"MAC!!!" I yelled again. Right then, I started to think the worst of the worst. As I began my third set of bangs on the door, it finally opened.

"Lil nigga what is your problem knocking like you the damn police?" It was Mac, looking like nothing was wrong.

"Man," as I tried to slow my own heart rate down. "After last night's talk we had, I was scared shitless about how I would find you. I'm sorry man. I just wanted to make sure you were okay."

Mac stared at me, and with a quick sip of whatever brown liquor he was drinkin, he uttered, "Come on in. Let's rap." I walked in and sat at the coffee table with my mentor. "Last night young blood, I was tired. I thought to myself, God hates me. He has put me through hell and back with this heart shit. I mean, even a hooker's pussy can tighten up, but my heart couldn't get back on the right beat." He paused for a long minute.

"I told myself, this was it. If God's gonna make me suffer, then I might as well lend the Devil a hand to ease it. I drank, and I drank, and I drank until I felt I was drunk enough to where when I finally took my last breath, I wouldn't feel anything. That boy Dockery, you know, the computer working muthafucka from the boat, look like DMX, he came thru last night. Asking can he crash here. I said cool. I gave him a room key and he was out and about doing whatever. It was about one in the morning when I finally closed my eyes. But right before I did, I said God, when I open my eyes, make sure the first thing I see is my grandma. I wanna see her in the same blue dress they buried her in, with her damn wig on straight. And make sure she got her shades on, cause she wouldn't go anywhere without her shades on." Mac started to chuckle before he got back into it.

"I went to sleep youngblood, thinking it was the last sleep I would ever encounter. Then, I woke up to a special on ESPN about the Chicago Cubs. Those sorry somma bitches I love that can't win shit, but I love em."

"Then...Carl," as his voice got real low. "I realized God had answered my prayer. I woke up to see my grandma. She loved her Cubs. I thought maybe they would win before she passed, but they didn't. I realized then that God showed me her, through her favorite team. I realized when I seen those boys on the screen, that I still had purpose on this Earth. What I'm trying to say to you Carl is this. This morning, I realized, life is like baseball. You strikeout from time to time. However, until the last inning is over, you're guaranteed another bat. I struck out. But when I woke up, I realized it was meant for me to crowd the plate again. Learn from me. And what I want you to learn the most from me is what not to be.

The good shit, yea everyone always harps on that. But when a muthafucka can exploit his own flaws, and bring em to the surface without fear of judgement, THATS, what makes a man. Not to mention sharing ass, as that somma bitch Dockery didn't do yesterday. Had me waking up to a naked white girl in the living room, and aint even have the **AUDACITY** to wake me up and ask did I want a piece. Aint that a bitch?"

As he sipped his brown, I could only bask in the amazement of what I had just heard. There was no sugarcoating of anything. It was all facts.

I learned something new today with this conversation. Another wound had been healed. That was the would of self pity. Mac had felt sorry for himself, and his bandage was alcohol. His wound was his soul. Who knew though that baseball could provide a healing effect of a mans mind? I didn't, but I truly knew now that The Good Lord indeed worked in mysterious ways. I was now less concerned about the rest of my time here, and focused on my next task at hand, which was returning stateside to California. A new chapter was beginning. My challenge though was who would write my story. Myself, or the world.

When wounds are fresh blood flows like rivers
through pores that scream out to be heard
cells rush to clot and stop life from being lost
but sometimes clots are impossible
blood must flow in order for one to grow
blood must flow in order for one to grow
blood must flow in order for one to grow
when you understand that, you will finally
understand life

I had now been back on American soil for about two months. I rang in the new year of 2013 hard as ever. California was unlike anything I had ever experienced. Shit was wild I tell you. I had linked up with some homeys on the ship from the Bay since being back and got a chance to hit up Oakland. Let me tell y'all something. Oakland aint nothing but a bigger version of Gary. Hood was an understatement. I mean, it felt like I could just walk up in someone's home, say I'm home and kick my feet up. That's how much similar it was to my hometown. All that stuff that folks see on TV with them ghost ridin whips and getting "Hyphy" as they call it, it's all true.

The funniest thing I remember was when I was downtown. I can't even remember the name of the joint we were in, but it looked like a Seizure convention. I saw so many heads and dreds shaking in there I swore that I would have to call the paramedics for somebody. Dreds, gold teeth and ebonics to the tenth power were the norm around those parts. I fucked with it though. They were down to Earth in the Bay. That was the major difference between Northern California and Southern California. In SoCal, it was every man for themselves. SoCal had SD, LA, Hollywood, stars, the big names, all that shit. It was fast paced and if you didn't keep up, your ass would be left behind wondering where in the world did everyone go. Northern California was more laid back and just chill to the tenth degree. You didn't have to deal with all the snobbyness and Hollywood acts put on by people. They were just human up there. It was truly humbling to have experienced the Bay Area. Also after the new year, I made my first major purchase, a black Mercury Sable. I know it wasn't much when you consider what young niggas drove around nowadays, but it was something.

After all the shit I had dealt with over the past few years, I was just happy to have something in my own name that was legally purchased. I whipped all around my new home of San Diego. This place was paradise to me. You were just a hop, skip and a jump to Mexico. There was something to do every single day of the week. Yea, life looked like it would be gravy over here. As far as work went, everything was going good.

I had my advancement test for petty officer third class in March, so I was really looking forward to trying to put some more money in my pocket. Don't even believe these military cats when they say they wanna make rank for responsibility. That's a crock of shit. They wanna put more money in their pockets, point blank period.

It was the end of January and the weekend had approached. Friday night was here and I had to get away from this ship. I was only an E3, so I was required to live on the ship. However, I didn't have duty this weekend, so I said to myself that I was gonna get me a hotel room down in Chula Vista. I had hoped to get off a lil early around lunch since it was Friday, but we had a huge ass clog in one of the heads on the ship where the Captain's Quarters were. It caused a major flood of shit water, so we had to get that fixed a.s.a.p. Unfortunately, it took the majority of the afternoon to fix and we didn't get off until around 3:30. Dead tired, I took a shower, got dressed, packed some clothes and headed off the floating piece of steel. The walk to the parking lot was a relieving one. It was about 4:15 when I got to the whip and threw my bags in the trunk.

"Hey Carl?" I turned around, it was Star.

"What's up Beautiful?"

"Ummm...are you doing anything tonight?" I didn't assume that she was getting at something, so I just kept my composure and responded truthfully.

"Well, I'm tired and I need a break from the boat. I was gonna get a hotel and just chill out for a weekend. You know...get my mind right.

"Ok," she responded, nodding her head in agreement.

"Would you mind if I spent the weekend with you?" I aint know what to think now. Here was the same chick who hated life it seemed when I first met her. Now, it was like somebody performed an exorcism on her and relieved her of whatever demon had possessed her.

"Sure, why not," I exclaimed with a smile. She smiled back as she told me to drive her to the ship so she could pack a bag. I waited in the officers parking lot directly out front as she went aboard to do her thing. In the meantime, a million thoughts ran through my head.

First thought was *where in the good hell did she come from.* It was just me when I was walking from the ship. That was like some ghostly shit. More importantly though, I was thinking *why in the hell were me and this girl all of a sudden connecting?* We talked a few times since we had been back home, but that was it. I couldn't front, shorty was cute as a button, but I still had my concerns about her. You just don't flip from the grinch to Mother Teresa. Not that fast at least. However, my inner voice in my head told me to go through with this. Right then Star knocked on my window, signaling for me to open the trunk. I popped it, she threw her bags in and we rolled.

It was kind of surreal heading off base, as she played with her phone and I didn't say a word. Crazy I talked to her freely any other time I seen her since Hawaii. Now, I had her all alone and I couldn't muster up a word to say to her.

"So…who's your favorite college basketball team?" *What the hell* I thought to myself. Of all the conversation starters I could start off with, and I ask a chick who is her favorite college basketball team. She put her phone away and looked dead at me.

"Kansas, and aint no other team in college basketball." I was shocked. This chick actually related to something most men do.

"You out yo damn mind miss lady. It's Hoosiers up, and that's all you need to know."

Aah man, that opened up a floodgate, as we had a hellafied debate all the way out the gate, over the bridge and to the 5 freeway. As we exited E street, the convo shifted.

"So where are we staying," Star asked.

"Right here," as I pointed to the Days Inn right off the freeway. "You hungry, cause I can check us in and we can get some grub? You know, get a good meal, get to learn each other." She looked at me while we were stop at the light.

"Wow...no one ever offered to even want to get to know me. That's cool." I could see the demeanor on her face change completely as the light turned green. I felt that I had hit a trigger down deep in her spirit, but I didn't know how deep. This night would surely tell. I checked in to the Days Inn, room 228. We didn't even put our bags in there. We were hungry and our stomachs needed to be fed immediately.

"What you gotta taste for?" I asked her.

"I'm simple. Wings or burgers will do," she responded. I drove down Broadway, the road going through all of Chula Vista until we hit a Wings-n-Things. I was glad they had one of these joints over here. I had some wings from there a few times since I been back and they were fire. We walked in to an empty restaurant, which was odd for a Friday night at only minutes before six o'clock. Each ordering a 16 piece with 6 breadsticks, we waited at the table until our order came and began in a convo that would change both of our lives forever.

"So tell me about Carl? The man, the inside person. The one who many people don't know?"

I was shocked. She had leaned in with this one. She was very interested. All I thought about was Hawaii when she didn't wanna open up. However, I wasn't gonna make this about the past. "Well...I came in after doing time for being involved in a murder. I copped a plea deal, and was released early when I decided to enlist. The warden hooked me up because he was connected with someone in the Navy. And now I'm here."

She sat back. She didn't say anything, but the look on her face said "I'm shocked." She then leaned back in.

"Well I'm Star. I was raised in multiple foster homes. My mama wasn't there. My daddy... There was a long pause, as I seen her head drop in obvious distraught. "My daddy...let's just say he wasn't what he was suppose to be in my life. I'm from Wichita, Kansas. I came in as a last resort. It was that or worse. Honestly, this is what's saving me right now. And that's me... Star."

I now was sitting back in disbelief. I knew this wasn't her full story, as she knew I didn't reveal all of mine. However, I now had a better understanding of why she was how she was. Our food came and we decided to change gears. We talked about college basketball again as we smashed these wings and breadsticks. It was like food brought us temporary comfort over our past hurts and allowed us to be free for a little while.

We finished up around seven and decided to go for a drive. Filling the whip with laughter, we headed back North on the 5, headed to the Coronado bridge. It was a clear night, so you could easily see into Mexico.

"What do you see when you see lights Star?" I don't know where that question came from, but I wanted to feel like my life was improving talking to this girl.

"I dunno," she said. "Too me, lights don't bring me joy. Life has kept me in the dark far too long. You think lights give you hope to escape to another side. For me...that's not the case." Things got dead silent for a minute as we caught eyes. Things all of a sudden didn't feel right.

"Can we go back to the room?," she asked. "I'm opening up to you too much and it's scaring me." I planned on turning around when we got to the bottom of the bridge in Coronado, but I had to make her feel comfortable. Right now, she was tense, and I didn't want her reverting back to that woman that was spiteful. "Just remember this. Like you, I'm broken. So I'm not tryna save you from whatever is troubling you. I'm just here to understand you. You came to me. I didn't ask you to come with me." I hit the bottom of the bridge and turned around. "However, since we're together, we might as well clear the air on everything. You like me. I like you. There it is. Aint no bullshitting about it. So if you like someone, you talk to them. You learn them. So the choice is yours on how you want this weekend to go."

There was an eerie silence as we drove back over the bridge. I don't know what prompted me to say what I just said, but it did come from my heart. Damn near back to the 5 South, she let out a deep breath.

"Ok…you wanna know Star…Then you'll learn tonight." We gave each other a quick glance and nothing was said all the way back to the hotel. Upon entering the room, the eerie silence continued. I just put my bags down and laid on the bed. She on the other hand sat opposite of me, at the table, a look of distraught on her face.

"Star, who are you?"

"I'M NOBODY OKAY! I'M NOBODY! SIMPLE AS THAT!"

Hot damn I thought. Here she was again with that crazy ass attitude I encountered when I first seen her. I could see where this was going, so I decided to comfort her with my own story.

"My mama's dead." She looked up at me, tears in her eyes.

"What?" in her muffled voice.

"My mama's dead like I told you. I did some ill advised things some years back with a group of people and it came back to bite me in the ass." I sat up and moved towards the edge of the bed to sit, nearly putting us face to face.

"She died because of my sins. My fuck ups." By now, I was shedding tears. "I grew up hard. Three brothers, now all locked up. Mama dead. Daddy dead. Little to damn near non existent family. I'm educated according to America. To myself though, I'm an ignorant fool. That's Carl. Now...who is Star?" I can tell that she wasn't expecting that, but I also seen that it kind of put her at ease. I wiped the tears away from her eyes.

"Thank you," she muttered. With a deep breath, she went into who she was. "Im Star Jennings. Born and raised in Wichita, Kansas. My mama was a drug addict. My daddy"...right there, the tears began to flow.

"It's okay beautiful," I told her. Right then, she looked at me with a surreal look.

"No one has ever called me that in my life. Not even my parents." I grabbed her hand. Why I grabbed it, I really don't know. I guess I felt she needed to feel that I was genuine.

"My daddy molested me since the age of five. He forced me to do all kind of things to him. My mother abused me, choosing dick over her daughter. I was the only child and I had no one to run too. Finally, when I was 8, my mama and daddy had a huge fight. I sat in my room, clutching my bear Junior, as I heard things crashing all over the place. I stepped out right on time to see my dad repeatedly striking my mother in the head with a meat mallet. He only stopped when he looked up and seen me.

'**COMMERE LIL GIRL!**' I remember those words as he grabbed me by the hair and drug me to him and my mama's bedroom. '**Remember what I told you!,**' he shouted as he pinned me down. '**The man is always right? Right!**' I was so scared that I couldn't even speak." She paused as her tears began to really flow.

"Then...then," as she fought her speech through pain, "he pulled out his dick and put it on my lips. He kept screaming the man is right. I finally managed out a yes, as he then threw me in my bedroom and shut the door. He was putting my mama's body in the closet. I thought someone would call the police. But in the projects, everyone minded their business. They didn't want to get involved out of fear of becoming a victim. He told me to c'mon as he got his keys and we headed to the car. I remember seeing people outside, not even paying attention. My daddy didn't care, nor did the people around me. We got in the car and headed to the liquor store. I didn't know where we were going after that, but I knew it couldn't have been anywhere good. He left me in the car. While in there, a police car pulled up. I took one glance inside the store and didn't see him. I darted out the car to the cop. Beating on the door, screaming, **MY DADDY KILLED MY MOMMY!!! MY DADDY KILLED MY MOMMY!!!** The cop got out the car along with his partner. Just then, my daddy came out the store. Liquor bottle in his hand. He caught eye contact with the cops. They all paused, and then he took off. The partner followed in pursuit as the other cop stayed there with me." At this point, I no longer felt bad for my situation. What this girl went through made my situation look like a bunch of nothing.

"I don't know when they caught him, but I never seen him again after that, and I knew my ordeal was over. I was placed in foster home for girls, but still scarred forever. I lost my virginity at 12. I opened myself up too many boys during my teenage years, looking for and wanting to feel loved. I'm the definition of a ho. I'm nothing more. I've had two abortions. I'll never be able to have kids. I'm not a woman. I gave myself up to so many men before the age of seventeen." She buried her face in her hands ballin as I reached over the top and hugged her. We just sat there. She cried and I consoled. This was the case for the next thirty minutes. Finally I told her c'mon and lay down. We got on top of the covers. I held her as she constantly cried harder and harder. Before I knew it, we were both asleep. I aint even realize we had fell asleep. The clock was about 1:22 a.m. Saturday now.

"Carl? Carl?" she whispered.

"Yea." The lights were still on, so my eyes were screaming.

"We both are broken. Can you promise to help me find Star? I'll help you find Carl." I was groggy as ever, but coherent enough to listen.

"Yea. Let's do that." I got up and cut the lights off. We both went back to sleep. I don't know what was going thru her head. As for me, another wound had been opened. This time, it showed us both how big of a bandage would be needed to heal us both. Time would tell whether or not that bandage would do its job.

Saturday morning came around and I was awaken by the light shining through the blinds. I looked at the clock to see it was 8:02. I turned back around to see Star awake, eyes wide open looking dead at me.

"Good morning," I said.

"Good morning." We embraced in a hug that seemed like forever. This here was starting to scare me. I never in my life had a connection with a woman, but I was slowly starting to feel like I was falling in love. I aint wanna think that far ahead though. I think this was my mind just messing with me. Star got up to take a shower. I cut on the TV, and went outside to bask in my thoughts for a minute. I really started to think about where I wanted to go in life. Truthfully, I was asking God very silently why was this woman put in my life? We had no talks about a relationship, but it sure as hell felt like one. I walked back in minutes later to see Star combing her hair. She cracked a little smile, but I was in straight awe. This girl had beyond an amazing body. She was in some basketball shorts and a wife beater. Oh boy, I had to keep my composure.

"So what are we doing today?" she asked while keeping a steady stroke of the brush going.

"You wanna go to base chapel so we can talk to Chaps?" She looked at me kinda strange for a minute until her demeanor finally shifted to a smile.

"Monday. We'll go together…Monday. For now, lets enjoy life. It's something that seems we haven't done ever." She knew just what to say at the exact moment to make me feel better.

"Okay, cool beautiful." I jumped in the shower to get myself clean. After that, I got dressed and we headed out to breakfast at the first IHOP we could find. The day was far more than amazing. Our conversation gave us both stimulation that neither one of us could have ever imagined. It was like this woman was trying to pick apart my mind in a good way. It was like she was attempting to break down my worse fears and put them out of my system. All day we stopped somewhere and talked. From the mall to the beach, we talked. As the evening came about, we descended back to the hotel room for a quick nap. Upon waking up around eight o'clock, I asked her a serious question.

"Can we have a redo of Coronado tonight? Maybe the lights mean something different now that we've talked."

Laying down looking at me, she smiled and responded "Sure." We took off around nine that night, hitting the bridge and cruisin with the windows down. Yea, it was January, but we were from the Midwest, so California cold nights weren't cold to us. It probably got down around 55 over here. That was gracious to us, seeing that in January back in the flatlands, winter nights would be like 20 degrees. Or, if you grew up on Lake Michigan like I did, you could be talking about 5 degrees, with a wind chill of -15.

"You ever imagined living in a place like this?" she said as we were stopped at Orange Avenue, waiting for the light to turn green.

"What you mean?"

"I mean look at this place Carl. This Coronado. Land of million dollar homes. An island all to itself. I mean, you can walk around here at one in the morning and not worry about getting mugged or anything like that. I always dreamed of that you know?" She really made me think with those words.

"Yea, I feel you. I wish like hell Gary could look like this. Seeing the house I grew up in. My surrounding area. This was stuff that we only got to see in movies. I could see myself getting married, raising two or three lil ones in an area like this. No worries about them going outside or anything. With a mama...and a daddy. That'll be my dream right there."

"Yea," she replied. "That would be good. Just us in a big house, raising a family." My head whipped around towards her at the speed of darkness. Fuck the speed of light, cause that wasn't faster than darkness. if you don't believe me, ask yourself why light cannot escape a black hole. It gotta be moving faster than light if light can't get up out of there, as the great comedian Eddie Griffin once reminded us.

"Oh, I'm sorry," palming her forehead in her hand, looking out the window. "I got caught up in the moment. Glad you were at the light. I don't wanna be the reason we fly off the road."

We both got a good laugh as I continued South towards the strand. "I always wanted that though Carl. I mean...even with everything that happened I wanted kids. I wanted to show them the love I didn't get. To give somebody the chance at life I never got. Now...I'll never have that chance. I...I messed up any chance with any man in my future. That's if someone would want such a broken person." She looked out the window as I hit full throttle on the strand headed towards Imperial Beach. I didn't know what to say, as it was obvious that she was beyond distraught. So, I did the only thing I knew how to do. Freestyle some spoken word.

"When a bird breaks its wings
it is told that it cannot fly
so instead of just laying down to die
it walks on two feet, trying to reach its destination
frustration sets in as it sees other flocks in formation
wishing it could hover above the clouds
instead, he hovers over soiled ground
fearing the ants will retaliate from all life he has taken
shaken, but not frozen, lost, but steady hoping
all of a sudden
his heart gains strength, his legs grow stronger
lungs almost out of breath
but its will to live grows longer and longer
all of a sudden its flies
reaching the sky to soar with the flock
non stop, the bird flaps its wings
as it sings tunes of freedom
even though it has never been imprisoned in a cage
however, its end is soon near
there is no fear of death

because it knows all that is left are dreams
dreams of flying, dreams of being free
dreams of being happy upon your last ride
because even when you're about to die,
your dreams can keep you alive
as the ants swarm
there is inner peace
it will rest in peace
even knowing it will become pieces to another"

Deep down, I figured that shit was corny. All I really wanted to do was try to make her feel better as we continued our drive on the way to the beach.

"That was beautiful." I glanced over to her real quick, thinking she said that to not make me feel so corny.

"What does the bird represent may I ask?" Damn, she was really into it to my surprise.

"Well, in all due respect, that all came off the top of my head. However, if you ask me, the bird represents you. I mean think about it. You expressed to me that you're broken down. Well, the birds wings were broke. However, instead of feeling sorry for what he couldn't control, he dreamt that he was with his flock, flying to wherever. He knew he was about to die, but he gained peace in his last moments, making it feel like he wasn't dead. What I'm trying to say Star is this. Healing can start with a dream. You dream about what you want in life. The kids, the house, the love. Then you make it a reality."

I didn't know if it made sense what I was saying, but I continued rambling on because deep down, I felt like I was striking a chord within her. "My grandma said once that we all have open wounds that we need to put bandages on to heal. From what you have shared with me, the bandage you need is one to cover up an open wound, which is your past. Don't feel guilty by it. Slowly, but surely, heal the wound."

That was it. I didn't know what to expect. I had hit the end of the strand and was turning towards the streets leading towards The Boardwalk pier.

"Well," Star expressed, eyes watery. "What if we both helped each other heal our wounds, like I asked you in the hotel?"

Right then and there, I started to think about my mother. With my eyes watering up, I let out a muffled "Yea." Star was a perfect example of how God can work in your life. She started off not liking or trusting anyone. I started off feeling guilty for what happened to my mother. It wasn't any kidding with this. We needed each other, and I would be boo boo the fool to think otherwise. We reached The Boardwalk pier in IB. From what I seen, it was just us and three other people out here. I understood, seeing that it was cold out here to these Cali folks. As we approached the multi colored arches that greet you upon your first steps to the pier, I grabbed her hand. What the hell was I thinking? I really didn't know. She gripped mine tighter as she glanced at me with a smile.

We continued a slow trot, no conversation until we hit the middle of the pier. I directed her over to the side, where I held her from the back as we looked out at the crashing waves that were enhanced with a sensual glow from the full moon that was out.

"I got a question Carl."

"What's that?"

"What is this here? Like, what we have right now. What is it?" I didn't even know truly, but I answered it the only way I felt necessary, and that was from the heart.

"The beginning of something great." She unclenched my hands, turned around and looked at me dead in my eyes. Her hair was blowing in the wind as she wrapped her arms around my neck. All I seen was a woman. Not the broken down female who was molested, abused and gave herself up to many men, trying to feel loved. Just a woman. She was more than beautiful. If God made a better pair of lips, he kept em for himself. She brought my head down to hers as we touched foreheads. I thought *wow. Here we are, about to share an intimate moment.* She slowly whispered "Can we pray?"

I let out a small chuckle. "I mean...sure. Why

not?" Her demeanor was so serious though.

"I never prayed Carl. I never believed there was a God. I never thought I would feel like I was genuinely cared for. I'm starting to believe that God is real again."

Man, I was now intrigued. A boy would be upset. However, I was a man, and I was grown enough to see that this was more intimate than lip locking.

"Let sit on the bench and do this," I told her. We walked over and sat down, and I immediately jumped it off. *"Dear God. I pray for the healing of Star and the guidance that you give me in order to help her with whatever she may need. Amen."* I wasn't much of a prayer person, but I always remembered that the few times I did go to church as a youngin, the pastor always stressed praying for others. So I did.

"Dear God. I pray that I can be what Carl needs to heal, and I thank you for putting him in my life to help me." With tears beginning to flow she continued. "I'm sorry that I distanced myself from you for so long…but I am ready to take the first step on the right path. Amen."

She grabbed me and we just hugged. In my young 21 years of life, I had never felt this close to anyone. I thought to myself that I put a bandage on another open wound. The wound was my emotions. I remember how I hid them in high school with my poetry, all because I didn't want the homies to clown me. Now, that bandage was taken off, as I was healed from what I thought was shameful. In reality, it was not. A real man shows his emotions. We hugged for what seemed like forever. All I remember was when I looked at my watch, it was 10:37 p.m.

We got up slowly and headed back to the car. The walk back was quiet, but we conversed through our hands. The power of our clutch said enough for the both of us. She said "I trust you." thru her fingertips. I said, "I'm falling for you" through mine. I just couldn't tell her that yet. We took the same way back we came. We were astounded by the lights and the view from the strand.

"Hey," I asked. "I'm a show you my singing skills."

"You can sing?"

"Hold on, hold on. I got this." I grabbed an old mix CD from the center console and popped it in. "Yea, that how it going down." Ja Rule's "Thug Lovin" was the shit, and I couldn't front. She was cracking up hysterically, and then Bobby Brown part came on.

"AND I KNOW YOU GETTING BORED!" I screamed that and she screamed back

"NOO!" That shit was funny. I knew I couldn't sing, but dammit it just kept our Saturday night going on the up and up. Man, this girl brought out the best in me. From the looks of it, I was bringing out the best in her. We made it back to the hotel sometime around 11:30. I showered first and she followed behind. Now, we were laying in bed different from Friday. Both clad in wifebeater and shorts, we could see what each other was thinking.

"Can you do something for me Carl?" she said in an oh so sexy voice. I nodded my head.

"Can you promise not to be mad at me for wanting to lay here with you?" Before I could even get a word out, she explained why. "Last night was one thing. Now, I wanna really make myself a woman. I don't know what you felt, but I felt comfort tonight. Promise me you'll be here through everything. Even when I'm weak. Be my strength."

The only way I could respond was by kissing her on her forehead and a yes. With a smile on both of our faces, I cut off the lights and we held each other. We drifted off into dreamland. No worries. No cares. It was us. We were together. She might not have said it. Neither did I. I just knew it. As we awoke the next morning, we were determined to spend our last few hours before checkout talking about goals. We left around 12, got us some surf-n-turf burritos and headed back to the ship. This weekend was over for us, but we were definitely just beginning.

CHAPTER SEVEN

<u>**VALENTINES DAY 2013: THE BEGINNING OF LOVE**</u>

Ever since our weekend rendezvous, things were looking on the up and up more in my life. Me and Star talked every night, whether it was face to face, or by phone. Nothing had changed between us. However, I felt better than ever as an individual.

The basketball games at The Warehouse on Naval Air Station North Island had even got more intense. I mean, me and the fellas always talked shit, but I swear I was Jordan now. All this renewed energy because of a woman. Aint that a trip? After finishing up an array of games the first Saturday of February, me and a partner of mine from GA called "Murk" sat back and chopped it up on the sideline.

"So where ya baby at?"

"Mannnn," I said in an oh so sarcastic tone. "That's not my baby man. We just close." I was lying my ass off, as I knew I had beyond deep feelings for this girl. Murk seen through that bullshit too. The words "NIGGA PLEASE" snapped off his lips at the speed of sound.

"A mane, I know I aint no relationship expert or no shit like that, cause all I do is fuck these hoes. But I see how y'all interact with each other and man....you got her ass to smile when before, all she did was walk around like her pussy stank." I couldn't help but laugh, as this dude was off the wall from his speech, to those bright ass Marvel super hero socks he always wore.

"Shit nigga, you told me the story between y'all two and Valentine's Day coming up."

"So what point are you tryna make?" I asked.

"What I'm sayin is this. You like her. Naw, scratch that. You love her and that's yo boo. The shit falls on a Saturday. The Captain giving everybody besides duty section Friday off so everybody can go skeet. You got money saved. Buy two plane tickets, take her ass to Wichita for two days, make her face her fears and be there for comfort. I **GUARAN-DAMN-TEEE**, she gone love yo ass for life and suck cancer out yo shit." Murk tone was funny as ever, but he hit me with some real shit.

"Like I said nigga, I aint no relationship expert by any means, cause all I do is nut on these hoes faces. But if you really love her and care for her, like I know you do, say fuck them cheap ass flowers, fuck that musty ass candy, fuck the teddy bears, fuck the hearts, fuck the dog with the fleas under its toenails. Give her ass something she won't forget. NIgga we just came back off of deployment, so don't say you aint got the funds."

He was right, even though I didn't wanna admit it. I was a grown man now, and if I wanted to obtain something, I had to do grown man things. I dapped Murk up as he went on about his day. Me, I stayed around to get in a lift session for about 30 minutes. With each lift, I thought about what Murk said. Honestly, I was scared. I didn't know to what extent Star would take me asking her to fly back to Wichita. Talking about it was one thing, but going back to where the pain started was a whole new ballgame.

I finished up and headed back to the ship to shower. I called Star, who was out and about in Diego. I told her to meet me at the bowling alley on base at six that evening for something major. I didn't know what her mindset was, but mines was shattered into a million pieces. Each piece represented an emotion. And right now, my emotions were everywhere like shattered glass. Six o'clock rolled around, and I was more nervous than a young boy walking into a cougar club. It was now ten minutes past and my nerves were on an all time high. I never knew her to be late. All of a sudden, I seen her car pull into the parking lot. My shaking right now wasn't cause of this chilly night.

"Hey you," as she greeted me with a hug, followed by a kiss on the cheek.

"What's up? What you wanted to talk about?" With one deep breath, I let it all out.

"Look…for Valentine's Day I wanna take you home. To Wichita I mean." A confused look overcame her face as I continued on. "I figured instead of a normal Valentine's Day…I'd take you back. Help you heal from everything."

She walked away a few steps, crossing her arms as if to be in disbelief. She stared up at the sky, not saying anything. She looked back, eyes watery, then whipped her head back around.

"I LOVE YOU STAR!" *Where in the hell did that come from? Did I just say what I think I said?* She turned around and just stared at me. Arms still folded with a look of disbelief. I walked up to her and placed her face in my hands. Chilly, our breath showing with each one we took, I kissed her. She kissed me back. I couldn't believe this was happening. Our meeting last year was in my rear view mirror. We were riding together now. Foreheads touching, tears flowing, she asked me in the softest voice ever,

"Did you mean it? Don't play with my heart. No one ever loved me." After a short pause to bring my heart rate back down to normal, I took in one deep breath.

"Yea...I meant it. Now, will you allow me to help you heal...love?" She began to cry lakes now as she nodded in agreement. One more kiss sealed it, and we hugged for what seemed like eternity. I looked up at the sky with her in my arms to observe the stars. I felt one of them was my mother, and that she was giving her approval of this girl. I grabbed Star even tighter. I now knew what it meant when a person would say that sometimes you have to decrease to increase.

I was decreasing the will to grow myself in order to help someone else grow. What I didn't know is that I was growing at the same time. I was evolving into a grown man. Age doesn't make one an adult. Their mentality and how they carry themselves does.

That Friday the 13th arrived quicker than we both imagined. We honestly wasn't supposed to be traveling this far without a leave chit. We just prayed like all to be damned that nothing happened between now and Sunday. She had duty on Monday, and I for damn sure didn't wanna get caught in some freak snowstorm in which she couldn't get back. Hell both of us for that matter. The day was already superstitious, so that added to my concern. We caught an early six o'clock flight out of Diego to embark on this 3 hour journey to the Midwest. She was sleep from the jump, head on my shoulder, looking like she caught a tranquilizer to the chest on National Geographic. Me on the other hand, I had my laptop open to a blank word document. I stared at it for a long minute, looking at the power of just a page. When we read, we sometimes fail to see the power of the words. It's not necessarily what they say. It's the fact that they are there. Remove them, and you just have a page. It reminds me much like life.

The people in our lives are like words. Whether they are bad words or good words, we Need them in our life to achieve our purpose. If you take away those words, in this case referring to people, we are left with just a blank canvas. An empty shell of ourselves. That why I hate it when people say "I dont need anyone but God." They are taking away His power of putting people in our lives to get where we need to be.

If you say you don't need people, then you are saying that you don't need God. It was about 30 minutes into the flight and we had reached cruising altitude. The flight was nowhere near full, as not many people travel from the hot to cold in February. I finally collected my thoughts, took one look at this beautiful woman who really didn't know how beautiful she was, and I began to write.

GRITS

Looking at the pot, empty with a hole that has to be filled, I pour water into it and slowly bring it to a boil, 100 degrees is its desired temp as I pour until I am satisfied with the proper amount to sustain my appetite, I can eat these all night and all day, see the key to good grits is to keep stirring, the grits that is, not the pot, you must not stop, as the spoon keeps em loose and gives it the proper texture, perfect food for the time of the year when sweaters and thick furs are needed, see I eat this so much but I still don't know where they are seeded from, it didn't matter, because they brought joy to my soul, whether in a bowl or in a plate, I embrace when I eat…....my grits, but as I reach for the salt and the butter, I realize I had none of em, I realize my grits are just plain, needing enhancement, but enhancement isn't available, see I thought making grits was simple, until I realize simple is when other parts are added, when you are missing pieces, things get complicated, and maybe that's why God has you in the position that you are in, because His enhancements he sent to you called friends, you pushed them away, all because you didn't need them in your way, and I realized, we are nothing more than grits, stirred up properly, but never properly being flavored, without our missing seasonings…called people

I really didn't think about it when I wrote it. However, I did think about how much me and Star needed each other. I closed my laptop and fell asleep, patiently awaiting when I could truly experience her world and absorb her pain as mine to digest it and shit it out. We awoke with about 45 minutes left in the flight. I put my laptop up and looked over at my girl.

"Hey Babe?"

I was answered with an immediate "Not now. I need me time right now." She looked dead out the window as she said that, as I knew us inching closer was stirring up emotions that she had built up for two decades. I couldn't even fathom the thoughts she was experiencing. All I could do was empathize. And right now, my empathy was telling me to shut the hell up and let her do what she had to do to prep herself.

We landed at 9:17 a.m. at Wichita Mid-Continent Airport. Exiting the plane was swift, as it wasn't anywhere near full. Star didn't say a word as we headed to baggage claim. There, I only placed my arm around her as if to tell her "I'm here." Still, no words, but I knew she felt some sort of comfort that I was there.

Our bags came around, and we headed to get our rental car. A red Ford Taurus was simple enough for this trip. There wasn't no need to stunt, as I know other cats my age would probably be concerned about that. We loaded up the car and I pulled off, headed to the downtown Hyatt that I had booked. It was only about 8 or 9 miles out, so we could get to the room and relax, possibly catch up on some sleep.

"Turn here," she said, staring out the window. I did exactly as she said. I kept driving under her direction until we came to a slew of old abandoned houses.

"Stop right here." I parked. From the looks of it, this was the Gary, Indiana portion of their city. This was the hood. Shit looked rough just like back home. Star got out, stood in front of this two story house and just analyzed it. I filed out the car about a minute later, giving her time to process her thoughts. I walked up to hold her from behind.

"I thought you grew up in public housing babe?"

"I did. This is my old foster home. If you wanna call it that." She broke my grip and walked up the stairs with me following close behind. She got to the doorway and just stood there, observing the caution tape over it, because that's all there was. She began to rip it down.

"You're going in babe?" She turned around, gave me the mean mugs of mean mugs and turned to walk in. I didn't wanna go, but I wasn't gonna leave her. I walked in, stepping over old furniture, trash and all sorts of other shit. Star continued to walk until she got to a back room and entered. I stood outside in the hallway for a minute before slowly walking up and peeking my head around the door to see what she was doing. She was knelt down, crying on an abandoned twin sized mattress. I walked over, placing my hands on her shoulders.

"This is it Carl," as she balled out her soul. "This is where I gave myself up so much, all in the name to feel loved by someone. I was stupid, naive, a young, dumb bitch!"

That's when I knelt down, grabbed her face and talked to her like a husband instead of a boyfriend. "Look, what happened, we can't take back. But I know *** damn well you aint what you just said. You're beautiful. Your soul is beautiful. When I look at this mattress, I simply see where a growth process occurred. This don't happen, you may not come to the Navy. You don't come, we don't meet. We don't meet, and I don't even wanna imagine what life is like."

She looked at me. Looked back at the mattress. Looked at me again. Looked back at the mattress again.

"You right Carl…it's over. I love you. Let's go." A faint smile cracked across her face as I picked her up and we walked back out the house. We made it back to the car, taking off for the hotel. Head leaned back, she shocked the shit out of me with her next words.

"My pain is dissipated
tucked away in a locked box
thrown under the sea
only to be found
by no one"

"I know it sucked Carl, but I tried for you. I tried to express to you how you expressed to me." I kept my focus on the road while responding to her.

"That was beautiful, much like yourself." I saw a smile out of the corner of my eye. She leaned back, closed her eyes and enjoyed the ride until we got downtown to the Hyatt. We got to the hotel after 12, which was cool seeing that we couldn't check in till 12 anyway. We went straight up to the second floor, entering into our poolside room. As we entered, bags were dropped and we both just flopped on the bed. Staring at each other, we talked through our eyesight for at least five minutes.

"I got one more end that I need to mend up."

"What's that," I asked. She clutched my hand.

"I need to go see my father." I really didn't believe what she had just said. She wanted to actually reach out to the man who molested, raped and scarred her beyond belief. If it was me, I probably wouldn't had given two shits about someone who did that to me. However, if the word if was a fifth, it would've been drunk already. Plus, it was not my forgiveness he needed to obtain. It was hers. More importantly, forgiveness isn't for the oppressor. It is for the oppressed. To support her with this would teach me more about myself than ever. In this moment I realized another wound was closing. It was the wound punctured to her soul many moons ago. This wasn't over by a long shot, but I could truly see that she was well on the way to internal peace.

We discussed that we would contact prisons across the state later tonight. As for now, we were dead tired and it was time for us to catch up on sleep. I awoke a little bit before four o'clock. Star was already up and on the phone across the room. I sat there and just looked at her for a minute, admiring her will and dedication to becoming a new woman, while in the process of making me a new man.

"Ok, Thank you, Bye. Carl!" she shouted. "I found him." I sat up in astonishment. I kind of felt bad for sleeping and not being able to help her in her search for her father.

"So where is he love?" She came over and sat next to me.

"Leavenworth. He's in Leavenworth. One of the officers was familiar with the case and remembers me vividly enough. He's gonna allow me to speak to him, but it can only be me in there. You'll have to wait in a room." I was cool with that, as I immediately kissed her and reminded me of how much I loved her. Tomorrow would be the day that would change both of our lives forever. In the meantime, we were hungry. We kept it simple and ordered a pizza, mashing it while watching movies. Time passed by fast as nine o'clock came around quickly.

"I'm going to take a shower babe."

"Aight," she responded, as she had already taken one about 30 minutes earlier. The water hit me in a different way it seemed tonight. It kind of felt like a baptism of sorts. The man was here. The fully grown man. The young, immature boy from Gary was gone. The temperature was just right. Hot enough to be comfortable, as I felt negativity burn out of my soul. I finished up and stared in the mirror as I dried off. I liked what I saw now.

"Carl!"

"Be there in a minute beautiful."

"Carl commere!" Damn, this girl wasn't patient. I aint know what she wanted, but I wrapped the towel around my waist and headed out.

"Babe what's up?" I stopped in mid sentence. It was Star like I never seen. She was standing at the edge of the bed, naked and bare. Now usually a man would be jumping on a sexy woman standing ass naked in front of them. I however, was in much shock. This completely caught me by surprise. I slowly walked up to her until we were face to face. She had a look of nervousness across her face, as I on the other hand was trying to maintain my composure, as my hand lovingly laced her right ass cheek.

"Carl," she whispered. "I've opened my legs before. But I never opened my soul to any man." Those famous tears started to flow down her cheek as she asked "Can you make love to me?" I stepped back, slowly dropping my towel, exposing my being.

"What do you see?," I asked her. "Don't say the obvious. I want you to really look at me and tell me, what do you see?" Her breathing increased as she looked me up and down.

"I see the man that has made me realize life is worth living......and the man I hope will accept my flaws and love me forever." I heard what I needed to hear. Star expressing her soul. We walked towards each other until we met. We shared a slow, passionate kiss as our hands explored the roads of our spine and our fingertips served as cars traveling long distances. Kissing became more intense as I scooped her up by those two plump cheeks she called an ass and put her against the wall. Kissing ensued until I stopped and just looked at her.

"I love you Star." She responded back with an I love you that spoke to my mental rather than my ear canal. I then literally threw her up while standing up, catching her and placing her legs on **my shoulders.**

"**OH WHAT THE FUCK!,**" she shouted. I could tell she never had this done to her in life. I ate her slow, as if she were a perfectly cooked filet mignon. Her juices were flowing. I could feel her breathing, and feel the vibrations her hands were causing as she alternated between putting them on the ceiling and clutching my neck whenever my tongue game got beyond vicious.

I turned her around, legs still on my shoulders and laid her on the bed, not missing a beat. It was turning me on with her noises and her running her nails across my neck and head. Damn the normal head games. I was trying to suck out every negative man who had been inside of her and replace her with me. The thought of those ignat niggas made me go into overdrive. Her legs were now quivering, as my tongue became a speedboat motor, charging up her lovebox until it was too much for her to bear.

"**GOD, FUCK, SHIT!**" she shouted simultaneously, as her head plopped back and her hands gripped the mattress. I thought The Leaning Tower of Pisa had fallen when she began to lose it and just shake uncontrollably. I was done with mission number one. It was mission number two. Make love to her soul. I slowly came up, greeting every body part with my lips. Clenching her hands, I kissed her everywhere except her face. I didn't want her to touch my lips, as I know that would do nothing but make her go crazier. Slow bites occurred as her moans grew louder and I grew anxious. Finally, the head of my dick was placed upon her clit. I kneeled on the bed, teasing her with up and down motions, sliding in little by little. She was beyond tight, and I could tell this girl had a lock on that box for quite some time. After what seemed like forever, I finally got all of myself inside of her. The shit felt like I ran into a summer rainstorm, which was crazy, because the way she explained her history to me, I expected it to be loose as a goose.

She felt great though, as we shared kisses with each stroke. Dirty talk only enhanced the moment as her nails began to dig for lost treasures in my back. From the back, I stroked her slow. I wanted her to feel me. Face down, ass up, she took it like a champ. I grabbed a handful of hair and slowly pulled it back. I could see her enjoyment as her eyes closed, a smile cracked upon her face and her tongue drapped out to lick her lips. I was giving her something she never had with a man. A genuine connection. What her heart was now pumping was called "No fear" and I was the reason for it. I continued to go harder and harder, until I exploded inside of her.

I laid her down flat, steady stroking until I went soft. I keeled back, covers all fucked up, my black ass laying in the wet spot, and I just looked at her. She laid there on her stomach for a minute looking like she had been in a Tyson fight from the 90's. After a few minutes, she turned her head, looked at me, let out a little chuckle and smiled.

"I don't know what to say," she said. I was confused like hell.

"What you mean beautiful?" With a smile, and flippin over to her back, revealing those beautiful ass C cups, she quelled my confusion.

"Its crazy. I first met you. The world. I hated you. I hated everyone. I trusted no one. You..I especially couldn't stand you when you attempted to talk to me. Damn sure hated you when you said I was ugly inside. Now...I look at you as the only man who will ever make love to me. Not the first, the only. I never had this. I never felt like a woman. This was the only time I didn't feel like I was trying to force love. It was given graciously. Not to mention ummm ya shit is thick and long."

We both laughed hysterically. Wasn't a better way to end that statement as I signaled for her to come here so we could share a kiss. Yea, I'll even admit, I got conceited like a muthafucka with that closing statement. Shit I must have gotten it from my daddy. He put four in my mama. If a woman give you four kids, you must have been in attendance at pipe shop university. We fell asleep. Right there in the wet spot. No covers and no cares in the world. Tomorrow was a big day for both of us. Tonight though, was the first of many for us as well. I no longer had the need for sweet dreams. Mines had indeed come true, and it was in the form of a Midwest woman from Wichita, Kansas named Star Jennings. Tomorrow came around fast as shit. Luckily, the military had programmed us to be some early risers, as we both shot up at around 6:30. We showered together. No fray business, but a genuine cleansing of each other. We each threw on some jeans and a T-shirt, headed to the car to begin this three hour drive to Leavenworth to where her father was.

"I wanna drive babe," Star said. I agreed graciously. This was her big moment in life. I wanted her to handle it how she saw fit. She told me to go head and rest up the whole way there. I really didn't want to, because I wanted to talk her through everything. However, I happily obliged. Who was I kidding. I was tired. I reclined that seat back and told her to wake me up when we were nearing the prison. I was sleep, but I wasn't sleep. I was too concerned about my love.

This lasted all of 30 minutes, as the sleep kicked in and the only thing I was thinking about was streets of gold, and peanut butter and jelly sandwiches. A dream did happen to kick in though. I was on a desolate road driving. Cornfields to each side of me. I was in the middle of nowhere, but close enough to the city as to where I could see the buildings emerging. I got a call on my cell. A voice said *"Get there, he's coming."* I didn't know where I was going, but I sped off. Doing 90 straight, I made it into this city. There was no one around. Only parked cars, green lights and birds filled up the scenery. I kept driving until I seen a building coming up directly in front of me that was a mere 2 minutes away. As I slowed down and got closer, I could see it was a hospital. I parked right there in front of the ER doors, as a doctor was signaling for me frantically to get inside. I didn't know what it was for, but I knew when something was urgent.

I literally blazed out the car, leaving the door wide open without a care in the world. Doc began to run and I followed behind him stride for stride. This looked like some Michael Johnson and Maurice Greene type shit. We raced down halls, turning and avoiding heavy equipment. I saw patients in beds, some suffering horribly. I noticed all the doctors staring at me with stone cold looks on their faces. We finally made it to an elevator, but doc stopped dead in front of me.

"**Press the button doc!**" I yelled. No response.

"**Press the button doc!**" again I screamed.

"**PRESS THE *** DAMN BUTTON MUTHAFUCKA!**" I was beyond pissed now. Just as I said that, his whole body disintegrated and the elevators doors opened up. I was stunned silent, with a look of awe and disbelief on my face. I looked at this open elevator, lights on, with that ol funeral ass music playing in it. I turned around to an eerie sight. There it was. A full hospital that I just ran through, cluttered with equipment and patients...now empty. Nothing was there. No people, no machines, no anything. Just bricks, empty chairs, signs and the few flat screen TVs that hung on the walls.

This shit was creeping me out. I walked into the elevator to an even freakier sight. There was one button. No number of floors, emergency stops, open doors, close doors, none of that. One button and that was it. I pressed it and the steel grey doors closed. I felt myself rising up. Nervously, I waited for it to stop, but this thing kept going. It literally wouldn't stop. I couldn't press any button to stop it, so I just endured the slow, dreadful ride up to wherever. Finally, after what seemed like forever, and at least five minutes, it stopped.

The doors stayed shut, not opening immediately. I didn't know what to expect. Suddenly, the doors slowly, and I mean slowly opened. There was a room. All I seen was light coming from the cracks. Having really no choice, I opened it up to a horrific sight. There she was, a lil girl. She could've been no older than five. She was sitting in her room, surrounded by stuffed teddy bears. All of a sudden, a man walked in.

"You know what time it is," he said.

"Daddy nooo," she pleaded as she backed up

off her bed and scowled over to the corner of her room.

"I SAID YOU KNOW WHAT FUCKING TIME IT IS!" The lil girl was begging and pleading for her daddy to stop, but it was to no avail. All of a sudden, he grabbed her by her hair and literally flung her on to the bed. At this point, I tried to run and stop it, until I realized that I couldn't move. No matter how hard I tried, I was literally frozen.

"STOP!," I yelled repeatedly. It was to no avail. He began kissing on his daughter. Groping her innocence and laughing as he was doing it. Finally, he did something so despicable I wish I could have killed him myself. He pulled out his manhood, demanding for her to kiss it.

"I don't want to daddy," she screamed with tears in her eyes. He grabbed her face with his right hand, forming duck lips on her.

"What...has daddy always taught you?" She couldn't answer as the combination of fear and her tears completely engulfed her.

"WHAT DID I SAY?," he yelled one last time as he began to rub his manhood across her lips.

"WHAT DID I SAY?" Then, I heard **"Carl... Carl!"** I shot up blanketed with sweat on my forehead and heavy breathing.

"Carl?" It was Star. "Are you alright?" I tried to gather myself as quick as I could. That wasn't a dream that you had everyday.

"Yea babe. I...I just had a bad dream that's

all."

"Ok love, cause we're here." I looked out of the window to see a fortress of buildings. This was indeed Leavenworth. It looked more like a 1300's medieval castle than a federal prison. We were met at the gate by two uniformed guards.

"Ma'am, your business for this visit today?" I was nervous with these big ass guns they were holding. More nervous on how the other guard was right outside of my window, looking like he was ready to pump a few shells in my ass.

"Reconciliation," she said in a firm, powerful tone. Just then, the guard on her side called in on his radio, gave her directions on where to go and waved her through. What the hell I thought. That was like some secret service type shit. Say a code word and you get through. Ahh man I thought. This was about to be one helluva prison visit.

We drove up to this huge lot to see a solitary man in uniform, waving his hand from side to side. This must've been the guard who remembered her case. I didn't know what the hell was going on. I was internally terrified, but I maintained myself for Star. Pulling up in front of the guard, I got even more nervous as I couldn't see his eyes behind his menacing shades. That was my thing. I never trusted anyone who wore shades.

"Ma'am, you're good right here. How ur doing sir?" He asked me how I was doing, while I wanted to ask him what the hell was ur? These ol farmland country mofos and their accent. "I'm doing okay sir."

"Good," he said in an even deeper accent and tone. "Come on out and follow me." We got out, joined hands and followed behind the guard. Once inside, we went through the whole metal detector and search routine. All that typical stuff that you go thru when you go into a federal prison.

"Ms. Jennings, I'm officer McNeley. Your friend can wait out in a designated waiting area. Only you can go in." I was cool with that, seeing that this was her battle and she had to deal with this personally. We embraced in a deep hug. She gave me a kiss and gave me a look of here I go. No words were said, as our grips released and she was on her way. I waited patiently for about an hour. It was so long. One lonesome TV with a few magazines. A guard looking at me thru the thick glass.

This was a federal prison, and they took no chances. I sat there, feeling like a prisoner myself. I felt trapped in a world that wasn't even mine, even though it was one I was now a part of. I couldn't even fathom what was going on between my girl and her sperm donor. I call him that because I refuse to call that fuck nigga a father. Finally, after what seemed like forever, Star came out with no emotion on her face. She thanked the officer who got her in on such short notice, and we exited. No words were said as we walked to the car and pulled off. Dead silence took over and the car ride was not enjoyable.

"Star?" She whipped over to the side of the road and hit the breaks. Both of her hands clutched the wheel as her head went down.

"Aahhh!!!" was this painful scream she let out. She flung the car door open and just went to the side of the road, keeled over at the waist, crying her eyes out. I got out the car and just held her. I had never seen her cry this hard ever since I've known her. It was like someone ripped her heart out and stomped it out right in front of her. I didn't utter any words. Right now, it was just time to hold her until she came too.

"I can't believe him babe," she screamed ballin. By now, I was ballin tears with her. Her pain was my pain.

"I'm sorry love. I'm sorry." I constantly repeated that to her along with what seemed like a billion "I love yous" and "I'm not going anywheres." All I could offer right now was reassurance. After about 10 minutes, I slowly brought her up to her feet. She cried in my chest as I was only hoping that my arms signaled to her my love was genuine.

"I'm driving back beautiful. Give me the keys." She slowly reached in her pocket and handed them to me. I took em, walked her slowly back to the car and we bounced. The ride home was silent as ever. She didn't even go to sleep. She sat in that passenger seat, staring out of the window the whole time.

I wasn't trying to imagine what that sperm donor fuck had told her, but I knew it had to be fucked up for her. Man, this was the hardest thing I ever had to face in my life. I couldn't even make the person I loved wholeheartedly feel better in her worse time. I felt like a failure, even though I knew that I wasn't. This was gonna be a long ass Saturday night I could tell.

We got back to the hotel around six that evening. Our flight back to the West didn't leave until three o'clock Sunday afternoon, so we both had time to calm our nerves before we got home. Walking in the room, she slowly followed behind. She dropped to the bed, face down, not saying a word. I walked over to place my hand on her back.

"**GET OFF OF ME!**" Star yelled.

"Beautiful," I expressed in a calm manner. "I'm just trying to help." Star had a menacing look as she raised her head off the bed.

"**STAY THE FUCK AWAY FROM ME! HE DON'T LOVE ME!!! YOU DON'T LOVE ME!!! NOBODY FUCKING LOVES ME!!!**" I backed off the bed and stood up, hurting deep inside. She slowly crawled up, tears in her eyes and walked over to me. She grabbed my shirt, pulled me close and looked at me with a deadly demeanor.

"I'm sorry," she whispered. "I'm so sorry." I

grabbed her and just held her. I could see the anger inside of her hours ago, but it all just came out in one fell swoop on myself. We sat down on the couch we had in our room, window open, revealing a lil mist of snow that was coming down. Before I could even ask, she ran down the conversation.

"I was sitting down, waiting at the glass. He came out, seen me and we just stared at each other. Right then and there the flashbacks came. It was like life had stopped for a good minute. I was back to being eight years old, seeing my mother's dead body and him taking advantage of me. I saw all of the pain he caused. It was like...like...I was in a time machine. I kept from crying, because I didn't want him to see the pain that he caused me. I didn't want him to see I was weak. I had to be strong, because not being strong is what caused me to have the life I had in the past.

He sat down, never taking his eyes off of me. He picked up the phone. The first thing I noticed were the few slits on his hand. I dont know when, but he had tried to commit suicide at some point in there. He put his ear to the phone, keeping his hand over the mouthpiece and just looking at me with a look of sorrow in his eyes. Finally, after what seemed like forever, he began to speak.

"I...I'm sorry" he told me. My blood began to boil, but I had to remember what kind of woman

I now was. There was an old saying I used to hear that said kill them with kindness.

"Why dad? That is all I want to know. Why?" I asked it in the calmest demeanor ever. You would've sworn I was Mother Teresa. He took a deep breath, droppin his head, only to look back up at me and give me the most shocking explanation ever. He said,

"I don't know sweetheart. I really don't know." And that's the worst part about everything, is that he said he had no reason for what he did.

"Karma has came back to me in so many ways. You can only imagine. I know why its done to me, yet I don't know why in the hell I did it too you. I'm sorry, I don't even know what I just said." Anywho, I wanted to burst out into tears. After all the pain he caused me. After all the scarring and torture he had me endure. **THE LEAST THE MOTHERFUCKER COULD'VE DONE…WAS GIVE ME AN EXPLANATION!**

"Well…Mr. Jennings I told him, let me give you my reasoning. I came to find peace. I came to let you know that you didn't destroy me. I came to let you know that you aint get your fulfillment. Pretty much, I went thru hell, sat with the devil himself and left out the flames. I walked barefoot thru fire and I'm here right now. Remember this face. Remember these words. I hope like hell you find peace within yourself. If not…my twin, which is a black soul who sits in hell, will be waiting for your ass, to torture you forever.

Goodbye…Mr. Jennings." I put the phone down and walked off, not ever looking back. As I got escorted to one of the rooms in the prison, Officer McNeley said my name and I turned around.

"It's okay to be angry," he told me. I couldn't contain myself anymore as I fell into his arms ballin. He comforted me in my worst moment. I knew what I was trying to do, but he could obviously see it.

"Thank you sir," I told him.

"No ma'am," he told me. "I'm not sir. My name is Justin, and we are friends from this day forward."

I hugged him and savored that moment forever. Justin McNeley. A man of such high valor and honor. I remember his look. A bald head, brown mustache and a smile that would light up the night sky. I only knew that because of the smile he gave me as he said some inspirational words to me. He told me to remember, even when we die, they can never kill our spirit. Have a strong spirit, and you will live forever.

"I remembered those words as he took me to their guest lunchroom to provide me with some food to comfort my stomach. And after I ate, I came out to you and here we are."

I just stared at her while rubbing her back, seeing that she was looking like a bunch of weight had been lifted off of her soul. She reached over to hug me.

"Thank You for giving me life Carl." I gripped her even harder.

"Your welcome beautiful, but it wasn't me. It was just God using me as a vessel." She lifted her head up and looked at me. I looked back at her, thinking another bandage had fallen off of a now healed wound.

"I love you Carl."

"I love you too Star." We kissed and just enjoyed the rest of our night with movies and some order in dining. The next afternoon, we were back on the plane to California. As with the flight here, she fell asleep, and I began to write.

FATHER

A woman never grows up
thinking that daddy will be the same man
who makes her call him daddy
sperm only creates
but sickness dissipates what once was
a solid lil girl
her world is supposed to be daddy
daddy and daughter dances
daddy pushing her on the swing
daddy chastising that thing
she calls a boy

those are her reflections and expectations of daddy
that's what they should be
but daddy sometimes confuses her
so call me father when my time comes
because I should only come to my daughters rescue
not inside of her

CHAPTER EIGHT

BREAKDOWN

MARCH 2014

"Jackson, in my office." That was my LPO. I aint know what he wanted, but from the tone of his voice, it sounded like I had did some stuff to piss him off.

"Yea boss man," as I walked in.

"A, they sending a team up to Bremerton to rip up two ships before they get scrapped. You wanna roll up there for a few weeks TAD and make some money?"

"HELL YEA!!!" I told him.

"Cool. I'll let Senior Chief know so they can cut your orders." I was on a high like never before. Man, I had never been anywhere else on the

West since I got here, so this would be refreshing for me. About an hour before I got off, boss man gave me my orders. I was leaving on a Monday with about 20 other cats from the ship. It was a Thursday, so that gave me a whole weekend to get prepped and everything. I looked up Bremerton on the internet to see what it was about. From the looks of it, it didn't look like much of anything. However, I knew that looks could be deceiving, so I paid it almost no attention. I hit up Star later that night on the ship's mess decks to let her know.

"So what about my birthday weekend?" Damn, that shit had completely slipped my mind.

"Well babe, I mean, they asked me and I said yea. Don't take it personal. We'll just celebrate when I get back in two weeks." What the hell did I say that for. The look in her eyes said *"Really nigga."*

"You know what....have your trip. I'll be aight." She flicked her hand at me and walked off. I was in the dog house I know, but she would be aight. I just chalked it up for what it was and continued on with my night. Man, women were so emotional I thought. I was so glad I was a man. Every holiday, birthday, made up holiday had to be celebrated by them. For men, give us a drank, a TV and maybe some strippers, and we were good. Flowers, candy, poetry and whatever else romantic I could think of was in my thought process, as I knew making up and sucking up would have to be instituted upon return. I went off to my berthing to head to sleep, figuring out how I would get it in this weekend. Friday rolled around and the work day went by without a breeze. Star wasn't talking to me, so I figured I would get out and about tonight. I booked me a hotel room at the hotel down in Chula Vista again so I wouldn't have to come back to this floating piece of ass. I hit the room about 4:30 after gettin it in on the court for a lil while. I showered up and was taking a good nap when my phone rang at 6:01. It was my homey Sleep from the Boot.

Me:"Sup nigga?"

Sleep: "A mane, what you on tonight?"

Me: "Dunno yet man. Why you got something poppin off?"

Sleep: "Its a few freaks out in Eastlake throwin a house party mane. Roll with a nigga.

Me: "Aight. I'm in the Days Inn off E Street in Chula. You gone scoop me?"

Sleep: "Yea, I'll get you round 8."

Me: "Fosho"

Sleep: "Gone"

This is just what I needed. A live lil house function to get my weekend started. I wasn't too much worried bout the freaks part, seeing that I had a personal one on my arm. However, I was always down to see a show. Sleep always had a bunch of females, so in my mind, there wouldn't be no worries tonight. I figured I'd get a few laughs, see a few thangs pop out and that was it. Sleep came and scooped me from the room at 8:30. I should've known when black people say 8 o'clock, it mean 30 minutes to an hour later.

We chopped it up on the 25-30 minute drive over some E-40 bout females and life in general. Everything was lining up to be a chill night from the looks of things. When we hit the 805, I just got a horrible premonition. Why, I don't know, but something was telling me that this was not gonna be my night. It was like that night I got in the car with Tez, JJ and Dant. I hurried up and shook that shit off, as I got back to being loose and enjoyin the time with the homey.

Finally, after what seemed like forever, we pulled up on a house in an affluent neighborhood. From the outside, it didn't look like much of anything was going on. I aint hear no music, see no folks standing outside or none of that. We got out and headed to the door, only to be greeted by some dark skinned chick with heels on. She hugged and kissed Sleep, and looked over at me.

"And who are you might I add?" "Oh I'm Carl sweetheart." She shook my hand with that "I'll fuck the shit out of you shake." "C'mon in, make y'all self at home." I walked into a house with all the house lights out, but strobes and exotic red lights gave it an eerie glow. There were quite a few females in here, giving me that look. I observed most of em were dressed in the skimpiest of clothes, looking like they were ready to fuck something. *Oh shit* I thought. This was gonna be a good night. I aint no anyone in here but Sleep, so I decided to just be the cool one who was laid back. Females seemed to be attracted to brothers like that. I sat down, sippin on a coke, when the host who opened the door and another banger came and sat on my lap.

"So why you so quiet?," the one I hadn't met yet asked me.

"Oh I'm just chillin ya know. Here with my mans Sleep, hoping to have a good time tonight." They looked at each other and giggled.

"Thats good boo. We might need the quiet dick later so gone enjoy yourself." They both rubbed me as they got off my lap and went back to the other side of the living room. I took another sip of the coke and said a silent prayer to God, asking him "Don't let me screw up tonight." I had a woman yes, but it looked like free meals would be handed out tonight.

As the night went on, more and more folks came in. It was now a good mix of females and bruhs. Everyone was choppin it up, the music was now blaring and everything was good. This is how its suppose to be. It shouldn't be no fighting in a house full of pussy and dick. No fighting, only fucking. I was in the kitchen chillin when the host yelled **"OK, EVERYBODY IN THE LIVING ROOM!"** I aint know what was about to go down, but I knew it was about to be something good. Just as I was about to walk out the kitchen, I looked out to the back patio leading from the kitchen. There was a girl out there crying. I really didn't care, seeing that I was possibly bout to see some action. However, I aint like everyone having fun and one person not. I opened the patio door and holla'd at her.

"Excuse me? A ya girl asking everybody to go in the living room."

"Just leave me alone please," she told me. I was like fuck it then. Just as I was shuttin the door back, she began talking to me again.

"Wait, can you come out here for a minute?" Man I swear, I didn't wanna be captain save a ho, but I was like whatever. I aint know anyone out here, so I was like whatever. I went out and sat next to her as she was steady crying.

"Well what's your name miss lady?"

"Capri," She responded. "Can I ask you what's wrong since its a whole party in there and you out here crying?" I know it sounded brutally honest, but oh well hell. I really wanted to be inside seeing what was going on.

"My man in here, and I caught him fucking ol' girl whose house it is upstairs." *Oh hot damn* I thought. I sipped my Coke like a frog did some tea. This meant this night was going to get more interesting.

"Well shorty, fuck it," I told her. "You gotta house full of fun, so don't let one dude make you feel like this. You too fine to be out here crying." True, I was just blabbin some stuff to make her feel better, but she was taking it hook, line and sinker.

"Thank you," she said. "C'mon, lets go inside." She grabbed my hand and walked me in. She was in front of me, and I was lookin at this thick ass in front of me. Man she was thicker than a bowl of oatmeal and raisins. Small waist and the titties were just the right size. Soon as we stepped in the door, I saw some dude on the other side of the kitchen, just staring at both of us. I aint pay it no mind, seeing that I would've been staring too if he had this thing on his arm. We chopped it up for about two minutes, just getting to know each other.

"A Capri," ol boy said as he grabbed her arm.

"Can I talk to you?" The funny shit was that he looked at me as he asked her the question. I let out a lil chuckle as I said "Do your thing playa. I'll see you later Capri," giving her a kiss on the cheek before I departed. Man I swear dudes were funny. I knew that was dude she was talking about. I let them handle their business as I walked into the living room. What I seen next damn near made me spit my drink back in the cup. It was four brothers on the couch, with four females all kneeled down in front of them. These hoes was having a dick sucking contest right here in the damn living room. I glanced around quickly for Sleep, but he was nowhere to be found. I just posted up on the wall, looking at these freak girls show off their skills. I aint no any of em like I said, so to get this type of entertainment was very enjoyable for me. Wow, what a Friday night. I was definitely diggin this until the **"FUCK YOU'S"** ensued. From upstairs, this light skinned chick and this dude got to arguing loud.

All of a sudden the sucking stopped, the music stopped and everybody and they momma it seemed was tryna calm them down. Ol boy stormed out the door, followed by ol girl and damn near the rest of the house. I seen Capri run past me as I headed back to the patio. Going through the kitchen, I saw ol boy in the corner, mean muggin me as if I hurt his soul. He should've controlled his chick. I was now on the patio with a few other cats. Sleep had came out to join us.

"What happened bruh?," I asked him. "I dont wanna talk about it man." I knew it was some serious shit. We could see the arguing clearly from the patio in front of whoever truck it was. All of a sudden, shit got real. Ol boy reached in the truck and pulled out a pistol. *Damn* is the first word that came to my mind. How in the hell could such a good night turn into a living nightmare? Eventually, ol girl calmed him down as he got back in the truck. He got in, followed by her, another cat and Capri herself. Everyone on the patio went back inside to really see what was going on. Me on the other hand, I lingered on the patio for about an extra one to two minutes. That premonition I had while on the highway all of a sudden came back into my thought process. This shit was not gonna end well and I could see that. I went back into the house to notice the majority of everyone outside in the front. I stood by the door, listening to the host talk as she had someone on speaker phone.

"STOP THE TRUCK!!!," was all I heard coming through. The host kept shouting back and forth with whoever she was talking to until we all heard a loud crash. My heart dropped as that sound echoed through my ear canal. Sleep scattered to the car along with everyone else's to theirs. I hurried up to the whip as Sleep damn near left without me.

"HOLD ON NIGGA!!!" I yelled, holding the passenger door open before he could accelerate and possibly run me over. Cars just started pullin out the driveway and off the street like someone yelled Jesus was down the street. This is why I always brought my own whip to places, so just in case some mess went down, I could be out. I definitely learned my lesson with this incident. We scattered up and down a bunch of random streets, not finding any truck in sight. The crash noise was obvious, but where were they at was what we were all wondering. Finally, Sleep got a phone call.

"I'M GOING!!!," he yelled, as he took that Ford over the Median and damn near broke it in half. I was now scared shitless as he was booking 80 down a residential. After what seemed like forever, we finally hit E. Orange Avenue. The sight I saw was enough to make the most hardened criminal shed a few.

There it was, a Red Chevy Suburban, flipped over completely on its top. Glass was everywhere. On the sidewalk sat the guy who was waving the pistol and the other male passenger. In the middle of the street lie a young woman, bloody as ever. Her homegirl was over her screaming and pleading for help. One by one, everyone from the house started to pull up. People were on their phones at random, screaming into their phones for 911 to come. Me, I just sat back observing it all. If this was fun, I really didn't want it anymore. Fun shouldn't include being out in the middle of the night, on some random street, hoping that a young lady could hold on long enough to get some medical attention.

"YOU MUTHAFUCKA!" That was Capri shouting, as she went after ol boy who was arguing with baby girl at the house. Everyone took off towards them both, trying to get in between them before she hit him, he hit here and all hell would break loose. It was too late though, she got at him and started swingin for the fences. Ol boy didn't hit her back, he just kept pushing her away until finally someone got a hold of her. The scene was very chaotic now. Luckily, this was an open road leading to the freeway, cause had this been a residential area, all of our black asses would've been going to jail.

After what seemed like forever, EMT's finally arrived on the scene. It took a collective effort of myself and about four other calm heads to keep everyone away from her while the paramedics did what they had to do.

"C'Mon Moni….C'mon!" One of the girls kept shouting that as a board and stretcher was brought out. She wasn't moving, but her chest was heaving up and down, so at least we knew she was still breathing. I got tired of all of this madness. I slowly slid back inside of Sleep's car and just waited everything out. All these sirens, screams and frantic people reminded me too much of back home.

This was your typcal scene for when someone got murdered. There was always the hysterical mother. The few friends who would get arrested for trying to fight the police to get across the caution tape. Then, you had the calm people who just sat back and observed everything as it was happening, doing everything they could to stay clear of what was going on. I pulled out my phone and hit my note app. Haiku poetry was made famous in Japan. It was a 5-7-5 syllable format that kept everything short and sweet. This is how I made myself a note to remember what this night did to me.

Truck crash late at night
young lady fights for young life
fun aint fun no more

They loaded her up in the ambulance and began to whisk her away. Mostly everyone was going back to their cars except the two young brothers who were inside the truck. They were busy talking with the police along with a few of the other crazies who were actually not making a scene, which was shocking to me. Sleep got in the car and followed everyone else to the hospital.

"Its my fault man. It's my fault," he kept yelling. I really didn't know what to say, seeing that I didn't know the story behind him and ol girl.

"Sleep man, it's aight. She gone be okay." It was like this the whole way to the hospital, as all I could do was be a friend to him right now in his time of hurt. It was sad to see one of my partnas like this. Combine that with an almost dead woman, and this was something that I just wanted to forget. It was well past one in the morning now as we finally pulled up to the parking lot of the hospital near downtown. I stayed in the car for a little while just to clear my head on things. This was one of those times in life where your bad luck streak kicked in. My lady was mad at me and for good reason. I didn't even consider her birthday. All I considered was getting myself to Seattle and making some extra money. A good night had turned into a somber one. *What else could go wrong* I thought? I was quickly about to find out. Sleep came back to the car after a lil while.

"Man we gone get those niggas a.s.a.p."

"What you talkin bout man?," I asked, confused as hell.

"They flipped that bitch over, Moni almost lost her life, we gone handle this shit." Just my luck. When I thought things couldn't get any worse, they were about to go there. I thought I left all this retaliation bullshit back home. I see it was out here too, even with the military niggas. I figured at least worry about ol girl first and her well being, then do what you gotta do. Nah, they wanted blood. I just got out the car and headed into the ER.

I figured the night would go by quicker being around people than being by my lonesome. In there, it was much of the same talk, except they kept it a little bit indiscreet on the payback tip. Soon after, the victim's father walked in, greeted by the host. It was obvious they knew each other and he was beyond heated. All I wanted to do was go home, but I couldn't even do that. I aint end up leaving that place until seven Saturday morning. I didn't even wanna go back to the room cause it was out of his way from the hospital. I just went to his spot to crash and get what sleep I could before he and those other cats decided to go rambo.

I'm not gonna dwell on the events of later that day, because it was to shameful to see things come to a head like that. I will say though that we did end up back at the house around four that evening, getting prepped to go to a pajama party at the club. I slept all the way until about 8:30 that night. I totaled maybe seven hours between the morning sleep and the sleep I caught there in the evening. Shit had been bad, but I couldn't see tonight going wrong. I mean, who would start drama at a pajama/lingerie party? Not no sane person I know. With all the cooch that was gonna be up in there, I expected nothing but a good time.

We got to the club around 10:30. Ooooh shit, it was packed with a lot of ghetto scattered ass up in here. I was in my beater and some shorts, and from the looks of it, I was overdressed. Man, this night was what I needed. Nothing bad was happening. There was ass shaking everywhere. They even had a twerk session for a couple hundred on stage. I was amazed by the cheeks that this evening was providing. I came in here needing a pick me up and I was about to leave this hoe sweating. The club let out at 1:30, and me & Sleep walked out laughing, feeling good and like we were both renewed. We were walking to the parking lot, about to head to Denny's and keep the night crackin.

"A man, who is these niggas?" That was Sleep saying that, as we both stopped dead in our tracks, observing the group of men leaning on his car and just scattered all throughout the parking lot. The females were oblivious to it, but being bruhs, we knew something was about to go down. All these dudes were clad in green, so I knew what time it was.

All of a sudden, the few that were on Sleep's car took off after someone. The rest followed behind. Commotion and chaos ran throughout the parking lot. Some dude was getting stomped out. I don't know what he did, but he pissed them off pretty good. We ran to the whip along with everyone else who was running to theirs.

POP! POP!! POP!!! You heard the shots go into the air. Where it was coming from, I didn't know and I damn sure didn't care. Sleep started up the whip. However, he had to be careful skidding out of here, seeing that everyone out here was runing round like a chicken with their heads cut off. While he was trying to figure that out, I noticed one of the dudes in green jumped on top of a car and started stomping out the windshield. The driver took off with him on top. He managed to jump down before he completely flew off. Meanwhile, Sleep had gotten enough room to reverse his joint. That's when I saw it. The driver of the car who got its windshield stomped out, they jumped the curb and smashed a young lady in between the car and one of the parking meter poles. Everything was in slow motion, as they reversed and kept going over the sidewalk. Time stopped as I literally locked eyes with a dead woman. It was scary to see the last vision of someone dead looking at you. I didn't even realize Sleep had made it out the lot and was on the street. When I thought it couldn't get any worse, it did.

"Man take me back to the room bruh. I can't take this anymore." Sleep just nodded his head in agreement and drove me back to the hotel. Once we got there, I began to get out. Just then, Sleep spoke to me. "A bruh. I'm sorry." I just stared at him, with one foot out the door.

"It's cool bruh. It's life. Sometimes, we can't control it." I got out, shut the door, headed to my room and went to sleep. If there was any night that I needed a good night's rest, it was tonight. Sunday came and went with a blur. The good thing was that Star was talking to me. The bad news is that she wasn't tryna give a brother none before I left. I just had to chalk it up as a L and get acquainted with my hand. Monday had now come. I was early to the air terminal, as in three hours early. They told us who were going to Washington to be there by 9:30, but my black tail showed up at eight. I was that excited to head up there. One by one, all the cats from the ship who were going filed in. Boy, talk about a diversified bunch. There was Chris, a Damage Controlman. He was a country ass hood white boy from the heart of Memphis. He dressed in the blues spirit with his Wranglers, cowboy hat and plaid shirt. However, he would still knock the dog piss out of you.

Then it was a Damage Control Senior Chief who were called "Po." I heard he could hit the bottle real hard when off of work, so I was hoping we had a chance to kick it. Throw in a couple of crazy bruhs from San Dog, Detroit and LA, and this was lookin to be a very fitting trip. We boarded around 11 o'clock for a flight that was well over three hours. I was gonna take this time to just relax and enjoy this two weeks of freedom that was about to come. Sure, we were gonna be working and ripping up some old ships, but I would be away from the typical folks for what seemed like forever. That was gravy for me.

Once we took off, I threw my headphones on to some smooth jazz. The song that I immediately cut on was Michael McDonald's "I Keep Forgettin." For my hip hop heads, it was the beat that was sampled by Warren G for his smash "Regulate." Jazz did something to me. It allowed me to put myself in a whole 'nother world. This time, it meant more than me than any other time. Back to back to back bad things happening around me had forced me to put my mind in a calm place. This was good, as we all needed to do this with ourselves. We may not think about it, but music can soothe our soul and heal wounds as well. This bandage that I now ripped off was over a wound of what I witnessed. The near death of one young lady and the death of another. We can never forget what we have experienced, but we can learn to move past it. Most importantly, we can learn how to enhance our own lives from the things we see, whether it's positive or negative. After a few more songs, I completely crashed out.

"A man, wake up!" My eyes adjusted to the light as I arose groggy, slob droolin from my lip. I was knocked the hell out.

"Bruh, yo ass was out." That was my dude Vic. He was the cool ass Mexican cat from Diego. Brother man was who I needed to hang out with while I was up here. He was married, had a kid and it was a lot that I could learn from a brother like him.

"We here?" I asked.

"Yea man, you the only one left on the plane. We almost forgot about you." We walked off and headed to the baggage terminal here at Whidbey Island, Washington where we landed. After getting our bags, to our surprise, we still had another two plus hour ride to Bremerton. I know I had fell asleep, but I was just ready to put my bags down and chill in a bed. We loaded up the van and began our journey.

"Hey!!!" Senior screamed at us from the front seat. "First rule up here. Nobody fucking shaves. Kiss my ass on regs. We're gonna rip this ship up, but make sure we rip everything else up." The whole van burst out into laughter. It may have been funny, but we knew Senior Chief was dead serious. He wanted us to let our hair down. I indeed planned too.

We made it to Bremerton Naval Base a lil after six that evening, and it was raining cats and dogs. Hell, matter fact, it had been raining the whole damn time we had been in Washington. I see why this state had the highest rate of suicide. All this greenery and water would make any man lose his damn mind.

We got to our rooms and I was luckily roomed up with Vic. We chopped it up for a while, cracking jokes on each other about our football teams. He was an avid Chargers fan, while I liked a real team in the Colts. That shit didn't last long though, seeing how tired and hungry we we were.

We left out and found the bowling alley on base, getting in a quick game and a quick bite. After that, was back to the room we went. Sleep was on the agenda, and I needed all of the sleep I could get.

BLACK VS. BLUE

We made our first day in Bremerton worthwhile work wise. We villaged, plunged, looted, tore up, whatever you wanted to call it. We picked apart toilets, engines, valves and everything else you can imagine that would make a Naval ship run. After that hard of a day, I went back to the room to catch me some sleep.

BOOM BOOM BOOM!!! It was a loud knock at my door. It pissed me off seeing that I was in a deep ass sleep.

"Who is it?!"

"It's P foo!!!" I opened up the door to see that big ass goofy grin he had. My dude was from Flint. He was gangster as hell, but he was also the biggest goofball you would ever meet.

"A man, we catching the ferry to Seattle in about an hour and some change. Let's roll." I was down like a mutha.

"Who we rollin with?"

"It's gone be me, you and Dee." Dee was from St. Louis. a country mofo with more gold in his mouth than a damn rolex. I knew it would really be on with him tagging along.

"Aight man, gimme 30 minutes and I'll meet y'all downstairs in the lobby." He was cool with it, and I hurried up and got a good, ten minute hot shower in. Luckily, I was always one step ahead of things. I had planned to be out somewhere tonight, so I ironed up a polo and creased some jeans the night before. I greased up the buttas, and ensured I was fresh from head to toe. That's one thing young brothers my age don't take into consideration. All they know is leaving the house in a tee shirt and some ragged ass jeans. They don't take the time to put creases in their joints. I refused to go out anywhere looking like a bag of ass.

From checking in the mirror, I was straight. No strings were dangling off this Chaps baby blue polo. The creases in my smoke grey jeans were so sharp that you could use my joints to slice up onions. As far as the timbs, they were sparkling. They were baby blue with grey bottoms, with my name engraved into the side. I gave myself the ok sign and headed downstairs to meet my partnas. We made the twenty minute or so long trek to the Ferry. Man, it would've been smart if I would've brought a jacket. It wasn't raining right now, but it was a lil crispy outside. I just manned up though and took it. We made it to the ferry and prepped ourselves for the 45 minute boat ride over to the Emerald City.

"A therre Carl," Dee spoke in that slurred St. Louis accent. "How yo folk and dem out thurr in Gurryy?" I paused because it kind of caught me off guard.

"To be honest mane.....I really don't know. I aint talked to nobody since I left to be 100."

"Oh damn folk," he said with a stunned look, eyebrows raised. "You aint even called yurrr mom dukes?" I leaned back on that ferry seat, looked at P real quick and answered my mans back.

"Both my parents dead mane. I aint got no family really except for a few cousins and shit. My brothers all locked up. All three of em. That's my life bro." I could see both of their eyes on me, but I could feel them even more.

"Well dammit folk, you family with us. I aint never been no big God type nigga, but I do believe he put people hurrr in other folk lives to get through things. Welcome to the fam bro." That shit meant a lot to a brother as I dapped it up with both of em. We continued to talk all the way 'til we hit Seattle. I found out we were more similar than any of us ever imagined.

Ol Dee was raised in the projects of the Lou. He never knew his daddy, and his mama worked two jobs to support him and his twin sister. Well, the year before he came in , his sister was shot dead, the mistaken target of a drive by. He felt he needed to get away from it all, so he joined to try to make something out of his life and hopefully one day, get his mama out of the jects.

As far as P, he had both of his folks in his life. However, his parents constantly fought and bickered, and he ended up always being caught in the middle of their arguments. He had enough of that and just wanted to get away from them both. As he explained, they did more damage than good, especially his pops. He said no matter how similar him and his pops were with some things, his ultimate goal was to not be like him in any shape, way or form. His pops thought he knew everything. He didn't. His pops was materialistic. He wasn't. His pops said one thing but did the opposite. He didn't. This was crazy. You sometimes get so wrapped up in life that you think you are the only one struggling. Then, you find out that your struggle is sometimes a good thing, because you couldn't even imagine going through the struggle of someone else.

We got to Seattle finally and I couldn't speak for them, but I was amazed by the sights. It really seemed like you entered the land of Oz. The stadium of the Seattle Seahawks was glowing. I had never in my life seen something so beautiful. I followed football a lot. The fact that I was looking at where greats like Shaun Alexander ran the ball relentlessly amazed me. I looked over at the other two, and they were just as awestruck as me. Here we were, three Midwest brethren, all from the hood, all experiencing life.

We caught a cab and made our way downtown and the rain began. It was a Wednesday night, and we didn't see anyone out and about. Granted it was just nine o'clock, but I think we had stumbled upon a dud tonight.

"Man hot damn dawg," P screamed frustratingly. "Aint nobody out and about in this muthafucka." The frustration kicked in as he kept walking and looking, seeing nothing. Finally, we stumbled upon a joint called Larry's. We heard reggae music blaring from the inside, so this was probably our closest shot to anything.

"Y'all wanna do this?", I asked both of em. We all looked. All in unison, we said, "Fuck it!" We stepped in, the bouncer checked our joints and hot damn. This muthaluva was packed!!! There was Jamaican ass, Haitian ass, you name it and it was in there. Truthfully, I aint know where any of these chicks were from, but you could tell just by the look of em, they all were either from the islands, or had roots that ran deep from them.

We made our way through all the twerking. The DJ was shouting over the mic, getting the crowd even more turnt up. As I made my way to the bar, I turned around to see those two nuts out on the dance floor, bending females over. That gave me a good laugh. I would be on that in a minute. Right now though, I needed my medicine of Hennessey.

"Two Henn and Cokes please" I told the bartender. As I waited for my drink, this sexy something crept up on me and rubbed her hand across my chest. I had my conceited moment as I looked down at her like yea, I'm the shit I know. She started slow grindin on me, as I flipped my hand back to the bartender with a full twenty, shooing him afterwards as my way of telling him to keep the change. This lasted all night. Dancing, good music, good drank. My partnas were well, the patrons in the club were well, the drinks were hittin, no one was fighting. Now this is how nightlife was supposed to be. We were parlaying real good, until I looked down at my watch and realized it was 12:34. The last ferry left at 1:45, and I didn't wanna miss that. I grabbed the other two drunk fools. Well, to be honest, I pulled Dee, but ol Pretty boy P was busy slobbin down some chick he had just met. I couldn't do that. She could've had H-I-V in her mouth for all he knew. He aint care though. He was faded just like the other crazy.

I was buzzed, but I was sober enough to know everything that was occurring around me. After pulling P from his future ex-wife, we all dipsetted out of the joint. To our luck, there was a cab driver right outside the club.

"To the ferry landing," I said, leaning thru his passenger side window.

"C'mon my friend. I take you all." *Shittt, coo beans* I thought. I hopped in the front and left the two drunk nuts in the back. As we took off, not even a block away from the club, the trouble started.

"A man?," a drunk Dee sputtered out. **"WHY THE FUCK YO PEOPLE BLOW OUR TOWERS UP?!!!"** I couldn't believe this dude just said that. The cab driver gave me a look, and I just gave the hand signal to simmer down and don't pay him no mind.

"A NIGGA?," Dee shouted again. Suddenly,

the cabby screeched on the brakes. He reached under his seat with the quickness. Everything was happening in a blur, but the only time someone reached under their seat in the hood, they were pullin out an equalizer. I fell out the car pushing that car door open. On the ground, I managed to see the cabby swingin what looked like a club. Him, Dee and P were going at it. This was the last thing that any of us needed. One big ass incident bringing discredit upon ourselves, and the Navy in general.

"STOP YO! MY NIGGAS..STOP!!!" I was screaming this shit. By then, they were all out the car scrappin. ***POP!!!*** Cabby had managed to strike Dee ass in the chest with that club, putting him on the ground. Now, it was P and the cab driver throwin blows. I was stuck. I aint no what to do. (**SIRENS**) Police patrolling downtown had now rolled up two cars deep. Dee was up now screaming obscenities at anyone he seen. P and the cab driver were now backed off, mugging each other. I was still on the curb barking out for everyone to calm down.

"PUT YOUR HANDS UP!!!," one of the officers yelled. No guns were drawn, but it was still tense.

"FUCK YALL!!!," P screamed as the cops continued to march forward towards him. He kept screaming it until he was hoisted in the air by two officers and slammed. All this was happening, and I barely noticed Dee mashed up against the police car, hand in his neck. I was scared as shit, but I was too amped up telling them to calm down to show it.

"What do you think you're doing?" That was said to me as another uniformed officer of the law grabbed me and basically force fed the side of my face into the hood of the patrol unit.

"Okay man, okay." I was telling him this basically to calm him down. Aint no reason he needed to do this to me. I was cool, calm and collective.

"You have anything on you I need to know?" He asked me this, smacking my pockets and trying to find anything he could to haul my black ass off to jail.

"No sir I don't." I guess the fact he couldn't find anything angered him more, as he put more force on the back of my neck unnecessarily. He snatched me up by my shirt, walking me back to the sidewalk.

"I WANT YOU TO SIT ON THAT CURB AND DON'T MOVE!"

"Yes sir," I responded, all while watching my friends handcuffed and just treated unlawfully. True, did the cops roll up on a fight, yes. True, did Dee verbally assault them, kind of. However, did any of us threaten them with physical harm? no. Especially me, I was on the sidewalk, trying to get my peoples to keep their cool. I ended up being forced face first into metal. And then they wonder why we say **FUCK THE POLICE** at times. This was the exact reason why. In the black community, the police were looked on as the enemy. Coming from the inner city, we felt that the police were never there for us. We call the cops when something happens, and they either take forever, or never show up. I know, I know, its not all cops. All of them aren't bad just like all black people don't act ignorant. However, the relationship between black and blue has been deep rooted since way back in the 50's.

I can't claim the experience, as I never went through hose spraying and dogs biting my ass. However, times may change, but so do tactics. I won't get into the rest of the details of the night, but just know that we avoided jail. We managed to make the ferry and make it back. Again, it didn't matter how we got back, just know that we got back. We were dead silent all the way back to our barracks.

I got back to my room at 3:17 on the dot. I had to be up and at the ship at 7:30, but I was nowhere near in the mood to sleep. I was highly pissed off and my blood was still boiling from the whole experience. Vic was dead asleep and snoring louder than a freight train. I didn't wanna wake him up, but I needed to vent something serious. Since I couldn't talk to anyone, I just grabbed my notebook, a pen and headed back out the room. I walked all the way to the end of the hall and just stared out the huge windows into the night sky. I saw no stars tonight. I couldn't even see the moon. It was like everything was dark as if to say God closed his eyes on the whole situation because it was simply fucked up. I sat down in the cushioned green chair and just closed my eyes in deep thought for a hot minute. Before I realized it, I opened my eyes to see it was 4:13. That sleep was starting to kick in, but I had to get my frustrations out. I just let my hand guide the pen and wrote my new piece in blood.

Dear Mr. Officer

This is my letter to you, Mr. Police Officer, see contrary to what the world says, me and you, we are more similar than you can imagine, see we both are hated for the uniform that we wear, yours in the form of blue cotton, mines in the melanin of the ones that picked the cotton, we are sometimes both labeled as rotten, dirty and filth of the earth, we both have a few bad seeds that overshadow our good deeds cause contrary to popular belief, there are those that actually uphold the law and patrol the streets, and there are those of us who actually do go to school and leave with degrees so you see, me and you, we are more like distant cousins that always met, but never recognized that we are family, and just like family, we have our own unique nicknames, they call you pig and they call us niggas, and its funny cause

*niggas are known to fuck up some pig on sight so I
see why you do the same to us, see this relationship
literally runs from the roota to tha toota, but much
like families we are disfunctional, you seem to harass
our ass for driving while black or come around us
lookin for that crack, all this because we're black,
severe beatings, constant mistreating or getting shot
110 times for holding up a wallet which you said was
a gun, maybe you do this for fun, maybe our distance
has upset you, maybe our family tree aint what it
seems, you branch out in different directions, while
the roots stay underground, the same place you plan
to put us for permanent dirt naps, Sean Bell and
Oscar Grant just to name a few, so when I hear that
song bad boys, bad boys, whatchu gonna do, I know
the answer is try to terminate me on sight, now
lemme clear something up, all of mines aint right,
sometimes, they do give you a reason to defend your
life, sometimes, you should arrest them for their
ignorance in the streets, sometimes, even niggas
deserve to get their ass beat, and if my wish come
true, you'll be locking up niggas that sag cause they
some undercover fags, and thats no disrespect to gay
men cause even they are more manly than those
clowns, but lets turn this back around to the subject
at hand, see as long as I remember its been blue vs.
black, nightsticks vs. niggas, 9mm bombs vs. black
men unarmed, yet you ask me to respect the long arm
of the law, the hell with that, and I know you thought*

I would holla Fuck the police, but when you fuck you come, and yall never come when we need y'all the most cause black people to yall are celibate, but you sell a bit of niggas to your federal cronies on charges that are phony, but for yall, its easy to holla fuck niggas, cause we fuck up and keep comin to y'all based off our own ignorance, so you see Mr. Officer, we are more related than you think, I just ask you to think the next time before you gun us down, cause like I said, we both wear uniforms, the only difference is, I can't take mines off

I wrote that piece and just looked at it. I stared at it. I really didn't understand what I wrote. I mean, I did, but I was so much in the zone that I truly couldn't even fathom the thought process. It was one of those so called out of body experiences. Yes, even us writers had em.

I walked back to the room. It was now 5 o'clock on the dot. I wrote Vic a letter and left it on the bathroom sink saying "Sick as all get out. Throwing up since we left Seattle. Please tell Chief." I know it was a bold face lie, but it wasn't no way in hell that I was gonna make it in. I know my other two partners would because they had the power to let shit go with ease, even while being angry. Me however, that was still a weakness of mine. I would hold on to things. Even if I was over them, I still wanted to resolve the situation my way. I was trying to learn to be at peace for myself, because letting negativity live inside of you was letting bullshit stay inside of your head rent free. I curled up under the covers, cut the fan on and dozed off immediately. Chief came by the room and checked on me around noon when they were on lunch.

"So how much did you have to drink?," he asked.

"Chief man...He saw right through the bullshit.

"Stop. Just stop. What happened?" I sat down on the bed and just poured everything out to him.

"Chie...you know who I went out with last night. We had a good time. We had fun. An incident happened in the cab, the police came and I felt we were treated unjustly." Chief sat back in the chair at the room desk.

"How?," in his deep voice. "They slammed us. I was put face down in the hood when all I did was scream from the side for everyone to calm down. They were too aggressive. The shit didn't need to go down like that. Yes, the alcohol caused one of us to say some things to jump it off, but the way the cops treated us...I didn't like it." Chief let out a lil chuckle. It kind of pissed me off, but I held my cool.

"You got a drink in the fridge?" *Was this muthafucka serious* I thought?

"Yea, it's a few pops in there." He got up,

reached in, grabbed a coke and took a seat.

"Let me explain something to you Carl," as he popped the top and took a sip. "You're Carl, I'm Michael. You're a soon to be Third Class Petty Officer. I'm a Senior Chief. You're black, I'm white. I have lived long enough in this world and been in the Navy long enough to see racism and stereotypes played out both ways. When Vic told me you were sick from some food, I highly doubted it. I figured you were drunk. Now, I know the real reason why.

Carl...let me explain something. I was raised in a small town in the Upper Northeast that was 96% white. I can count on two hands how many black people I seen in my small town from Kindergarten to twelfth grade. Honestly, I grew up with people who loved every race and creed. I grew up with people who were disgusted with any other race besides theirs. Me, I chose to love a person for a person. I dont care if you were white, black, green or yellow. If you were an asshole, I didn't like you. If you were a good person, I did like you.

I don't know how it was growing up in Gary, as I know this from glancing at your record during ranking boards. But, however it was, I ask that you don't let one incident make you define a whole genre of people. I'm not just talking about white people. I'm talking about cops too. As with any occupation, there are good seeds and bad seeds. The Navy has them too. What I need you to do is not be hostile towards the next man because of this. It may have been race related. It may not have been. All I know is if you let someone anger your soul, they've won. On the other hand...you have to be smart. You said something was said that triggered the incident. I don't wanna know what was said, how it was said, none of that. All I will say is this. Know that your actions have a consequence. If whatever was said wasn't said, you guys would've made it back with no problems. I want you to think about that as well. An elephants shit attracts beetles. Remember that." He got up, walked towards the door, turned around and said one more thing.

"Also, its a damn soda. The only pop I know is a ring pop, and thats cause my daughter loves those things. " We shared a laugh as he exited the door and I laid back on the bed to just think. That was very informative, as he gave me both sides of the game. I could do nothing but respect a man like that. Right then and there, and it was hard for me to comprehend but I healed and closed up another wound. The bandage was off the wound of excuses. Yea, it was easy for me to bring the race thing into this situation, and by all accounts it may have played a factor. However, I had to look at the incidents that led up to everything. If me and my peoples control our liquor, shit like that doesn't get said in the cab. If that's not said in the cab, no fight occurs with the cab driver. No fight with the cab driver, and we aint gotta worry about the police tossin us up. I see my people all the time using the excuse of "the white man did it." When truth is, we do a lot to ourselves. We have too many wanna be militant folks who wanna scream through computers and cameras, yet put no real action in the street. When you tell black people something like what I'm thinking, many will label you a coon, sellout or whatever other funky name they want to give you. However, a coon doesn't tell the truth. A coon conforms to everyone else's mindset.

I mean, look at a raccoon. A raccoon has a black stripe going across its eyes as if it is wearing a mask. The only people who recognize people wearing masks are those who are wearing them themselves. So when I hear that term coon being thrown around by so many of mine, I figure they are either one misjudging someone because they don't conform to what they think is black. Or two, they wear a mask themselves and also recognize their fellow family members.

That's just how it is. The two weeks up here wrapped up quickly, with no other major incidents occurring. Well, let me take that back. I told y'all about my hood country guy Chris. Well he had to knock a cat out from the USS Abraham Lincoln. The night after my little fiasco in Seattle, he went to the bar with a few of the guys, including Senior Chief. Long story short, a young boy got liquid courage and approached Chris on some bullshit. Chris tried to defuse things and avoid confrontation, as did the rest of the guys. Eventually, dude hit Chris in the head with a beer bottle, but that thick ass country dome of his was hard as a rock and didn't phase him. Chris got him with a one hitta quitter, and that was all she wrote. If it's one thing Navy guys can do, it's fight. If they don't know how to fight, they will damn sure learn, especially with all the scraps and brawls we get into overseas.

CHAPTER NINE

HEAVEN AND HELL

Time had passed quickly between our deployment which ended in November of 2012 and now. It really surprised me, cause it seemed like I was having so much fun for these past ten months. Now, it was time to go back out to sea to get ready for these strenuous work ups to get ready for our next deployment which was to occur in May of 2014.

Our first out to sea period was scheduled for five days, just floating around the Harbor of San Diego, making sure that our systems were up to par and that this old son of a bitch Nimitz wouldn't break down on us. We were going out on a Monday and coming back on a Friday. That Sunday prior, me and my beautiful Star decided to go out and just indulge in each other. Everything had been copasetic with us. I blew her out of the water with a birthday celebration she would never forget when I came back from Washington. Trust me, I had to seeing that I missed her 23rd birthday. We had our little miscues, spats or whatever, but we continued to have each other's back. We started counseling with a church group, trying to enhance our spiritual along with everything else.

Things were indeed on the up and up. We kept it simple on that Sunday and got us some Jack in the Box and headed to Shelter Island down by the airport. This was our little spot to just get away and clear our heads. We sat under a tree like little kids and began to just wonder about everything.

"Carl...would you consider me wife material?" I looked at her kind of nutty. I mean, I loved her like all hell, so I don't know why she would ask me that.

"Why would you ask me that??? You see all that we had been through. Why wouldn't I?" Her expression didn't change as her hair blew in the small breeze off the Pacific.

"I didn't ask for that. I asked because you know my past." Her head leaned back against that tree and her eyes started to water as she always did when she got emotional. "You gotta pay for my mistakes. I had two abortions. Because of them, I'm messed up inside physically. I'll never be able to bear children for you, for me, for us. It hurts like hell. All my life I wanted to be loved. I never got it. Now I do have it, I'm actually becoming a better human and I can't even give you the basic thing every couple in love wants. Family."

Her head went back down, staring at the ground. I was kind of in awe too. That had never really crossed my mind. Maybe because I was still young. However, I did want to have a family one day. All I could think about at this moment was how I grew up. A drug dealing daddy who wasn't married to my mom. Three brothers all locked up. Two parents both six feet under. Truthfully, I had no family. She had no family. We could never make a family due to her mistakes. I did the only thing I thought that was right at the moment.

"Marry me Star?" She looked at me like I had lost my ever lasting mind.

"You wanna repeat that?" she said.

"Like I said, marry me." She saw how serious I was as she wiped the tears from her eyes.

"You remember when I first saw you...and I took a risk to say Hi to you? You didn't wanna even be bothered with me, nor anyone else. You remember when you took a risk to share your past with me? We flew to Kansas and you confronted everything you went through with me. Well why not take another risk? That's what life is about. It's like being in a plane. You jump from it. You take the risk of your parachute not opening. You take the risk of it not opening up when you want it too. However, you never know what can happen until you take that risk. Let's take that risk? I love you. I fucking love you. Fuck the past. Fuck the abortions. Fuck what you went through. Fuck, what I went through. We are each other's family, and who ever God puts in our lives, they will be our family. I'm not gonna miss out on something great. So again...I ask you...marry me Star?"

She just sat there, ballin her eyes out. Man if my girl didn't do anything else, she most certainly cried. She leaned on my shoulder as I caressed her head ever so gently.

"Yes," she whispered. She then wrapped her arms around me as we embraced each other's souls. This wasn't your typical wedding proposal I know. At the same time, we weren't your typical romantic couple. As we sat there, we saw a sight that symbolized both of our lives. As long as I had been in Diego, I had never seen Geese. I seen Pelicans on a daily by the water, but never any geese.

Well these two geese appeared out of nowhere, making their squaking noises at each other. What their head movements symbolized, I have not the slightest clue on Earth. Suddenly, they took off together, just the two of them. I grabbed Star's hand at that very moment. Our grips brought together 23 years of agony, grief and the fulfillment of life for her and 22 for me.

"Let's Pray Star?" We then brought our heads together and I said a prayer like never before.

"Dear Heavenly Father, I come to you as a man. A broken man. A broken man who you are constantly rebuilding on a daily. Lord, the day you brought Ms. Jennings into my life, I didn't know it then, but you were laying the foundation for the both of us to learn, grow and heal. Lord, as a future husband and as a man in general, I ask that you guide my hand to make the right decisions for our future family, kids and all. Yes Lord, I said that. Kids and all. We will have a family, no matter what I have to do to ensure that happens, my beautiful future wife will become a mother. Lord, I ask that you guide her heart in support of me and the comfort when I may need it. Overall, I thank you for everything that has occurred in my life. Even the negative, because it has now lead to the positive upgrade in my life that I so desperately needed. In your son Jesus name I pray...Amen."

I genuinely felt a rush come over my body when I was saying that. I clutched Star as if my life depended on it. She clutched me back as if she was about to lose me forever.

"Carl...motherhood to me will be special. If you spoke life into it, then I believe it. I never in my life imagined myself being a mother, ever since my mother met her end. I thought...if that's how mothers are treated in this world, then I sure as hell don't wanna be one. You make me look forward to it though babe. I love you."

I looked her in those beautiful brown eyes, gave her a kiss and we continued to look out into the water. We stayed out there so damn long that we managed to see the sunset over the horizon. August 18th, 2013 would go down in the memory banks as the day that I officially grew up into a full fledged man. I was young yes, but way ahead of my years. All this due to the meeting of one woman. We got back to the ship that night, kissed in the parking lot and got ready to get these next five days over with. As I hit my office to sit back and watch some TV, I wrote on today's greatness.

???

How does a man survive his toughest challenge
when the battle is against his norm
How does he conform to something he is not
accustomed to
when he never accepted it, Why does a man see a
bigger picture
even if it causes him to lose his own frame
Why does he still put blame on himself
even when it is not his responsibility

How does he find humility in situations like these
How can one ever question his heart
How can he stay on a path
when even the path he's on can lead him astray
or towards the right place, just at the wrong time
How does a man put himself beneath the next by his
own free will
How does lookin up at the sky and saying yes ensure
his treasure will come at the end
Its hard
I aint gone even lie
but I indeed found mine

I closed my notebook and ended up falling asleep in the shop on our couch. The next day we took off, preparing for world journey #2 in nine months with these crazy sea trials. I aint gone lie. It actually felt kind of good to get my sea legs back. It had been a long time since deployment, but life on the water wasn't all that bad. I was on a carrier man. This wasn't nothing but a floating city when fully occupied.

6,100 people would be sleeping on this thing when full. I mean look at what we had. 1,092 feet front to back. A brother had a choice of four weight rooms on this joint. I aint never have to wait around for a bench, machine, treadmill or whatever else that I had to use. I had two huge mess areas where a brother could eat anytime.

We had some bomb ass cooks, including two of my guys John and Jeff, who were both from the East Coast. Boston and Camden, New Jersey respectfully. Them dudes always made sure I had a good meal in my stomach. While I'm at it, let me not forget my dude Lopez from Louisiana. He was a short, stubby, fat boy from down in the bottom of the boot in Louisiana. I couldn't remember the exact city he was from, but I know it wasn't anything major. He lived in the backwoods wrestling alligators and shit.

We had two stores on the ship. We had a main one, which provided everything we needed to make it through like deodorant, t-shirts, draws, all that good stuff. Then, we had what we called the JetMart. It was like our version of 7 Eleven. It gave you everything except the slurpies. When I wasn't working, fixing toilets and unclogging tampons out of the lines because of nasty ass females, I just cut loose.

The ship would have crazy ass karaokes on the mess decks that we called ice cream socials. Eating God knows how much ice cream while watching people from the ship making a fool out of themselves on the microphone. I remember my boy Drew from Arkansas swore he was Montell Jordan during those things. HALO and Madden were a religion on the boat. Hell, on deployment in the Persian Gulf, that's all we did. Once work was over, those X Boxes and Playstations were getting dusted off and put to work. I was a king on Madden with the Colts. That tax free money in The Middle East was a fool, so we were always betting money on the game like we didn't have bills to pay. I had my partna Reggie from Tennessee who was in my shop and we stayed going at it on one of our three televisions. Shit, the HT shop was the shit. Behind that big weld curtain, we knocked out spades and poker games in the back of the shop. My dude Juan from Bakersfield always called his Mexican homeboys up at night, and it was card games every night. They reminded me of the cats off of Training Day with Denzel. The only thing missing was a token white boy and the bathtub.

Our hangar bays were live at night time when the planes were up topside on the flight deck. In one, you'd have cats hoopin on the puzzle courts. The next, you'd have cats playing football. You'd just pray that no one ran a route to far outside and slid over the side when the hangar bay doors were open.

In the last one, well...you had some of everything. You had the B boys of the ship who would be break dancing on pieces of cardboard. You had a couple of cats trying to relive their high school days and get wrestling matches going on the mats. Hell, I even had a country ass homeboy I worked with named Josh who did some over the wall top shit. He was from Wyoming, Riverton to be exact. Him and a couple of other HT cats took some scrap metal pieces and welded it into the form of a makeshift bull. Every night damn near, they would come up and be roping the bull. I was amazed, as being from the hood, I aint know anything about horses, bulls or any of that. It was cool to see the diversity of everyone on board. Different backgrounds, different places, different cultures, all that.

This was the best workforce alive and this was simply the life man. So many people have this misconception that all we do is work, work, work. In truth, we chillax most of the time and let our hair down. Especially in The Navy. People wonder what I do. They rarely believe me when I tell them not a damn thing. Yea, we have jobs, as does everyone. However, we really aint goin thru no major stressing.

We're on a ship. If we got beef, we got people to press a button. We got planes flown by pilots who drop bombs and come right back. Then, we go party. Yep, that's the life of a squid. Sailors belong on ships, ships belong at sea. Haze, grey and underway is the only way to be. That was our saying and we lived by it.

We got back from that quick five days early Friday morning and headed straight into the weekend. I aint have duty so I was beyond gravy. I was waiting for Star in the parking lot in front of the ship, fiddlin with my phone, when an incoming call came in. It was from back home, but I aint recognize the number.

Me: "Hello?"
???: "Waddup. This Carl???"
Me: "Yea, who in the hell is this???"
???: "Hold on nigga" **(Speak nigga!!!)**
???: "Cuz?"
Me: **"SNAP!!!"**
Snap: "Yea. I'm...I...I"
Random: **"HE DEAD NIGGA!!!"**

POP!!! POP!!! POP!!! POP!!! That's all I heard and I was stunned silent listening to my phone. I heard a total of 24 shots. They had got my family.

"And by the way, **GD NIGGA!!!**" *POP!!!* Cuz phone went dead and I literally lost my breath. I walked over to the solid bar fence between the lot and the ship and just sat down. I couldn't even cry. What were the odds of this. The last real family member I had, he was now gone. I tried to really grip my hands around what I had just heard. I was hoping someone was gonna call me back in five minutes and tell me they were fucking with me.

"Baby, Baby?" I looked up and saw Star. She saw the pain in my eyes.

"What's wrong babe???" I didn't say anything. I just got up and started walking.

"Carl, Carl?" I heard Star, but I didn't care. Now, I really had no reason to live life I felt. I walked across the street to the little makeshift park. **"CARL!,"** as Star snatched me by my shoulder and spun me around. "Tell me what's wrong with you???" I stood there looking at her. The build up was evident in my eyes, and before I could drop one tear, she grabbed me and hugged me. I cried deep in her shoulder as she pulled me to a bench. I hadn't balled like this ever since my mother died.

"Baby, what's wrong?," as she was now crying with me. I wanted to answer her, but I was in my feelings right now and nothing but anger was building up inside of me.

"Carl…talk to me?," she pleaded, as her tears were now overcoming mine. I looked up at her.

"You're what's wrong with me." She backed away. "What...What...me?"

"Yea you!," as I stood up. "I lost everything! My mama gone!!! My daddy gone!!! My cousin gone!!! My whole fucking family is gone!!! I have nothing!!!"

She slowly got up with a pissed look in her eyes. "Then what do you call me Carl??" I just stared. "What in the good hell do you call me???" I wiped my tears.

"Wasted time." It looked like the breath had left her body completely. She was beyond stunned and couldn't believe what I just told her. I calmly turned around and walked towards the big parking lot where my whip was at. I didn't even turn around to look at her. My feelings to anything and anyone were numb at this point. What was I gonna do? I had no idea.

<u>MEETING WITH DEATH</u>

It was 8:57 p.m. I was back here at the Days Inns off E Street in Chula Vista. My phone had been buzzin with nothing but missed calls from Star. It was about 30 of those missed joints. I didn't wanna talk to anyone right now, nor associate myself with anyone either. I knew I had hurt her, and I was dead wrong. However, I didn't care. I had a room full of liquor. Hennessey, Crown, Jack D and Coke. I couldn't take it anymore.

My whole family was gone. Either they were dead or in jail. Aah fuck, this shit hurt. I was fucked up on the inside. This drink wasn't doing anything but killing me even more, but it felt like a friend right now. How could this be happening to me? I thought my grief was over. Of course though, it only suited me right that bad news come back around. I was tired and felt that I had nothing left to give this world. I grabbed my car keys, drunk and all.

11:20 was the time. I shouldn't have gotten my drunk ass on the road, but I was beyond out of my right mind. I somehow managed to swerve my black ass to the 5 freeway and head South. I was drunk, but I still had some sense of what was around me. The freeway was eerily empty.

It was a Friday night, and I only seen one other whip on the road with me. Nothing was in my rear view either. It was like someone was telling me its time. I had no music on or anything. It was just me and my thoughts at this time. I was tired, and I didn't need anymore pain. It was time to end it all. I made it to the Palm Ave. exit headed towards Imperial Beach. Again, I was at the light and it was just me. No other cars or anything. Either the whole world had died, or somebody was seriously fuckin with me.

I made that right and caught all damn greens. This shit was getting more strange by the minute. I booked a hard left down whatever the hell street until I got my ass to the strip where the boardwalk was. There were literally no cars on the street as I double parked in my drunken mindstate. I got out stumbling, groggy and feeling at the lowest of lows. It was August, but the night was beyond breezy. It felt more like a November night out here. I stumbled slowly over to the beginning of the pier. I looked at the pretty lights of the boardwalk sign. The red and yellow. It kind of looked like a bootleg ass golden arches. I stood there and gazed at it for a minute, until all of a sudden, the lights went out.

The shit got even stranger now. I focused my eyes as much as I could down the pier. There wasn't a soul in sight. The only other life I seen were two pelicans. I slowly started my drunken descent towards the middle of The Boardwalk. I had nothing else to live for. Everyone was out of my life and I had no other reason to continue on. I got to the middle of the pier and walked over to the side, leaning against the old wooden sides as I watched and listened to the waves crash. The moonlight gave it an eerie glow. I began to cry as I looked up at the star lit sky.

"Mama, I failed. It's time." I reached in my back pocket, grabbing the little notepad that I always kept on me. I pulled out a pen and wrote my final thoughts for the world on there.

"TO THE ONE WHO MAY READ THIS, KNOW I LEAVE THIS EARTH UNFULFILLED, KNOW THE THRILL OF LIFE WAS A ROLLER COASTER THAT GOT STUCK AT THE TOP, SO I TOOK THE PLUNGE, RATHER JUMPING TO SEE HOW THE GROUND FEELS, INSTEAD OF WAITING FOR SOMEONE TO RESCUE ME, BECAUSE FOR THEM TO SAVE ME, MEAN THEY WILL TAKE ON MY BURDENS, SEE I'VE BEEN HURTING FOR TOO LONG, STRONG IS WHAT THEY TELL ME TO BE, BUT WEAK LINKS IN MY DNA BROKE THE CHAIN, AND I AM SIMPLY......A LIFE NOT WORTH LIVING"

I tossed that green notepad to the middle of the pier. This was it. **"GOODBYE WORLD!"** I yelled, hoping that someone would hear my last cry and be witness to my last hoorah upon this

Earth. I placed both feet on the middle beam and got my balance. I simply closed my eyes and outstretched my arms as if I were Jesus Christ himself. This was it. 10…hitting Richard with that rock flashed in my mind. 9…helping rob a man flashed. 8…Sitting in a prison cell flashed. 7…Boot camp flashed. 6…Landing in Bahrain flashed. 5…Talking to Star for the first time in Hawaii flashed. 4…Making love to Star for the first time flashed. 3…Getting slammed face first on the hood of a police car flashed. 2… Loving life on the ocean flashed. 1….Carl Lamell Jackson flashed.

I flashed in my own mind as I leaned and fell. **THUMP!** My head hit the hard, cold surface.

"CARL! CARL!!!" I was delirious. I wasn't in the water, but my head hurt like a muthafucka. Opening my eyes, with blurred vision, I saw Star.

"BABY! TALK TO ME!!!" I heard her, but I couldn't focus because my head was throbbing so hard.

"B-B-Bae." I couldn't even get out a word.

"C'mon, lets go," she told me as she tried with all her might to help me up. She threw my arm over her and we made our way back towards the street. I wanted to talk, but I was so out of it that I couldn't even make out what to say to her. Finally, after what seemed like an eternity, we made it back to her car. I aint even know I was in her car. That's how out of it I was. It was dead quiet in there until I asked her one simple question.

"How did you find me?" I mumbled out, head throbbin as hard as ever. "Remember that night you brought me here?" I looked at her, as I remembered, but still wasn't coherent. "I asked you what was this that night and you said the beginning of something great. So I came back to our beginning, hoping that it wasn't your ending." I heard her, but I couldn't believe it.

"How did you know I was here though?," I muffled out.

"I didn't," she said. "I just followed my heart and my heart was you." I leaned my head back and just soaked that in. This whole time I thought I had lost everything. In reality, everything I needed was to the left of me.

"Carl...the only other time I have ran in my life was when I tried to escape my dad. I was trying to save my life. Tonight, I ran again, with the same intentions...to save my life. My life is you. I saw you standing on that beam. I called out your name as I ran and ran and I ran as if someone was chasing me with a knife. You began to lean and I just dove out, managing to grab the back of your shirt. I flung you back and fell with you. I saved you because saving you is saving me. I need you Carl. I need you. I love you and I don't wanna love any other man."

I nodded in agreement, looked at her and gave a faint smile. "Let's go home...wife." She smiled, teared up and we headed back down the road. She cut on her IPOD to some old school Mint Condition. You don't have to hurt no more was the song to be exact. I think that was the song that simplified both of our lives. Two imperfect people becoming perfect with each other. I was laid back, just thinking about what would have happened had she not shown up. Rather, what wouldn't have happened if God hadn't shown up. That's all it was. He led her to me through words. It's amazing how words you say so long ago can come back and save your life.

I truly was grateful for Star and everything she had done for me. We made it back to the hotel. She helped me up the stairs and trust, I needed it. We just lied on top of the bed, staring at each other. The caressing she gave my head reassured me that she wasn't going anywhere. Nothing was being said. I slowly started to drift into dreamworld, until she pulled out a piece of paper and began to speak.

"Intimacy
The first word is in
that's where you must be to complete the process
timacy is the root for timid
something you shouldn't be with the one you love
its put in there to remind you there's no room for that
she with a random, its just sex
with your best friend, it is something much deeper

much, much, much more deep rooted
its lookin into the eyes of your mate and having full
blown conversations without even saying a word
its touching their skin in the faintest way and telling
them you are mine
its hugging them and connecting your hearts through
your chest to the form of one beat
strawberries, cherries, berries, oils and hot candles
are just extras
but in this movie, there are no extras
only two actors who aren't acting out a scene
they are simply playing it out in real life with no
breaks in the action
Hollywood couldn't even write a better script for this
and if you want this
you have to stop playing with love and embrace it
because it is truly worthwhile"

Those words made me rise up out of my drunken position. I just looked at her. I swear I had sobered up.

"You wrote that babe?"

"Yea I did. Just for you." She put her head down and I was stunned. I don't even think she knew the power of the words that she had just read me. She got up and walked in the bathroom, shutting the door. I didn't know what to do. My gift had always caused me to affect others personally. Now, I was getting a dose of what I always did. I don't know what time she came out the bathroom, but I fell asleep, gone to a different world.

I arose the next morning around 6:30. There she was, my baby, clad in a sleek, white lace full body lingerie piece. She was asleep in the next bed, all by her lonesome. I think she was trying to send me a message. She looked so peaceful. I felt bad about the previous night. Hell, the whole day to be real. I told her to basically stay out of my life. Yet after all that, she still searched me out when I was at the lowest moment in my life. I just plopped back down on the bed. I felt like the ugliest piece of shit any man could ever be. How she forgave me, I have no idea.

I got up to take me a shower. The water hit me a lil different this time. It woke me up and cured me for one. Two, it felt like a baptism that was unofficial. I guess a near death experience will do that to you. I finished up, threw on my shorts and walked out to a wide awake Star just staring at me.

"Come here," she said. I went over and laid with her. We locked hands and ended up falling back asleep. This was the message she wanted to send me I believe. She just wanted the man who helped her heal back. The man she fell in love with. She didn't want the sex. She wanted to look her best for what she considered her best. This was Intimacy like she said in her poem. Snap was dead, and it was messed up how I had to experience that. However, I was still complete. Right then, another bandage fell off. My wound of self pity and feeling sorry for myself had been healed. It almost wasn't. Me taking the bandage off almost caused me to not be here.

However, almost doesn't count, because my bandage came in the form of a light skinned beauty from Wichita, Kansas. 9:31 a.m. rolled around as I couldn't sleep anymore. My movement awoke Star, as she just gazed at me, eyes glossy from still being sleepy.

"Star...babe, I'm sorry about la...She put one finger over my lips. "Carl you taught me to not to pick at scabs or open up wounds once they are healed. This wound is healed. No more talk about it." She grabbed my face to kiss me, and proceeded to head to the bathroom. I could honestly tell me damn near taking my own life affected her deeply, as it was written all over her face. She still forgave me though and proceeded to be strong. Once she came out, a rush came over me.

"You wanna go to the courthouse on Monday?" She stopped the brushing of her hair in mid stroke, just staring at me, not saying anything. "Star? Seriously? Do you want to go to the courthouse on Monday?"

"Nah," she said in a low tone. "You got some healing to do, and marrying me won't complete the process." She walked over to me as I was stunned beyond belief, placing her hand on my right shoulder. "It's one thing to not feel like you should be living. It's another to stop living when you know someone loves you." She sat down next to me.

"The difference between us is this. I felt like I shouldn't have been living because of all the trauma I endured, with some of it caused by me myself. You were surrounded in love, by the one whom you taught how to love. And in the moment where it was my job to comfort you, you pushed me away. You shunned me. You blamed me for your downfall. I'm not the smartest woman on Earth, but I know real love doesn't do that. This isn't Star from years past. This is Star. Here. Now. You gotta heal internally before we cross any threshold of love again. You hurt me… deeply. Yet I'm still here riding with you. Maybe you need to find out who Carl is before you can call yourself a husband."

We stared at each other for what seemed like eternity. I had no words. "I love you," she said, as she kissed me on my forehead. "Get some clothes on so we can go get your car." Again she got up, walking over to put on her clothes. I quietly threw on my Crown Royal smelling clothes from last night. I was sober, but I was hungover by anger and sorrow. In life, we do sometimes push those who love us away. In times of hurt, the ones we love are the ones we need the most. Anyone hollin out that bullshit of I don't need anyone but God is a fucking fool. God places people in our lives. You don't need people who love you, then you don't need God.

What I needed was her. I just now had to prove my worth to her all over again. Crazy, when I first met her, she wanted absolutely nothing to do with me. Now, she wanted everything to do with me, but she wasn't sure if I wanted to do anything with her. That's a sad feeling to feel like you aren't loved. Its an even sadder feeling how I felt like a piss poor excuse of a man.

We made it to Imperial Beach on the most silent trip ever. She left the car running after she parked. "Star, what do I gotta do to show you that I love you and that I will never hurt you like that again?"

Head down, not even looking at me, she said, "Heal yourself." I glanced at her for about ten seconds before I got out.

"I love you beautiful."

"I love you to handsome," with no eye contact from her. I got out pitiful and distraught. Immediately, she pulled off. I stood still and watched her all the way until she disappeared. It was crazy how The Boardwalk was now full of people again. Last night, there wasn't a soul. I decided to walk down the pier as not only a refresher, but to face my demons head on. I walked out to the middle once again. This time, there wasn't any breeze, nor darkness. It was broad daylight and wind was damn near non existent. As I walked over to the side, my foot kicked something. I looked down and there it was. Sitting in the cracks of the wood was my green notepad. I reached down to pick it up and saw that it was intact.

"TO THE ONE WHO MAY READ THIS, KNOW I LEAVE THIS EARTH UNFULFILLED, KNOW THE THRILL OF LIFE WAS A ROLLER COASTER THAT GOT STUCK AT THE TOP, SO I TOOK THE PLUNGE, RATHER JUMPING TO SEE HOW THE GROUND FEELS, INSTEAD OF WAITING FOR SOMEONE TO RESCUE ME, BECAUSE FOR THEM TO SAVE ME, MEAN THEY WILL TAKE ON MY BURDENS, SEE I'VE BEEN HURTING FOR TOO LONG, STRONG IS WHAT THEY TELL ME TO BE, BUT WEAK LINKS IN MY DNA BROKE THE CHAIN, AND I AM SIMPLY......A LIFE NOT WORTH LIVING"

Those words were still there. No water or wind damage. They were clear as day. I read them over and over a good seven times before closing it. I began to think seriously of the spiral my life had taken in one fell swoop, and how I almost sentenced my soul to a lifetime of burning. I couldn't do this anymore. I couldn't allow my past to dictate my present or my future. I called the only person whom I felt could help me in this situation.

(RING,RING)

Mac: Waddup young blood?"
Me: Mac I need your help. I need to talk to you face to face, man to man. Please brotha.
Mac: Come on up. I'm home.
Me: I'm on my way.
Mac: Gone

It was a good lil drive to Encinitas where Mac stayed from here, but it was well worth it. Hell, he was a lot closer than most of the cats that stayed outside of San Diego. Encinitas was maybe a 25 minute drive from downtown. You had some cats though who traveled to work all the way from Temecula and Murrieta, which was about an hour and some change drive. Throw in traffic, and they were looking at a much longer commute.

Even worse than both of em, I knew one Chief who stayed all the way out in Victorville. Two hours both ways….fuck all that. I cruised all the way out there bumping some old Gangstarr. "Mass Appeal" to be exact. I needed some old hip hop to get my mind right. I'm glad I was born when I was born, but those 80's babies were lucky cause they heard a lot more real shit. I came out in 91, so I had a lot of catching up to do when it came to real old school hip hop. I got to Mac's house and just sat there in front for about five minutes.

Encinitas was so different from Diego. It was just open and chill. I mean, Diego was the lick, but out here, it was just like you were in your own world. I went up and knocked on the door of this simple, yet decent sized house.

"Well, well. if it aint young blood, happily in love." We both laughed as we dapped up and he invited me in. "Whatchu wanna drink youngster?,"as we sat at the kitchen table, his medicine in front of him.

"You got cranberry juice?"

"YOU GOT LEGS NIGGA!" Yep, that was Mac. Once he invited me in, I was fam bam. If I wanted a drink, I could get up on my own and get it. I mixed up some cranberry and pineapple juice. I didn't need any liquor after last night's episode.

"What's on ya mind youngblood?" I took a deep breath and just told him everything. I'm talking literally, I didn't skip a detail. Before I realized it, I was talking for a good twenty minutes. Once I was done, Mac just kept looking at me. He would sip, stare, sip, stare, sip, stare.

"Are you gonna say something Mac?" He took one more sip.

"Look around youngblood. Tell me what you see?"

"I see a nice house." He nodded his head.

"Right right, a nice house. A nice house that I couldn't have if my black ass was dead. Remember how I tried to drink my sorrow away in Hawaii? Well, I was a stupid son of a bitch." His medicine sippin continued. "When life hits you in the mouth, you gotta punch back and knock the shit out of it. And right now, that woman needs to hit you. You think I don't watch nothing? I see everything. I'm old. I aint got shit to do but observe. I have seen it all. You changed that girl from nothing to something."

He sipped again. **"AND FOR YOU...YOU MUTHAFUCKA**...to push her away when she trying to be there for you and blame her...... you'z a stupid muthafucka."

I could do nothing but take it as he was telling the truth. "You got one choice," as he pointed at me. "You gotta make that woman fall in love with you again. Now, that's all I'm gone say." As he took his last gulp and went to the sink, I asked him something serious.

"How do I do that Mac???" He laughed, looked and told me three words:

"Prove her right...Now, negro you stink. We bout the same size, so gone head and grab you some shorts and a shirt out the hallway closet and rest up here tonight. It's a store down the street if you need some draws, cause you aint wearing my draws." He walked off into the living room as I continued to sit at the table.

"AND TAKE ANY ROOM UPSTAIRS AND RELAX. YOU GOT A TV NIPPLE!" What in the good hell a TV nipple was, I had no idea. That drink was really starting to stir his head up. I fixed me another drink of pineapple and cran and headed up. There was a shower in the room I chose so that was gravy. I sat on the bed for a hot minute and soaked in everything Mac had told me.

No matter how crazy it sounded coming from his mouth, it was true. My phone was in my hand, constantly going thru old text messages between me and Star. Lowkey, I was hoping that she would text me and just say I love you. However, I hadn't heard from her since she dropped me off. I was hurting inside. I needed to drive. I went to Walmart which wasn't to far from his house. I know I was a lil tart, so I was hoping the basketball shorts and dingy t-shirt I had on made it look like I had came off the basketball court.

I grabbed some boxers, deodorant, a few lil things to eat, some miscellaneous stuff, some drank for Mac and I was on my way out the door.

"You're cute." I turned around at the whip to see this nice lil brunette white girl. She was bangin. Definitely not your typical white girl body either.

"Thank you," as I continued to put my bags in the car.

"So you from around here?"

"Well...I stay in Diego. I'm just up here for the weekend with a friend."

"Good," she said, as she approached me, placing her hand on my chest. "Well, some of my friends are having a party up here and I would love it if you met me there. Take my number." I was stuck between a rock and a hard place. I loved Star, but hot damn this girl was bangin.

"Aight coo." I gave her my number. "By the way, whats your name?," I asked.

"Dani. Yours?"

"Carl."

"Nice to meet you Carl," as she grabbed my face and planted one on me. "See you later tonight." She walked away and all I could think was what the fuck just happened. She aint even look back. That was some pimp shit. Oh boy... this was gonna be a long night. I aint know what to do. Random white girl, with ass I might add. Man...I needed to pray.

I got back to the house and headed upstairs with the quickness. The shower and a nap was calling my name something serious. I called Star, no answer. I didn't even leave her a voicemail. I aint even wanna hear her message. I wanted to hear her live and direct. Damn shame she wasn't picking up, but I completely understood. I cleaned up real good and checked the clock as I pulled the sheets back. 4:13. Cool. I could get at least three or four hours of rest before I got my night started.

"YOUNGBLOOD!"

"YEA!"

"JUST GOT WORD FROM THE SHIP THAT THE C.O. WAS SO IMPRESSED BY THE FIRST UNDERWAY WE GET MONDAY OFF!"

"AIGHT COO BEANS!"

That's just what I needed to hear. I had duty Tuesday so this worked out perfectly for a brotha. I set my alarm for eight o'clock and drifted off to sleep. When I awoke, I felt like I had slept for seven days straight. Thats how tired a brother was. I looked at my phone. No call or text from Star. However, I did have a text from Dani. She texted me the address and told me to come thru at about ten. That was cool with me. At the same time, it wasn't. I already knew what was going down.

I aint wanna creep on my girl, but I needed a release. I debated for about the next hour as I watched TV and ate me a bowl of ramen noodles with a cracked egg and some green onions. Yea, yall know black folks can make a delicacy out of anything. 9:30 came with the quickness. Fuck it I thought, I was going. I went downstairs to let Mac know I was bout to bounce, but he was passed out on the couch. However, he left the key on the living room table with a note. *"Wrap it up youngblood if you go out."* All I could do was crack a smile as I grabbed the key and dipped out. I put her address in my phone and swung over to Jack in the Box first. A nigga had to get two supreme croissants and a drank before I swung up over here. I followed the road, winding thru the hills. I was excited and nervous at the same time.

White girls, yea I knew they got down with the freaky shit. Especially when they had some black snake to play with. I had a homeboy from the Chi Blocks named Lashawn who always told me about those white girls, but now I was about to see first hand. I had to block Star out of my mind. I didn't want to, but I had to. I pulled up to a huge ass crib. I aint know if it was hers or her friends, but I could tell this was gonna be something to remember. I took a few deep breaths and jumped out the whip. There were a few females outside conversating. The looks they gave me as I walked up let me know what type of night this was gonna be. I heard their lil chuckles as I rang the doorbell. The door creaked open as I was greeted by Dani.

"Hey handsome," as she happily greeted me by toungin me down. "C'mon in." She grabbed my hand so joyously. Man this girl was oooh weeeee. She had on these little ass boy shorts, with a wifebeater, no bra and all that hair was hanging down to the middle of her back. We got to the big ass kitchen. This was slut heaven in here. It was a few sistas in here, but these white girls just looked like they were ready for some dick. She walked around, introducing me as her friend to everyone. The white boys were funny, as every one of em called me dude. That shit was funny.

"Let me show you upstairs." Oh man, this was about to get crazy I thought. I wasn't in the house ten minutes and I was about to smash I thought. "Now, we got a huge play room up here. I want to introduce you to some more of my friends." We walked in and it was much of the same as downstairs. This room had a big ass chandelier, plush couches and pure tan colored carpet. She walked me around introducing me to the same. Girls, dudes, you know.

Finally, we came to a sister who from the back was magnificent. That phat ass sat in those boy shorts so nice. She had on an airbrushed cap with some pink and white AF Ones.

"Carl, I wanted you to meet my good friend.," as she tapped her on the shoulder. Baby girl turned around and her eyes got big. "Star, this is my friend Carl. Carl this is Star."

What in the fuck were the odds of this? Oh boy, I could shit bricks right about now.

"Ummmmmm...how are you," I said, trying not to show my nervousness. She stood there analyzing me up and down, not saying a word, with a stone cold look on her face.

"Do you two know each other?," Dani asked her.

"Yea, I know him. We used to be tight, Real

tight. But umm...times change. Aint that right Carl?" I didn't know what to say. Dani was looking confused as ever.

"Excuse me y'all. I'm a go outside and get some air." Star walked out the room.

"So Carl, what happened between you two?" I really wasn't tryna pay Dani any attention anymore.

"Excuse me shorty? I gotta go handle something." I aint even turn around as I ran out the room and shot down the stairs. Fuck that pussy I thought. God definitely intervened. This was probably my one shot at reconciliation with the girl I loved. **"STAR!!!" "STAR!!!"** I shouted her name as I got outside. I didn't see her anywhere. I looked all around from the front to the sides of the house. No one was in sight. Finally, I came back up front and walked to the street, just fast enough to see Star down the hill and almost to her truck.

"STAR, WAIT!!!" I ran towards her as if my life depended on it. **"STAR!"** She finally stopped as she was opening her car door. By the time I reached her I was out of breath. Panting, on my knees keeled over, her standing with her arms crossed, I tried to get my words together.

"Babe...just gimme...one minute to explain." Damn, a nigga had to get back in the gym. "Look...I know I fucked up. I can't revert back to the past. I can't change anything I did. Last night, I was messed up in the head. I-I-I thought life was over. You've been there for me, and I can't deny that. I dont care how things started between us, but I know where they are right now. This afternoon, when you left and didn't even bother to look back, my soul was crushed. You made me feel what you felt. Trust me, it didn't feel good. This afternoon, I went to a friends house up here to get wisdom. Right now, by the grace of God, I'm executing this wisdom. Please... Star... please... give me another chance?" She stayed in the same position, staring a hole through me.

"Did you kiss her Carl?" "She kissed me babe. I met her at Walmart earlier. I was lost, hurt and confused. I thoguht I had lost you. I thought you never wanted to see my face again. She gave me the invite, I came over and I had plans to smash. Once I seen you, I was brought back to reality." I dropped to my knees. "Star, I love y...and I'm beggin you, I am literally beggin you...to give me another shot at love with you?"

She looked up at the stars as if she didn't know what to do. "Remember Kansas. Remember Leavenworth. Remember the first time we kissed at The Boardwalk. I don't wanna throw that away. I love you Star." She looked back at me, teary eyed and all.

"How do I know this will never happen again Carl? That you'll just toss me aside like trash when you get angry at the world?" I really didn't have an answer great enough to make her feel better.

"Here." I reached in my pocket. "Read this." I handed her the paper and watched her open it under the street lights. It was the Life poem that I wrote on my way to the airport before I flew out overseas. I always kept it on me to remind me of my journey. As she was reading it, I just spilled my heart out.

"I don't know why I wrote that poem Star...but I do know my life didn't start until I met you. I love you." She finished up reading, and looked dead at me. She folded up the letter and just stared at me. Her hand warmly rubbed my face.

"I love you Carl." I started to cry, as I leaned in and we embraced in a kiss for the ages. This was like the ending of Love Jones, minus all of the rain. This was poetry in motion. This right here. This love. What we had. This was love. We stopped for a minute, looking in each other's eyes, under the lights, back together again. I began to speak:

"Say baby, can I be your slave
I've got to admit girl, you're the shit girl
And I'm diggin' you like a grave
Now do they call you daughter to the spinnin post, or
Or maybe Queen of 2,000 moons
Sister to the distant, yet risin' star
Is your name Yimmy-Ya
Oh hell nah, it's got to be Oshun

Ooo, is that a smile me put on your face child
Wide as a field of Jasmine and Glover
Talk that talk honey, walk that walk money
Hound legs that'll spank Jehovah
Shit, who am I?
It's not important
But they call me Brother to the Night
And right now
I'm the blues in your left thigh
Tryin to become the funk in your right
Who am I?
I'll be whoever you say
But right now, I'm the sight raped hunter
Blindly pursuing you as my prey
And I just wanna give you injections, of sublime
erections
And get you to dance to my rhythm
Make you dream archaetypes, of black angels in
flight
Upon wings, of distorted, contorted, metaphoric jism
Come on slim
Fuck yo' man, I ain't worried about him
It's you who I wanna step to my scene
Cause rather than deal with the fallacy
Of this dry ass reality
I rather dance and romance your sweet ass, in a wet
dream
Who am I?
Well they all call me Brother to the Night

And right now, I'm the blues in your left thigh
Trying to become the funk in your right
Is that alright"

Star started to laugh her ass off. "Love Jones huh?!" I couldn't help but laugh.

"Yea baby. I thought this would be fitting. All we need is the rain." That smile came back that I loved so much.

"Well, baby," as her finger glided across my chest. "Before things get wet...I've been practicing to get on your level. So tell me how does this sound? I call this, A Blues for Carl."

I sat there, big ass smile on my face, waiting on her to spit. I kept standing there, but she wasn't saying anything. "Are you gonna speak girl? She kept looking. The, she smiled at me.

"Look at how I am looking at you Carl?"

"Ok...I see this. Are you gonna spit?"

"You aint getting it. Sometimes, the best words that are spoken are the ones that are never said. The look I'm giving you should tell you everything that you need to know." That shit right there hit me like never before. She was on some other shit. However, she was right. I saw a mixture of I love you, fuck me and make this last forever. I placed her face in my hands, kissing her ever so softly. "Lets go," I told her. She grabbed my hand and led me to the back seat of the truck. Kissing and groping led to the boy shorts sliding off eventually. We were now indulging in all out, blow out sex. We were in the back seat of her truck foggin up the windows. I thought I would have to call the fire department in this muthafucka. It didn't even matter that we were in one position. It just felt great being intimate with my love again.

We went at it with grunts, bites, nails in the skin, all this until she began bouncing like a mad girl, and we both came at the same time. It was the greatest orgasm that a brother ever experienced. We were both there, taking deep breaths. Hell, we were out of breath to tell you the truth.

This shit was sweaty, raunchy, kind of slutty, but good. Who in their right mind would fuck under the streetlights in a residential neighborhood, with many having the chance to catch you? Hell anyone! That spur of the moment type shit is the best. Hell, let this would've been a bedroom session and I would've pulled out the refrigerator. Pineapples, cherries, grapes, strawberries, all that.

We sat there for a minute sharing laughs and kisses, until she was ready to go back with me for good. I told her I was staying at Mac's house. She nullified that quick.

"It's a Best Western right up the road. Let's go. We need another round. I'll pay" I was with it, but I had to give flare to this upcoming moment.

"Lets umm run by Vons before we go

beautiful. I wanna get some crazy wild shit going on. She just smiled.

"HURRY UP AND GET TO YOUR CAR NIGGA!" I damn near broke my neck trying to run to my whip. I started my joint up as she pulled up next to me and signaled for me to let down my window.

"Meet me at the store!," she yelled. I followed behind my babe as we made our quick drive to the store. They were open real late so we were straight. As I pulled up next to her in the parking lot and got out, she had an idea.

"Tell you what. It's 12:12. You sit in the car and write as many erotic poems in twenty minutes as you can. I'll come out at about 12:40. Food, poetry, bomb ass sex. How about that?"

"I'm down beautiful." She smiled, giving me my kiss and I got back into my whip. I pulled out a notebook that I kept in the glove compartment. I swear that I kept too many of these things. I told myself I was gonna go super sand and write three of these hoes before she got out. I was trying to get some beyond freaky shit going in this room. Me and my pen went to work:

FOOD FETISH

This is for those who orgasm when they sleep, those who are what they eat, my like that late night snack type peeps, see they say you shouldn't eat after midnight, but that's only in movie scenes, cause behind these scenes we get uncut, I direct and produce that fresh produce you love delving into for your late night appetite, see Adam may have been punished for taking a bite of the apple, but me tasting her Snapple has no consequence except fulfilled thirst, cause it is indeed made from the best stuff on Earth, and she wants to quench from the drench of my shaft alley, so I indulge on pineapples and watermelon, to sweeten up her taste buds, pomegranate gives it a lil bite, these cherries and grapes are shared mouth to mouth like resuscitation, and I'm basting her with tongue flicks saturated in coconut oil drips, see she is my grocery store, every aisle I explore, purchasing her goods free of charge, the only cost is the time it takes for me to deliver her the goods, her food is never out of season, and being full isn't even a reason for me to exceed and lust for greed, yea its one of the seven deadly sins but so is her mouth, her breasts, her pechs, her tongue, her back, her feet, her hands, she claws deep in my back to leave a carved canvas as if I were a slave man who tried to escape the fields, and our fill is only mere appetizers, the fruits of our loins are washed for stock, and we only drop when its time to rotate off the shelve, see she is my shell, I am her turtle, filling her inside when in fear, and I nibble a lil bit on her ear to calm myself down before I drown in her fruit juice, 100% Vitamin C for me while she gets 200% vitamin D, highly satisfied and sustained, taste this love here, cause its far from simple and plain

MR. LATE NIGHT CREEP

How can you deny her that intimacy, her every wish should be your command, so how can you as her man not be her genie in a lamp, she rubs you down three times to make you pop out, but you don't wanna put out, you'd rather tell her get out, sleep on the couch, you're too tired, and she is tired of this lack of love, cause even with love you need lust, that woman wants to feel that thrust, that poke, you should be her pope, blessing her with the dick, doing what the Romans do as if you were in Rome, your tongue should roam her every crevice, your fingers should created highway maps across her back, your mouth and her clit bangin like bloods and crips, her mindset flipped because she never had her pussy ate while being sat on the wall, balanced on your shoulders, she never knew the thrill of stand up 69's, she never knew face time wasn't only on a computer until you downloaded her software as she rode her program on your keyboard, you were part female cause you are what you eat, pussy, and then you stopped, so she set her clock for 1 o'clock to call me, Mr. Late night creep, majoring in between bed sheets with a minor in fitness, she witnessed my bench press, those body curls as I made her toes curl, her leg lifts would sift out the rift of you every time they would vibrate, her squirts released the hurt of the pain you caused and she would eventually fall to received a treat she shoulda been receiving from you, see this aint about cheating, this aint about creeping, this is simply about watching your woman teething like a baby, crying tears because I have quelled the fears of rejection that her man had once given, and now she is driven to drive my stick and adjust the clutch from when she wanna go from making love to downright fucked, she don't want your automatic, cause your transmission went bad, stuck in the repair shop, meanwhile, I popped her top, changing her oil every three thousand miles, removing your clut from her engine and while you were her beginning, I became her ending, and don't worry, I'll be sending you a bill for my service, cause I don't repair broken hearts, unless its your lady

BACK SHOTS

Could you believe this started in the back of my whip
as I slipped your panties to the side and let the top
back
and you hopped on top and threw yo back into it
we weren't finished though
I cruised the whip to the crib
as you tested the back of your throat
and you passed with flying colors
soon, we were under the covers
you on top as I caressed your back
and you started to arch your back and get into it real
well
I started to swell even more as you got wild with it
and then you begged me to hit it from the back
and as I stared at that back
I could do nothing but high five the sky
asking God why did he choose such a prize for a wife
I entered that split slot and hit you with back shots
until your back shot out and your face was buried
deep into the sheets
and as I started to creep to the moment of expectation
I went ham inside of you with deeper penetration and
then..........
POW, POW, POW, POW
BACKSHOTS
then, ya back dropped

and I backed out knowing that I satisfied you once again

I couldn't believe how fast my pen had bled across the page. By the time I looked up, it was 12:29. I really couldn't believe that I wrote all that in 17 minutes. I was on one. I knew I had skills, but damn. This was how love was suppose to go though on some real G shit. You had to spice it up. I know I was young, but I remember the talks I had with couples who had been to together 10, 15, some even 20 years plus. When it came time for the bedroom, they did new and amazing things to keep their sex life spicy. People can front like intimacy in the bedroom doesn't matter, but it does to an extent. I patiently waited for my baby to come out. My heart was beating as if it was my first time meeting her. Time hit 12:36 and I seen her coming out. She looked at me through my window, waved and hit the whip. She had a huge brown paper bag. Its contents remained a mystery, but from the look on her face, I could tell that she had some plans. We arrived at the Best Western on a spontaneous tip. They had a room available so everything was gravy. We chuckled like lil kids playing in the park as we headed back to the car to get the bag.

"What's in it babe?"

"Damnnnn.....be patient. I got this." I couldn't

help it though. I was super anxious. It had been one hell of a 48 hours. I went from losing my cousin, to almost losing my life, to almost losing my girl, to almost losing my sanity, to having everything come back around full circle again. I recognized in that moment as we laughed, smiled and joked, that a bandage fell off another wound that us at humans fail to see at times.

That wound is the scar left by not realizing that we need help. We scar ourselves physically and our spirit when we shun those who genuinely loves us and push them away. What's worse is that we take out our frustrations on them when they did nothing to harm us. That bandage had fell off and I was now healed. There was no more of that. Now, it was time for reconciliation at the highest level.

We made it to our room on the 3rd floor. Room 303 to be exact. *Go take a shower* were Star's words as soon as we hit the room. I happily obliged as I rushed to the bathroom and put the water on damn near scalding. A nigga had to get purified. I was gone boil the remnants of any dirt, or Dani that were left on me. I cut that water off and just stood there for a minute. I knew what was coming, but wondering what was to come besides the obvious was mind boggling.

I came out to Star laying down in her boy shorts and pink laced bra. Food was placed out on a tray. Grapes, strawberries, peaches, a bottle of coconut oil, pineapples, with a pile of whip cream in the center.

"Come here and lay down," she said ever so sexy. I obliged and tried to be smooth as hell as I laid next to her.

"What's funny, may I ask?"

"You tried to be sexy when you laid down, but you were low key corny." All I could do was laugh because she was so right.

"So what's up beautiful?" She smiled those pearly whites.

"Okay. Go in my purse and there's a piece of folded paper. Pull it out and read it. I got up and reached in there, stealing a little bit of her Carmex before returning to the bed. I couldn't have my lips crusty, looking like I was kissing goats. I came back, held it and just looked at her.

"OPEN IT CRAZY!" I laughed as I started to flip it open. What I read next…

To the love of my life…Carl,

You met me as an angry, broken down, unfit person who could not call herself a woman. I bottled up every piece of anger and hurt I ever encountered and took it out on everyone else. I didn't like anyone, including myself. When we were on that plane for the first time, I felt like the pinball in the machine, being bounced around from the energy of everyone around me. I saw no one really but an enemy.

Remember the first time you attempted to talk to me??? I just stared off at you I know. I didn't like you. I didn't want to get to know you. I just wanted to get to this ship, do something with my life a lil bit and get out one day. I wanted to escaped all the pain that my life had endure, even if just for a lil while. Then, out of nowhere, we talkin in Hawaii. I went back to my room that night for the first time in a long time with a smile on my face. I can't lie, I was scared at that very moment, because all throughout my life, everytime I smiled for someone, they turned it into a frown eventually. I'm not gonna go into every detail because you know it all. My main message is to let you know that I Love You with everything, I am truly in love, whipped, sprung, all that. I look forward to growing my life with you. LOVE, a lost soul who you found.

-Star

A smile cracked over my face. I folded it up, placed it on the nearby nightstand and slowly proceeded over to kiss her. We embraced in deep, passionate lip locks as our tongues wrestled as if it were the main event on PPV. Our hands created paintings on each other canvases, as I allowed my fingertips to tell her how much I loved her.

Slowly, I unstrapped her bra, as we both got

excited and started to lose clothes. She started to control me, pinning me down in the bed, looking at me as she grinded slowly on me, my hands with a firm grip on her breasts. She bent down, grabbing a cluster of grapes with her mouth. She fed me, as I fed her skin rubs all over. Man my shit was about as hard as a fresh stiff laid out in the streets.

Kissing ensued, until she slowly slid down, taking my shorts with her. She flung em, then proceeded to stand up on the bed, slowly removing those boy shorts and exposing that juicy clam in the middle. It was well shaven, just how I liked it. With a slow wind, she came back down on top of me, teasing me with tongue flickers all over my chest.

Busy playing happy lick with my body, she grabbed the whip cream can, rising up to spray some in her mouth and around her upper torso, rubbing it in ever so sexy. I couldn't control myself anymore, as I sat up to meet her mouth, cream just dripping from our lips. I gripped her in my arms, telling her with touch that she wasn't going anywhere. Food was now off the pan and everywhere on the bed as I rolled her over, placing me on top. She was wetter than Niagara falls right now and to me that meant dinner was ready to be served. I had never in my life ate coconut, seen a coconut, none of that. However, I grabbed that jar of coconut oil and just poured it all over her until she was soaked. Before she could even feel the full effect of this intimacy, I was down.

I was down there, burying my face in it. Fuck all the slow flickers and fingering. She was ready enough and I was trying to suck cancer out of her soul if she had it. Her moans, shits, fucks, uno, dos, tres, quatros and all out spanish let me know I was doing the damn thing. Man, I don't see how grown men didn't eat pussy. I mean hell, we were made in em, so why not eat from em. If a baby could grow in this muthafucka, my tongue could sprout new seeds. Man if I would've known it was this good, I would've started eating at thirteen instead of eighteen.

"MI AMORRRRR!!! FUCK!!!" She shouted that as she came like I had never felt her come before. I backed my face up, slick ass look on my face because I knew I was that dude. My baby shot up, kissing me, pinning me, licking me until she just inhaled me.

"HOLLY FUCK!," I shouted. She straight up made my shit disappear. When I say disappear, I mean disappear. Crazy thing about it, she just held it there for at least a good 7-8 seconds. Star was on one, swallowing me as if I were her last meal before she left Earth. She grabbed that can again, spraying whip cream on my shit while still blowing me. I was a bitch right now. I wanted to cry tears, but I couldn't. I had to maintain my manhood somehow. I was laid back, eyes closed when she jumped on me and slid myself inside of her.

Baby was going to town. If this was called riding, then I really didn't have a clue on earth what in the hell she was doing. This was some next level shit. I really had to control myself as she talked so much dirty shit to me, bouncing harder and harder as if she was tryna make me come.

"COMMERE!!!," I yelled, as I just pushed her off and got on top. I fucked with her for a minute. Kissing her and playing with her clit with the head of my dick. I had to slow her ass down. This was a move bruhs used so they wouldn't bust. Either lick it, or play with that shit til you got your powers back. I got my wind and got back inside of her. Her legs were higher than the Eiffel Tower, as I began to go Transformer on that pussy.

"FUCKKK!" was all I heard from her. I was knee deep in this shit. It was tight, wet and felt like pussy heaven. I knocked the bottom out of that shit until she let out an orgasm so strong she could've shook King Tut awake from the dead. Her nails had dug into my skin, so I could imagine that my back looked like a hot wheels race track. I was pushed off of her. She was out of breath, but she did something crazy.

"COMMERE!!!," she yelled as she pulled me by my legs to the edge of the bed. Star dropped to her knees and put that human vacuum cleaner to use. I couldn't help but to scream. I wanted her to be easy. I still wanted to give her some more, but I knew it wasn't gone happen. *BAAM!!!* I nutted dead in her mouth and do you think she stopped one bit?? Hell to the muthafucking no!!! I was sensitive and twitching like I was having a seizure or some shit. I tried to mumble some words, but all I got met with is

"**STOP BITCHIN!**" and more sucking. She blew me until I was all the way soft. I was exhausted, sprawled out and I felt her kiss my dick and jump on top of me. I looked at her with my blurred vision. That's what some fire ass head will do. I observed that long, pretty hair of hers and that nice smile. I also noticed the sweat dripping off of her forehead. Yea it was hot in here, but we gave two shits. Sweaty, dirty, tired and satisfied. The tell tale signs of some over the top, bomb ass sex.

We embraced in a kiss for the ages. Who gave a fuck that a minute ago she had just swallowed my kids. I was in love with this woman. If she was woman enough to drink me, then I was man enough to kiss her after she finished. This was love. We finally got back upright on the bed, looking at the mess we made. Food, whip cream and coconut oil was everywhere. I couldn't believe we did this. We really tore some shit up. We just looked at each other. Man I tell you, her body was beyond gravy. I loved it because it was all mine. Most of all and most importantly, her heart was all mine.

I'm pretty sure she looked at me the same way. Matter fact, I know she did. It was amazing being in love at this tender age, recovered from everything you went through. We didn't even say anymore words to each other. She placed her head on my chest and we dozed off into wonderland. How in the good hell did I get so lucky, I had no idea.

CHAPTER TEN

HALLOWEEN: BEHIND THE MASK

Time had passed and life had stayed on the normal course. More workups out to sea, More good times, fights and make up sessions with my girl. You know, it was the usual things going on. However, I started to take my grown up intellect that I was processing from experience and apply it to something real.

Me and Star had decided we were going to get married on December 31st in Vegas at the stroke of midnight. I had taken into account all that we had been through and everything that led up to what we both felt was nothing but divine destiny. We didn't care about rings, huge entertainment ceremonies, cakes, pies, dresses, suits, inviting a million muthafuckas who at the end of the day wasn't gonna help pay our bills, none of that shit. I'm not knocking the people who did it, but I know as a man, I was more concerned about the marriage portion and not the oh my goodness show portion that people just wrapped themselves around. Star felt the same way. We both didn't have any family outside of us. We were each other's backbone.

It was now Halloween, and it was time for the looney tooneys to come out. This would be sort of our pre marriage party. We decided to kick it off different from everyone else. We were gonna do it big on a yacht. 800+ people, acting plum crazy on a boat for about three and a half hours.

"Babe, what in the good hell are you supposed to be?," as she laughed hysterically in the parking lot of the Bowling Alley.

"Baby I am what they call Julius Ceasar…De Negro." She laughed even harder, as all I wanted to do was drop kick her in her chin. I was in a white toga, sandals, with a green leaf around my forehead.

"YOU GONE BE FREEZING YOUR ASS OFF TONIGHT!!!" Like I didn't know the obvious, but she had to remind me. She stayed laughing as we got in the whip, ready to leave the base bowling alley where we met up. As much as I wanted to come back and roast her, I couldn't. She was catwoman for the night. Hot damn boi. She made Halle Berry look like Halle Scary. That full body leather suit of hers did her no justice, seeing that I knew what was underneath it. Yea, this was my lady. We got down to the pier on Harbor Drive a little bit after nine o'clock, waiting for the 9:30 p.m. board time. They had a lot of characters out here. They also had a lot of skut buckets. Y'all know who those are. Those are the girls who are sluts, dress up as their normal selves, but try to pass it off as a Halloween costumes. Me and Star just laughed and joked the whole time while waiting. Moments like these were what life was all about.

"AIGHT FOLKS...LET'S GO!" That was security announcing it was time to get on this boat and cut the plum fool. All I was concerned about was getting to the bar. I wasn't planning on drinking, seeing how SDPD were hounds downtown. However, some cranberry and pineapple mix would do me just right. We got on this joint and went straight to work.

The second deck was poppin with hip hop. Me and babes got our dance on something fierce, all while white people moved around with no rhythm whatsoever. The night was definitely on point. My mixed fruit drink was good, my baby was having fun, one lady had cursed her husband out for falling asleep on her birthday, folks were drunk dancing and it was no drama. That was the best damn part of the whole thing. Time crept by fast as ever because it seemed like as soon as we stepped foot on board this big ass yacht, it was time to get off. It was closing in on 1:30 the next morning. We were up top on the outside deck when some crazy foolio in one of those full body green men suits jumped his happy pappy ass in the water. Everybody was aww struck and laughing their ass off. My girl mouth was down to the deck.

Me, I was just knowing how cold his ass had to have been. Yea, this was California, but it was winter time out here. Night time got chilly as shit. It wasn't any Midwest freezing temps, but you damn sure didn't wanna be in the water at this time of night. Harbor patrol was waiting for him as soon as he hit the pier. They pulled him out, cuffed him and walked him off. As they did, the crowd let out a huge applause as to say "Thank you dumb ass for the entertainment." He happily acknowledged us by making it hard for the cops as he nodded his head to us vigourisly and kept trying to walk slow as possible.

We exited the pier, happy and joyous as ever, oblivious to the chilly night air as we walked to the car across the street. I cranked up the heat and the Ludacris "Chicken-n-Beer" album as we headed off. We had to work tomorrow on Friday, but that was national military get off early as ever day, so we really wasn't trippin. Plus, we were young, so give us a good 3-4 hours of sleep, and a red bull, and we were gravy. We were jettin down Pacific Highway, laughing plenty.

"So Baby?"

"What's good love?" I answered.
"So when we get married, lets say we...

"When time stands still
It is only then we see true value
How the clock hands stop Reaching for the
numbers
And come to a halt
Hoe the ticks and the tocks stop
Their every second talk And just stay hushed in
silence
How numbers now dont have the
same value they once had
See I used to just look at the clock For what it was
A clock, then I realized it's not
I realized it is an hourglass in a Spherical form
Ticking from the time we are born
And stopping
Ultimately at our demise."

"Mr. Jackson? Mr. Jackson? Mr. Jackson?" I felt a nudge as I struggled to open my eyes. My body was in some serious pain. I didn't know what the hell was going on, nor did I know where I was at.
"Wh...wh...wh...what's going on?"
"You were in a car accident sir. You were very lucky you know." I couldn't comprehend what

doc had just said. He was some lil Asian dude saying a bunch of jibberish to me. My head hurt like all to the damned. I glanced around, noticing the other two ladies in the room with me. I saw lights. Hell, thats all it seemed like I was seeing.

"Doc what happened?," I managed to mumble out.

"Well, let me tell you. You were struck by a drunk driver and you were very lucky. You have a concussion, a sprained wrist and a whole helluva lot of soreness. Other than that, you're fine. No internal bleeding. You'll be on your feet in about three weeks." Out of all this confusion on what I was hearing, Star finally crossed my mind.

"What about my girlfriend?"

"Well sir she managed to pull through, but she was banged up pretty bad. Her leg is shattered. We had to place some rods in there. Like you, she suffered a concussion, but she also suffered a bad chest contusion, and some bad bruising. Her rehab for her leg is going to be extensive. We're going to do everything in our power to see that she makes a full recovery. And I'm going to need you to stay by her side through it all. Rest up sir." He patted me twice on the shoulder and exited the room. I couldn't even remember anything that happened that night. I didn't even know what day of the week it was. I drifted off to sleep and everything all of a sudden crept back to me in a horrendous dream. There we were, driving down Pacific Highway. We were laughing, joking, having the best of times. Then, all I remember was seeing lights. I think Star was asking me something about marriage. I don't even know. My eyes shot open. I was drenched in sweat. I glanced up at the clock.

12:48. The lights were out, and the beep from the heart monitor was the only sound that comforted me. I was alive and happy. Where in the hell was my baby though? What fucking day was it? I needed answers. Right now though, sleep was my only answer, as my head was pounding harder than the Packers on the lowly ass Chicago Bears.

I arose the next morning with my DIVO, the CO, The Chaplain and a few of my division peoples over my bed. "How ya feeling Carl?," my Captain asked me.

"Sir, what's going to happen to me?"

"Well son, you will be alright. We talked with your docs. You will make it through the concussion just fine. All you need is rest. The ship funded you a hotel room near the beach on North Island for your recovery. 30 days of convalescent leave. Personnel will bring you food, the whole nine." That sounded cool, but I wanted to know about my lady.

"How about Ms. Jennings?" The Captain took a huge sigh, looked around at my DIVO, Chief and a few others. He turned back to me.

"Well it looks like her career may be over. That

leg injury will make it hard for her to be onboard ships." I started to shed a tear as I got into my feelings. All I could think about was all the shit we went through. All the shit we put each other through. All that, and then we finally came together as one. There was only one thing left to say.

"Chaps…Sir?"

"Yes sir Mr. Jackson. What do you need?" I really hope Father Dan was ready for what I was about to ask him.

"Can you marry us? Me…and Ms. Jennings…on December 31st? We were planning that. We fell in love. We helped each other get through our troublesome past." Just then, Chaps stopped me, yet continued to look dead at me.

"Gentlemen, can me and this great young man have about twenty minutes to ourselves?" Everyone happily obliged, as they yelled out well wishes leaving the room. Chaps turned around back toward me, pulling up a chair next to my bed. "Carl, I know a lot more about you than you think. Star came to me a long time ago. Matter fact, it was after you went back to Kansas with her, to help her heal from her past. She told me everything. Everything from her, to you, her father, everything. One thing that I learned over time in my work is that God makes no mistake. It was no mistake for you to go to prison and end up in the Navy. It was no mistake for her to end up in The Navy. It definitely wasn't a mistake for you to say she was an ugly human being, which ultimately brought you two together. I have seen a lot of couples meet in The Navy, get married, and then dissipate faster than they got together. I seen them marry for the housing allowance, the benefits or whatever absurd reason. However, when I look in her eyes, and now into your eyes, I see The Lord. I see God really healing through togetherness. You two are meant. IT WOULD BE MY HONOR to marry you two!" Chaplain Dan smiled and one cracked on my face as well.

"Thank you sir." We shook hands and I felt like another bandage was released. It was the wound of solitude. You think that sometimes you and another person are the only ones involved in a fight for their lives, whether it be literally, emotionally or spiritually. Chaps was that person who saw both sides, and saw the good in both of us. He knew about me, and this accident, bad as it was, brought us two together for this very moment. For that, I was very grateful

DECEMBER 31ST: D-DAY

LOVE IS

I once said that I don't know what love is
thats until love hit me directly
its fist landed right in my sternum
taking my breath away in one swift punch
love almost killed me then rebuilt me
love had me doing crazy shit
I was so infatuated in love that I learned Spanish
In a country that talked Chinese
and spoke it with a British accent
yes, love did that
see love aint just bedroom crushin or suckin
real love makes that a bonus
love is cookin grits for dinner
love is washing her panties
love is goin to the store for her cycle needs
throw them on the counter
look at the clerk and say
you got a problem with this
love is laughin at hair in the sink
love is looking at the mask on her face
still saying damn you're beautiful
love is when she eat your cap'n crunch
and even though you wanna kill her
you just smile
love is her inch extending your life miles

love is her television shows

There it was. December 31st was here. I hadn't been this nervous since the day that I lost my virginity. We were in the base chapel. Me, Chaps and Star. There was nothing else, or no one else. It was just us and stained glass windows. We all sat on the front pew, having a moment of prayer, followed by a conversation.

"Now, you two have been through so much, and look where the Lord has you both end up. Right here, on this altar, about to be united in Holy matrimony." Just then, the doors of the church opened, no pun intended. We all looked back.

"You aint about to get married and not have me see it." I stood up to see Mac.

"Mac, How'd you know?"

"Boy please! I know everything. Chaps, I'll be the witness." Chaps just smiled, looking at me and Star.

"You see how The Good Lord works? Let's do this." Chaps raised up, followed by myself. As he waited on the altar, I slowly bent over to help up Star.

"You ready for this babe?" With a huge smile, she said "This is the day I never thought I would see in my life." Steel cane in her right hand, I helped walk her over to the altar. She was getting stronger everyday, as the Navy doctors were doing a great job rehabbing her. All I seen was a strong and beautiful woman. The visible scars that remained and a limp in her walk did nothing to deter me. As a matter of fact, she was even now more beautiful than the first day I met her. Oddly enough, I thought the visible scar remnants of the stitches she once had over her right eye made her look a little bit more sexy. We got up there to Chaps, stared at each other and joined hands.

"Dearly Beloved, we are gathered here today in the presence of these witnesses, to join Carl and Star in Holy matrimony commended to be honorable among all; and therefore is not to be entered into lightly but reverently, passionately, lovingly and solemnly. Into this, these two persons present now come to be joined. If any person can show just cause why they may not be joined together, let them speak now or forever hold their peace."

We all glanced at Mac in a joking way. "What yall looking at me for? If you aint interrupting my drinking, I don't care." Well all burst out into laughter, as those words would ensure we would never forget this day. Chaps got back into it.

"Carl, do you have your vows for your soon to be wife?" I stood there, looking at this beautiful woman.

"Chaps, Star once told me that sometimes the best statements are made with complete silence. I don't need to say anything, because regardless of what I say, it still wouldn't be enough to tell her how much I love her." Star didn't cry to my surprise, but she just smiled. Before Chaps could ask her, she began to speak.

"Chaps, don't ask me for vows. Don't ask us for ring exchanges. We don't need that. We know exactly what this love is. So I do." Chaps gave a head nod.

"Well alrighty then. Carl, do you take this woman to be your wife. To have and to hold, until death, do you both part." I stood there for a minute.

"Sorry Chaps, but no. I take her for much more than that. Now, ask me to kiss my bride." My eyes never left hers.

"Well, I must say, this is a first. And you better believe, this is the best ceremony I have ever been a part of. You may now both kiss your lifelong partner. As we kissed, my life flashed back to that fateful night in Gary, all the way to this moment. My bandage was off. My scar wasn't even visible anymore. I was fully healed, and Star Jennings was now Star Jackson. At that moment, somewhere, I felt my mama smiling. I was indeed healed and feeling good about it.

<u>MAY 5, 2014</u>

Deployment day was here. It was a clear, crisp Monday, but I was leaving my wife for the first time. She was out of the Navy now. Medically discharged for her leg injury, but still contributing to our nation. She took a job with Fleet and Family Services, running a class for sailors with troubled pasts, helping them adjust and adapt to a new life. We hugged outside of that ship, crying tears with each other. It was 5:53 a.m., and we had to be inside the gate by six.

"I have something for you Carl." I stepped back, wiping my eyes.

"What's that babe?" She handed me a small jewelry box. "What kind of jewelry you get me babe?"

"Open it. You won't regret it. Funny I was about to be gone for six months, and she got me some jewelry of all things to remember her while I was gone. I opened the box to one heck of a surprise. I just stared at it in amazement.

"Baby, two lines are you telling me what I think this means?"

"It's God baby. He had the final say. Looks like we'll have the family we always wanted." I cried my eyes out as she grabbed me and hugged me tighter than she ever had. She then grabbed my face.

"I'll see you when you get back. You got two minutes. I love you, and Jr., or Jaliyah, loves you too. We embraced in one last kiss and I walked to the gate. As I got up to the MA's, I turned around one last time. She rubbed her stomach. I rubbed my heart. That was the last eye contact, as I proceeded to head on the boat. Six months would seem like an eternity, but I knew who I was now. Carl Lamell Jackson, a grown ass man. Hmmm? I wonder what's next...

ABOUT THE AUTHOR

Joe McClain Jr. is more than just an urban fiction author. He is fastly becoming a name that the black community can be proud of. Coming from one of the roughest areas of this country, he is just one of many shining examples who shows that just because you grow up in a negative atmosphere, you do not have to stay there, physically or mentally. You can stay in tuned with Joe and his many written and spoken word works on his website:

www.uprockpublications.com
www.joemacuncut.com

IF YOU ENJOYED "BANDAGES" PLEASE
LEAVE A REVIEW ON AMAZON.COM
HTTP://OW.LY/JGGVZ

ALSO AVAILABLE

When his father passed at 12, Mr. Terrelle Washington grew up fast and survived the dangerous streets of East Chicago, Indiana. After finding out his deceased father left him a large inheritance, he decided to leave for California and achieve his dream of becoming a published Author. However, the land of Hollywood stars was soon transformed into a maze of unforeseen obstacles he never expected on his way to the top. How will it play out??? Will he achieve his dream, or will it be shattered into a nightmare of failure.

Ricky Walters grew up in the gritty streets of San Diego California. Upon quitting his security job, he meets an ex pimp name Trust who teaches him everything about the pimp game. Ricky ends up turning out a young Asian girl name Yuki, changes his name to Jackpot, and jumps knee deep in the pimp game. Jackpot makes a conscious decision to become the biggest pimp to ever play the game and goes cross country. Here, is where Jackpot finds himself getting money, ducking the police, feuding with haters, vindictive females, snitches, and eventually doing time in the penitentiary.

Let Me Pimp Or Let Me Die 2, tells the story of a few female workers in the "Game," told through their lives as you see and find out what motivates a woman to start ho'n and sell her body. Re-visit some of your favorite characters from part 1 and see what drove them into the lifestyle that they chose. Each story different but ultimately the same.

Graphic and not for the faint of heart, the scenes take place in a realistic setting with many twist n turns you won't see coming. Find out how F.A.B Killed Sunshine and what happened in those last moments. How Green Eyes got hooked on drugs and the real reason she left Jackpot for dead in prison. Or the number one question...Will Jackpot Return To The Game?

Xavier Sands and Danielle Seville meet at the grand opening of Xavier's nightclub, and it happens to be his birthday. Not to be left out, Danielle is celebrating her birthday as well. As the two grow closer, wedges are driven between them behind the scenes, by their own mothers!

Xavier and Danielle both work for King Kole Konners, in different venues, but when the King is shot, all bets are off. The kingdom having just survived the Chase St. John mutiny in South Nubia, is rocked once again. The assassin begins picking off the King's top people, leading to Danielle being kidnapped.

Xavier vows vengeance on the person, or persons responsible for the shooting of the King. During her kidnapping ordeal, Danielle learns a horrible, life changing secret. Just as her world is rocked, Xavier learns the same shocking truth from his mother.

COMING SOON

"Freeze mother fucker!" a cop spat, but the Skyline hardhead wasn't trying to hear it. He blindly reached on the floor for his gun as he slowly regained his eyesight. Jail wasn't an option for the young rida. He knew he had done too much to turn back. Fuck it, he was gonna hold court in the streets. As he placed his hand on the gun that laid dormant on the floor, that would be as close as he got to picking it up and letting off a shot...

- Website: www.uprockpublications.com

- Emails: uprockp@gmail.com

- Facebook: uprockpublications

- Twitter: uprockpub

- Contact: (619) 259-0298